WE CAN ALWAYS TELL

This anthology is dedicated with love
to every member of the trans community.
You are seen, you are valid, and you are loved.

TABLE OF CONTENTS

The Wicked Ways We Writhe

By A.L. Davidson

"**B**aby... I've changed my mind."

Marcus stopped dead in his tracks, nearly slipping across the muddy ground from the sudden force of the motion. He shoved his hands into the tight pockets of his admittedly outdated skinny jeans and gazed over his shoulder at his boyfriend with a coy smile. A twinkle glistened in his whiskey-hued eyes as he scanned that enthralling frame. His sweet, bite-sized partner looked dashing in the moonlight.

"Are you... *scared*?" Marcus inquired playfully, putting such an emphasis on the word that it sounded a bit silly. Jo perked up a bit, huffing in response as he tried to hide a little smile.

The wind rustled Marcus' soil-toned curls and sent a shiver down his long spine. He should've opted for something warmer than his leather jacket. He hadn't realized the walk from the car would take so long, but it made sense in retrospect. It was safer to park where they had, even if it made the journey a bit lengthier—though it wasn't uncommon this far out of town for long stretches of space to feel even longer with the nothingness between stops. The anticipation was building, and he knew he'd warm up soon enough, so he didn't mind it. It felt like autumn had finally arrived, which meant it was time for bonfires, cuddles, and horror movie marathons with his adorable little goth boyfriend.

Not as enthused about the situation, Jo pulled his shoulders in taut and looked around the quiet, lonely graveyard. Behind the beveled lenses of his designer glasses, his sharp blue eyes appeared uncharacteristically worried. His wavy, luscious, wheat-gold locks fell in front of his eyes—only slightly pinned by the woolen beanie over his head—and the decorative, cross-covered chains that hung from his spectacles threatened to tangle in his hair. Cute, but impractical for what they were about to do.

"No," Jo replied firmly after a beat of faux contemplation.

"We've been plannin' this for months. You wouldn't shut up about it, you were *so* excited," Marcus reminded. His tone was gentle but somewhat playful as he tried to keep Jo from shutting down. The southern twang of his accent hung on certain words.

"And now I'm not."

Marcus took long, exaggerated strides back toward his partner's side and tilted his body to look into those beautiful blue marbles. That damning smile crept over his face again, one he knew Jo couldn't ignore.

It made Jo's heart skip a beat as he bashfully pursed his lips and turned his nose up in retort. Under the waxing moonlight, in the quiet of it all, Jo couldn't help but second guess his second guess after seeing how excited Marcus was. Too much guessing and questioning and musing over something meant to be fun. It was borderline insanity, but it thrilled him. Still, he worried that Marcus may not find him attractive after this, worried he may be too disturbed to want him after this twisted dream became a reality. He didn't know if it was worth it, worth losing him. Marcus was the first good guy he'd met in what felt like hundreds of years.

"What's the point of bein' a cute little goth-gay with an overzealous Labrador boyfriend —one who will literally do anythin' your morbid li'l heart desires—if you ain't going to take full advantage and do some spooky shit?" Marcus proposed with a soft peck on Jo's cheek.

"It's embarrassing. It's weird! I'm weird!" Jo explained with a pout.

Slowly, Marcus circled him and approached him from behind. "It's *kinky*, and you're *cute*," he whispered as he pulled Jo in close, close enough for his ass to press against him, to prove a point with his super obvious erection pressing against his tight denim. "And I've had a massive hard-on since we got in the car 'cause you got me so riled up about it."

An involuntary gasp shot out of Jo's throat. He quickly clamped his hands over his mouth, and all Marcus could do was chuckle as his younger boyfriend tried to hide his embarrassment.

"I like you, Jo. Don't know how many times I can say it. I

like you, this is fun. And I ain't sayin' that t'get in your super expensive designer pants that are immensely impractical but oh-so-perfectly fitted to that ass of yours. That's just a fun bonus," he said with a low growl. "C'mon, it's after midnight—on a school night, no less—and the parkin' lot was empty. Ain't no one gonna be out here, and I want to wake the dead. Let's go cause a ruckus."

Jo swallowed hard and tilted his eyes to look up at Marcus. "You devil."

"*Your* devil," Marcus corrected as he kissed the tip of his nose.

He softly took Jo's hand and urged him down the hill. Jo sheepishly followed, keeping his head down to try and hide the embarrassment etched into his cheeks with the high collar of the peacoat over his body. That intense pressure against him, the warmth of Marcus' body, and the excitement in the way his strong hands gripped him sent his thoughts spiraling.

Keeping to the shadows of the towering tombstones along the worn, wobbled path, they made their way with stifled giggles and Cheshire grins. Guided by the moonlight, they carefully walked through the tall grass so as to not dishonor those lying beneath them. The area was unkempt, they didn't want to accidentally trip over a marker or damage a tombstone. They would do enough *damage* in the coming moments, they didn't need the dead finding more reason to be angry. It felt eerie, especially with the only sounds being their laughter and the wind, but it reassured them that they wouldn't be stumbled upon. At least, not by anything human.

The trees in the beautiful old cemetery were covered in Spanish moss, a light layer of fog rolled down the dipping hill and coated the slanted tombstones with a haze. It was a southern gothic dream, and Marcus—though a bit disturbed by the overall weirdness of it—couldn't help but stand in awe of it all. It was scary, yet beautiful, and he couldn't believe that such a place existed only a few hours north of his home. He really needed to get out more, and a part of him hoped that Jo would take him on more weird road trips like this.

Fingers interlaced, the young couple approached a slightly off-kilter mausoleum that sat at the bottom of the hill a short ways away from a beautiful courtyard with a statue of a female-bodied angel at the center. She'd long since lost her head, one of her wings was chipped. The mausoleum was one they scouted a few weeks prior on a trip out to the cemetery when talks of planning this excursion started over cheap Chinese, a classic Universal monster movie, and the question of '*how far are you willing to go?*' came up. The old structure had blue-paneled stained-glass windows on the front, the entry was covered by iron bars without a lock. It was haunting in the moonlight and looked massive compared to how it had in the daylight.

The gate swung softly on its hinges in the harsh autumnal winds, as did the bouncing leaves that scaled the exterior with grace and fervor. The name atop its entryway had begun to fade with time, but Marcus could make out an STR. Nearly illegible, it was crumbling and forgotten, like most things in this place. The cemetery was historic, neglected, and far enough out of the nearest town that no one would come wandering through.

As they approached the structure, Marcus turned and quickly wrapped Jo up in his arms. His hands found his boyfriend's waist and gripped tight to plant a soft kiss on his cheek. He loved the extra weight Jo carried in his midsection. Loved the slight tremble of his body whenever he first took his hand—especially in public. Loved the harsh gasp that escaped his throat whenever they kissed, as if it still surprised him even after almost a year together. No, he didn't just *like* him, he loved him, and Marcus was going to tell Jo that tonight.

"Shall we?" Marcus asked, his lopsided grin prominent.

"Are you sure?" Jo questioned.

"I ain't never been more sure of anythin' in my life."

"You won't be too weirded out after? You won't…leave me?"

"I ain't going anywhere, Jo. You're stuck with me."

Jo gnawed on his lip with anticipation and urged his partner toward the crypt with a beckoning gesture of his finger. They quietly opened the metal door and walked inside.

As Marcus pulled his backpack off his spine, his eyes were immediately drawn to the stone slab in the center. The ceiling was tall, dark, and cast a long shadow that made the mausoleum look endless. The back of the structure was obscured by a pitch-black veil from the lack of light. A beautiful string of ivy broke through the concrete flooring and crawled up the wall, aiming for the broken window that let in a slight breeze by the door. Out of the corner of his vision, Marcus noticed a few of the shelves on the wall meant to house bodies were empty, but many held large, dust-covered caskets. It was a big family.

The reality of the situation settled in. Marcus knew there would be no going back once they started. They were going to fuck atop someone's grave. A literal handful of inches of concrete would separate them from a corpse while he was buried in his lover. Lord above, he was in *deep*.

He pulled a rolled throw blanket from his pack and handed it to Jo, letting him take the lead in this situation. This was Jo's night, his fantasy, and he would bend to those desires despite his nerves. *Focus on Jo, focus on Jo*, Marcus told himself as he let his eyes adjust to the dark. It was hard to discern, but saw a name etched—and dark splotches he immediately worried was dried blood—into the top of the slab before it was covered by the blanket. J—STR—. He silently apologized to the poor corpse with the lost name for what they were about to do.

As his lover unfurled the linen and laid it atop the stone resting place behind him, Marcus composed himself and tried to find the best place to start. All thought and logic left him when Jo locked eyes with him. Setting his hands against the tomb, Jo leaned back and let his legs spread. Marcus felt his breath hitch in his throat. He watched wordlessly as Jo popped the top button of his dress shirt and beckoned him once again with his finger, giving him an open invitation to come close. The blood-red polish on his nails looked black in the ominous space. Ensuring the gate was closed, Marcus faced Jo with a flood of hormones hitting his system like a shot of liquor. He could feel his dick react against the restrictions of his jeans.

With a seductive grin, he pulled a mini bottle of red wine from the gas station out of his bag, eliciting a laugh from Jo.

"I figured you'd pounce on me, I didn't expect wine and build up," Jo noted with a genuine spark of surprise.

Marcus unscrewed the cap of one of the plastic bottle. "This is a special night, I'm allowed t'spoil you for your birthday," he stated as he pressed the opening of the plastic bottle against his boyfriend's lips.

Jo took the slightly chilled container from him with a soft thanks, then watched as Marcus grabbed some cheap black taper candles from the dollar store and struck a match. Marcus' tan face was illuminated by the soft warm glow as he lit the slightly bent wick. How endearing, how lovely, how smitten he was with this man. Damn it to hell, Marcus Santiago was nothing if not a charmer. One well-aware of his actions, too. The sly devil.

With a cheeky grin, Marcus set the candles on the empty casket shelves—mindful to keep them away from cobwebs so he wouldn't accidentally set fire to the already desecrated tomb. The final touch, the last desire his beloved wanted from this night, was the camera. He booted it up and attempted to balance the readings in the darkness so it could get a clear shot. Jo teased during the planning stage that it would be a waste of Marcus' gear to *not* use it, so he obviously had to. That it would be the most beautiful piece of cinema he'd ever record, and the aspiring documentarian had to agree—even if it would only be for their eyes.

Once he was satisfied with the framing and the red light was blinking, he returned to his partner's side. Jo had slid up onto the blanket-covered stone and continued sipping his wine until Marcus pulled the beanie from his head, freeing his golden locks in the process. They rustled in the soft breeze that slid in through the gate. Marcus let his fingers trace down Jo's skull, tangling in those soft curls and playing with the little black studs that lined his ear. He kissed him, gently pressed his tongue against Jo's lips until his boyfriend opened and allowed it inside to explore. They knocked teeth, Jo bundled up Marcus' shirt in his hand and shifted his head to better taste the lingering tobacco on his boyfriend's lips.

Breaking for a breath, Marcus snuck one last soft kiss then threw him a wink. With tender motions, Marcus removed Jo's glasses and safely tucked them in his pack. Everything was done with care, and it exhilarated Jo.

"I think you're more excited about this than I am," Jo said as he offered the half-drunk wine to him. He slid out of his peacoat and set it to the side, then kicked his heeled vegan leather boots off onto the floor while his boyfriend indulged in the drink.

Marcus took a swig and set the bottle down. He cupped Jo's face in his hands and kissed him again. He slotted himself between his spread legs, pressing up against the concrete that was cold enough it could be felt through his pants. Jo fumbled the heavy buckle that kept the leather belt around Marcus' waist and let out a soft giggle as his boyfriend bit his lower lip and tugged with a desperate moan. Marcus wriggled out of his own jacket, the heat in his athletic frame was rising to an uncomfortable level despite autumn's arrival on the winds.

"I am excited. I…" Marcus steeled himself, "I love you. Just thought you oughta know."

Jo felt his cheeks grow hot, his eyes widened with disbelief as he attempted to register those damning, powerful words. He set his hand on Marcus' chest, felt the aggressive thump of his heart, and knew in that moment he had to believe him. The way the wannabe documentarian gnawed on his lip ring nervously, the way his whiskey-hued eyes glistened in the candlelight, proved it to be true.

"You're so fuckin' cute," Marcus said with a throaty growl as he untucked Jo's dress shirt with an aggressive tug.

Jo let out a soft, shocked gasp as Marcus slid his hand into his pants.

"Oh… hell," Marcus mumbled as he lowered his head, "Is this what I think it is?"

He playfully pulled on the black lace band around Jo's waist. Jo only replied with a coy nudge of his knee into his boyfriend's groin. The floral-patterned garment was moist as Marcus' hand continued to creep downward.

"You're already dripping wet," he teased, with both his words and his hand.

Jo's head fell back as a visible, satisfied shiver overwhelmed his body. Marcus' fingertips were rough, hot like matches, and eager. He looked thoughtful, contemplative in the candlelight as he stroked, as his free hand palmed Jo's waist to keep his urges in check. His nerves got the better of him and he shakily reached for the wine, only to topple it with his unsteady fingers, sending the sticky red liquid running down the concrete box.

"Why are you… so nervous?" Jo asked with a soft groan.

"I just did somethin' stupid," Marcus whispered.

"I love you, too."

Jo wrapped his arms around Marcus' neck and kissed him.

He descended to the slab with slow motions, the small of his back was cradled delicately in Marcus' palm. The pressure of his taller, stronger boyfriend lying atop him, of their groins grinding against each other with Marcus' fingers refusing to relent their teasing against his flesh, caused Jo's spine to arch. Still firmly touching Jo's back, Marcus traced the motion, the curve, and studied the ridges of his vertebrae with his fingers as he wiggled and writhed. Desperately, he wanted to grab hold of those bones and seize control of his frame, control every breath and motion. Dig his nails into the flesh and sinew like an animal.

"M-Marcus—fuck!" Jo gasped.

Marcus' teeth bit into the strained tendon along Jo's neck and his tongue danced circles along his jawline. The wind picked up a bit, it brushed by and sent a few of the candle's flames bouncing. Jo's trembling fingers finally undid the button on Marcus' tight black jeans and shakily released his twitching dick from the bonds of cotton and denim. The heft of his cock never ceased to amaze him, nor did the way his liquor-colored eyes snapped closed at that first touch. As if they hadn't done this dozens of times, as if he wasn't aware of what was about to happen.

"Don't let me... have all the fun," Jo chided playfully.

"Trust me, sugar, this is only round one. Let me treat you right," Marcus taunted.

"Round one?!"

A sensual, harsh scream echoed out into the mausoleum as Marcus penetrated him with an eager finger. Jo's thighs compressed against Marcus' body and his hands clawed at his back. Sweat formed from the friction of their frames.

Jo took Marcus' dick in his hand, tightened his grip and pressed his thumb against the head as he tauntingly traced circles over the slit. This was the most turned on he'd ever seen him, and the thrill of it was something otherworldly. Something wholly lovely. Something wicked. Marcus hadn't been kidding when he said he was into this, Jo wished he'd believed him. Wished they'd done this sooner. They were both royally fucked in the head.

"Put it in, Marcus, please!" Jo cried.

"Nope, you can wait," Marcus said with a throaty laugh.

As Jo went to plead again, he slapped his hand over his mouth. Marcus stopped his grinding, stopped the motion of his hand, and listened. Footsteps. The sound of the autumn-kissed earth being crunched beneath heavy footfalls. Marcus exhaled, sweat rolled down his scruff-covered jaw onto Jo's face. The breeze wasn't enough to curb the hormones and lust despite the way the candles flickered.

They listened as the unknown presence wandered in the darkness, through the old tombstones to somewhere unknown. Marcus, looking over his shoulder, studied the windows for movement, for a security guard's flashlight or the dashing motion of an animal being stirred from the pleading of his boyfriend beneath him. As quickly as the noise disrupted them, it seemingly vanished.

With a devious motion, Jo shifted and rubbed his thumb over the head again. Marcus grunted, then he retaliated by sliding two fingers inward, pushing through the lips into the soft, fleshy inside of Jo. The younger man nearly yelped.

"Better keep it down, unless you want an audience," Marcus whispered, shooting a devilish gaze Jo's way.

"S-stop..." Jo mumbled.

Marcus leaned down and placed his lips near Jo's heavily pierced ear. "I can't wait t'bury myself deep inside you. Feel how tight you get from the anticipation of someone findin' us here. The only thing you gotta tell me, sugar, is which hole you want me t'pleasure t'night."

Jo slapped him on the chest. Marcus laughed as he thrusted his hips. His cock slid freely in his boyfriend's soft palm as his own fingers scissored against Jo's warm, moist skin—moving in time with the blinking red light of the camera that bounced on and off. On and off. Up and down. He used the unending tempo of it to guide his own.

Desperate to keep himself from screaming, the birthday boy pulled Marcus close and kissed him, hoping the contact of their lips would be enough to stifle any surprised sounds that could echo out into the graveyard. The flicker of the candlelight turned Marcus' warm eyes into desperate infernos, and Jo found himself intoxicated by that liquor-like color. He could feel him stiffening against him.

Damn it all to hell, he was so into this.

"Let me ride you," Jo begged.

Marcus grinned and wrapped his arm around his partner. He lifted him from the slab and held him close, never once letting his eyes drift from Jo's dreamy gaze as he turned and sat down atop the crumpled blanket, swapping their positions with effortless ease. He clamped down onto the remaining button of Jo's shirt with his teeth and pulled it free, revealing his pale flesh. The beautifully designed floral-lace tattoos that covered the curve of his chest, hiding the surgery scars that allowed him to be the man he always knew he truly was, drove Marcus crazy. They were lovely, gothic, and perfectly framed his ribcage like wounds slicing through his skin. Revealing a lovely garden of magnolias and ivy.

Delicate, devilish, and dizzying—just like Jo.

Jo dropped his shirt to the ground and slid out of his jeans, leaving nothing but bare skin and lace silhouetted by the shadowy moonlight. He kissed him as they prepared themselves for that sweet, powerful moment of connection—mouths tinged with the lingering taste of tobacco and wine. With a sly grin, he slid his leg up onto the slab. Marcus set his palm against Jo's thick thigh and helped hoist him up as they got into a comfortable position atop the concrete box.

Once he was fully prone with Jo atop him, Marcus grabbed

hold of the saturated lingerie and pulled, opening him up like a door swinging wide for a most welcomed guest. In the flickering candlelight, the happy Jo's pale, specter-like body burned an amber hue, akin to fire raging across untouched snow. Beautiful and deadly.

Jo took Marcus' erection in his hand and moved it between his spread legs. The rocking of his hips as he sat down on his cock was intoxicating, and Marcus found himself stifling his own pleasured noises. Biting into his knuckles enough to draw blood to keep the sounds to a minimum. They'd be in serious trouble if they were caught like this.

Trembling, Marcus' hand clamped onto Jo's waist, and he let himself succumb to the pressure, the pleasure, and the restricting feeling of his boyfriend's vagina pushing through the pain until he bottomed out atop him. Quivering around his throbbing cock. The satisfied '*ohhhh… fuck*' that left Jo's mouth caused him to tense. Jo's nipples were perky in the cold, he reached up to touch them, to trace the lines of those top surgery scars and the lovely inks that cut through his pale flesh. Then, he gave an approving not, letting the happy birthday boy do literally whatever he wanted tonight. If his boyfriend asked, he'd do it in a heartbeat, no matter how unhinged it may be. It was his big day, after all. He'd do literally anything to see the man he loved smile.

The cold chill of the slab beneath Marcus stung, the feeling was at war with the rising heat that swelled from the friction of their bodies. Jo's sweat rolled down his rounded cheeks as he fully took control of the situation. He shifted a bit until he found a comfortable place to sit, legs spread and hands placed behind him on Marcus' muscular legs.

"Fuckin'… hell, you're so tight," Marcus mumbled, eyes closing and head falling back.

With Marcus fully engrossed in the experience, he didn't notice Jo's eyes were locked onto the darkness behind them as he rocked. He saw the shadows of figures, cast by the moonlight, trace up the mausoleum walls. Someone was approaching the tomb.

Slowly, he leaned over, sending surges of ecstasy through his spine with the shifting of positions as his thrusting allowed Marcus' dick to find the perfect arc. His knees grazed against the worn concrete, pulling skin away and trailing ripped pores and speckles of blood along its surface more and more with every inch. To add fuel to the fire, Jo set his palm over his boyfriend's eyes and blocked the night from his gaze.

"Do you know why I picked this place, Marcus? Picked this concrete coffin? This tomb?" Jo asked.

Marcus' hands followed the motions of Jo's shifting—desperate to hold onto something as his vision was blanketed by those soft hands. One wrapped itself around his boyfriend's sweat-licked flesh, the other slid between the slits and pleasured with precise strokes, and he began thrusting his hips in rhythm with Jo, unable to stave off those primal desires. The aggressive thump of his heart and the passionate pants that shot out of Jo's throat drowned out the sounds around him. He swore they would break the stone beneath them with the force of their bodies. Jo was relentless.

"Do you?" Jo asked again, his lips dancing close to Marcus' ear.

"N-no... fuck..."

"It's *mine*."

Marcus chuckled, "What're you—"

Jo slid his hand upward, tangling his fingers in the thick, sweat-saturated chestnut curls like roots through soil. Marcus snapped his head up when he realized his lover was gazing at something in the darkness behind them. As he tried to scramble and sit upright out of fear and a need to protect his boyfriend, Jo rocked his body and pressed the full of his weight down upon his hips, locking his ability to move.

"You're *early*," Jo said angrily, peering at the forms in the shadows.

Marcus, trying to catch his breath, watched as robed figures moved into the glow of the candlelight. They were surrounded, but he was more panicked about the fact that Jo seemed calm than the fact they'd been found. A monstrous, shrouded individual stood over him. Antlers protruded from the hood that obscured the stranger's features, but Marcus could see a fiery, burning yellow hue in his eyes. He was massive, inhuman, and held an aura of maliciousness unlike anything he'd ever felt before. Jo set his elbow on Marcus' chest and placed his hand on his head. He continued to thrust, writhing atop Marcus despite the eyes upon them.

"Jo—"

"Shhh... it's okay, they're family," Jo assured with a playful hush and a soft tap of Marcus' nose.

Marcus twitched, causing a pleasure-filled sigh to escape Jo's throat. The young blonde lifted his head with a pout. The cloaked figure at the head of the slab raised his hand, nails sharpened like daggers, and placed it under Jo's chin. The man slid his thumb into Jo's mouth and pressed down upon his tongue.

"Enjoying yourself, my dear?" the tall figured inquired, tone booming like thunder across a field. Marcus swore the windows rattled from the intensity of it. He tried to scramble away but he felt so heavy, so numb, in a way that was beyond the sexual. Fuck. The wine.

"Yes, daddy," Jo replied, a look of sheer satisfaction on his face.

Two of the cloaked strangers approached the slab. They set their hands upon Jo's chest and groped him, tracing the tattoos with sensual motions and a familiar intimacy that sent a flood of jealousy through Marcus. One even joined Marcus' trapped hand, still set firmly between Jo's legs, and added extra pressure with his ice cold fingers that caused Jo to moan. Marcus gazed upward, catching the lifeless eyes of one of the men staring blankly at his boyfriend. Through the darkness, he could see his lips were sewn shut. Someone held down Marcus' legs against the slab, pinning him to the stone with such strength he thought his ankles might break.

"The fuck is happenin'?! Jo!" Marcus wailed. He tried to release his hold on Jo's waist, but the two stone-faced strangers held his hands firmly in place, forcing his palms to connect to Jo's sweat-slicked skin and continue pleasuring the birthday boy despite his pleas for them to stop. The strangers pressed him down atop Marcus' lap with relentless strength. He felt like his dick would break.

"My birthday party, Marcus," Jo replied innocently, licking his lips with a loud moan of desire as he wiggled.

"Cut it out, Jo," Marcus pleaded, tone soft and tender.

"Why? You feel so fucking good!"

"Jo—"

"You promised," Jo reminded, "You promised me you'd stay once you realized how messed up I am. You love me, right?"

Marcus nodded. "I do…" tears welled in his eyes. He was afraid, but he was also aroused and close to climaxing.

Jo nibbled on his ear and whispered the words back. Words Marcus had been so desperate to hear, for so damn long. '*I love you*' had never sounded so sweet, so vile.

Unable to fight off the overload, Marcus grunted and emptied himself into Jo. His body jerked violently; with such intensity the cloaked enigmas nearly lost their grip on him. He saw Jo extend an arm with wiggling fingers, saw the antlered man above hand over an item, but his eyes snapped closed as Jo continued to writhe and overwhelm every nerve in his body.

"Jo—"

Unimaginable pain halted his speech. The severing of his

vocal cords throttled his ability to cry out in agony. His fear-filled eyes—if only for a moment—saw Jo's handsome, sweet face become painted with a spray of blood but he was unable to focus as the jolt from his ejaculation rocked him on a soul-deep level. His lover's satisfied cry echoed out into the night, but all Marcus could hear was the gurgle of his own throat. The sticky warmth of blood ran down his neck onto the slab, slipped from his lips down his jaw, and coated his skull with a flood of death.

He couldn't breathe.

Jo traced a black blade across his tongue, licking up the blood from the freshly opened wound he inflicted during climax. Marcus' body continued to writhe, the receptors in his brain were unable to focus on the pain with the immeasurable pleasure. His vision started to grow dark, and a soft whimper followed. The cloaked figures finally released his limbs and Marcus shakily lifted a hand in a desperate attempt to find sense in the madness, to touch that beautiful face and hope it was all a bad dream. The documentarian stroked his boyfriend's bloody face and tried to speak, but nothing could be heard over the sound of the wind winding through the cemetery.

"Shh… it'll be over soon. I love you," Jo promised before he kissed him. He gnawed on Marcus' lip until the skin tore and his piercing ripped. Marcus went limp beneath him.

Jo nuzzled his face into the wound, licking up the blood and painting his golden curls red as he listened to Marcus struggle for a final breath. The would-be documentarian's hand slipped down Jo's face and fell onto the bloody concrete. The soft whine of escaping air through the wound was a sweet melody that preceded his death rattle. The birthday boy turned his eyes up to the antlered figure above and smiled a childish, cheeky grin.

"Can I keep him?" Jo asked as he stuck his tongue into the wound. He dug into the slit, Marcus' Adam's apple shifted from the pressure as Jo lapped up the mess.

"You already have so many."

"Yes, but he *loves* me, this one loves me. And he's pretty, and he came so willingly, and his dick is *so* big. Please?"

The large figure laughed; the sound boomed like thunder. "Alright, little one, if you insist. Anything for your big day. Let papa handle it. Go bask in the moonlight with your siblings. Bless this new year with the gift this sacrifice bestowed upon you while the night is still young."

Jo giggled and scooped up the hot, thick blood that pooled around Marcus' head. He let it drip over his skull, creating a syrupy waterfall that replaced the October chill with warmth. Marcus' eyes stared motionless at the ceiling; his plasma-filled mouth sat agape. The heat of life was already leaving his corpse. He placed a final kiss on Marcus' lips. "I really do love you..."

As the towering, shrouded man began to chant lowly, Jo stood over his lover, dripping sweat, blood, and semen onto Marcus' chest. He breathed in the fresh scents of autumn and revival that filled the desecrated space. The sound of his Maker preparing his lover for rebirth pounded like war drums in his ears. It was exhilarating. The silent figures opened the mausoleum door and offered a hand for Jo to descend off of the empty coffin onto the uneven mausoleum floor.

Stepping down off the slab, Jo looked back and saw his lover's blood fill the faded name atop the concrete and couldn't help but smile at the thought of the person he had once been, and all of the accomplishments that had come after his rebirths. Jo Strauss had died many times, in many different ways, but he came back stronger every time. Happier every time. Truer to himself every time. How exciting it was to know that his beautiful Marcus would come back alongside him this time. He'd finally found someone worthy of his happily ever after.

He snatched up the expensive camera and walked out into the chilly air through the rusted gate of his mausoleum. Leaving bloody handprints around the device, he turned the recording off and pressed it to his chest with glee. What a cherished experience to relive again and again. He was truly blessed this night.

Basking in the glorious light of the waxing moon, Jo felt the coagulating blood cling to his body. Bare naked with nothing more than a hint of lace, the birthday boy entered the hunting grounds of the old cemetery and listened to the bloodcurdling chorus of wails and screaming. His siblings, broad in numbers and powerful under the ever-watchful eye of their Maker, drug the fresh corpses of their sacrifices out into the night.

This unholy, glorious time only came once a year, and this was by far the best night of rebirth Jo had ever experienced in the several hundred years he'd been a part of it. My, how the world had changed so drastically since that first time, and yet this simple sacrificial event remained steadfast in its narrative. The carnage was beautiful. Draped over tombstones, hung from mausoleum entryways, and littering the tombstones, the heads and limbs of the deceased decorated the historic cemetery with blood, guts, and the stench of sex. His siblings danced naked in the cold light of the moon, around the bonfire in the center courtyard that rose higher with each new body tossed into its embers, engulfing the statue of the decapitated woman whose outstretched hands and wings now held entrails. How poetic.

It would be a good cycle, one full of vigor and vitality, and he craved the dark deeds that awaited him over this next cycle. Craved the next soul he'd seduce and bring back to this space to do it all over again in a year's time. How fun it would be to do so with a fresh new puppet in his clutches, with love in his heart. The excess of blood twisted his hair, coiled it like snakes ready to strike, and his once sharp blue eyes held an unholy yellow in their surfaces.

"How funny," he mused to himself. "I feel alive."

When he heard the crunch of footsteps behind him, he looked over his shoulder and smiled. His Marcus, how handsome he looked covered in red. The floral-patterned lace now sewn over the wound that slit through his muscular throat curled from the saturation of blood, turning the white cloth black with the presence of death. His once warm, whiskey-hued eyes were pale and motionless, and those slender lips—so full of laugher and love that had haunted and excited him for nearly a year of Jo's long life—were forever silenced with the stitching of black thread. He seemed lost and scared.

"Come here, love," Jo called.

Yes, he was scared. Yet he knew. Marcus knew his lover, and his body craved him. So he walked, unsteady as a newborn babe, and moved toward the man he loved. He was perfect. What a delightfully perfect gift his Marcus was.

Jo extended his arms with a smile and tears in his eyes, and felt the rejuvenation of a much-needed rebirth sew itself into his skin. He beckoned once again with that simple gesture of his finger.

"You said you'd stay, you said you loved me, and you do! You're still here!" Jo cried as his boyfriend, enchanted by the thoughts of nothing but his master, embraced him. Marcus' powerful and protective arms held him close under the long shadow of a tombstone coated in gore. Marcus groaned, buried his face in the curve of Jo's shoulder, and mumbled something inaudible. But Jo knew he was professing his love. Of course he was. What else would he ever need to say aside from that sweet, simple phrase?

They connected through the blood, the sweat, and the shared experience of wicked death, and bathed in the satisfaction and pleasure that came alongside the sensual motions of their frames. They writhed together in the first hour of a new year that joined them in such an unholy matrimony, and Jo knew that it would indeed be a good year.

Transymbiosis

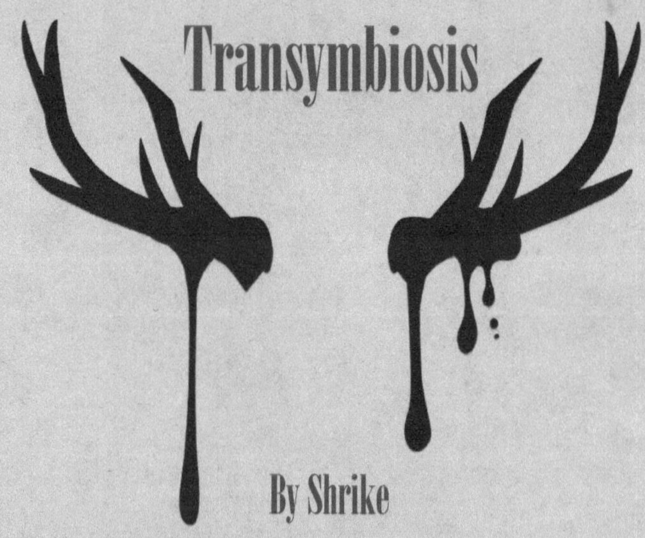

By Shrike

Transformation is a seductive sin. Tracy holds this knowledge soul-deep; transformation is his lifeblood. More accurately: his life, their blood. Semantics.

Generation upon generation slip through his chapped fingers. How beautiful, this destruction. This creation. Rebirth beyond nature's intentions. Inconsequential things repurposed, reimagined, reformed to fit man's image. Tracy wishes the soft creatures had enough awareness of their station to be grateful to live on as art, in tapestries woven of death. He watches, mesmerized, as fleshy bodies boil away into new shapes. The cogs turn, cold and callous and creating.

Do these silkworms know they only exist to unravel at his fingertips?

Tracy imagines himself a god of pathetic, writhing creatures. Their primitive neurons cannot fathom his intentions, cannot understand his divine designs for their short lives. All the more tragic that Tracy knows he is no god at all outside of this tiny domain.

Real power eludes him, but still he searches. Magic exists in whispers. Tracy is not the first to crave abilities far beyond sanctioned bounds of humanity. His heart aches to imagine arcane knowledge lost to time, rotting away in some moldering private library. Or, worse, destroyed by those who fear what their simple minds could never comprehend. For his own sanity, Tracy holds onto hope.

Tracy remembers the exact moment he first felt the pull of forbidden magic. On his tenth birthday, his mother gifted him a book: a collection of fables for young girls. Her eyes glistened with bittersweet nostalgia as she relayed how her own mother read it to her when she was his age. The book's well-worn edges bore out the truth of its provenance. Tracy pored over the colorful pages, devouring the text well into early morning hours. Over the coming years, Tracy kept returning to one tale in particular: *The Seed of Jealousy*.

Once upon a time, a handsome male suitor sought the affection of a reclusive Witch. All the townsfolk swooned at the very idea of their coupling. After all, he was the most dashing man in the land, and she the most beautiful woman. One day, the man came calling at the Witch's door, arms full of fresh wildflowers. When the Witch laid eyes upon him, she was indeed swayed by his charms, but her heart held no love for him. She coveted the suitor's striking visage, the blemishless blooms held to his breast. The Witch lured him into her abode under the guise that she was but a lovestruck, blushing maiden.

Weeks passed without the gentleman's reappearance. Steamy rumors chilled into anxious speculation. At last, a brave neighbor rapped at the Witch's door, demanding to know the suitor's fate. What greeted her was a horror beyond comprehension. The Witch, in her lust for beauty beyond her biology, had cast an awful Transformation spell upon the man and his bouquet. She stole them away into herself, warping her body into an inhuman amalgamation of masculine, feminine, and botanical. Unable to bear this slight against nature, the townspeople banished the monster to languish in the consequences of their hubris. The Witch's envy and vanity cost them their humanity.

Even as a young child, Tracy recognized the intended moral of this story. He gleaned that he was to rebuke the Witch by practicing humility and gratitude for his lot in life.

Yet, all he saw was possibility.

His parents did not understand. The stricken look in his mother's eyes when he confessed his desires seared forever into the back of his skull. She weaponized her tears, crying that she had failed him. As if she had any part in his physical form beyond conception. His father was worse: he looked at Tracy with such grief, like this fantastic revelation was somehow something to be mourned. He feared that by changing his form Tracy would lose some vital part of himself that made him their child. The very people meant to love him unconditionally abandoned him before he could abandon them. For a time, Tracy languished in self-pity, believing himself at fault for their betrayal.

Tracy never hated his body and refuses to believe the Witch hated theirs. Far from it: he loves his body so much that he sees its infinite possibilities. Should the potter hate their unformed clay? His family was too simpleminded to understand. They thought that his desires, his needs, his truest self unnatural. Although their doubts broke his heart, a crucial revelation has long since sutured his fraying ventricles. His heartbreak evolved into something more akin to pity. His parents are as misguided as the hands that wrote the Witch's fable. Such a shame that most people never realize they are not confined to random acts of nature. They have power, agency, hands to mold and make. Instead, they avert their eyes and cover their ears to his truth. They are slaves of their own narrow minds, shackling their own wrists. Unfathomable, tragic. His body from birth holds untapped potential. He needs only the means to uncover it.

Seeds of doubt occasionally work their way into his skull. He speculates whether losing oneself to this fabled Transformation magic is possible, after all. He surmises it would depend on where the "self" resides. Is the soul bound within fragile neurons, snuffed out the moment the brain quiets? Is it an organic thing that transcends the human mind, woven into a sapling's matrix of cellulose? Perhaps the self nestles poetically between the pulses of the human heart. Tracy's rational mind threatens to balk at exploring this nigh-uncharted territory; however, his heart knows the reward is worth the risk. He is intimately familiar with the beauty that blooms from destruction. If he succumbs to a spell, he will die in the name of divine discovery.

Tracy hunches at his back porch workstation, lost in his musings. Calling it a workstation may be generous. In truth, his setup is little more than a water-warped writing desk, a creaky secondhand reel, mismatched pots, and frayed baskets of scavenged dyes. He thrives in unbridled creative chaos.

His little projects have caught the eyes of hobbyist and professional textile artists alike over the years. A select few make an annual pilgrimage to restock. His work is far from as clean and refined as the mass-produced stuff, or even professionally handmade materials, but his patrons hardly seem to mind. They do not seek to purchase perfection, they come seeking a story. Provenance is everything in the arts.

Fibers spun by Tracy's fingers become embroidered shawls with lofty price tags hidden behind quaint little placards: *Handmade with Local, Artisanal Silk.*

Silkmaking serves a dual purpose: keeping his hands busy and his thoughts from wandering. Tracy rocks from side to side on the creaking old stool, separating the worms' goopy remains from their cocoons and harvesting the fruits of their labor. His tawny braids sway, a sweat-streaked pendulum keeping time to his labor. Each worm is tossed out over the back of his battered desk, sailing through the air before plummeting to their final resting place in his overgrown garden. When Tracy took ownership of his land, he staked out a garden to plant exotic vegetables and herbs. He pictured himself in worn workclothes, sun-kissed and strong-armed. Too late, he realized he only had the wherewithal to maintain a few tomato plants and a miniature forest of potted mulberries. The remainder of his land hosts his silkworm swarm within a motley canopy stitched from textile shop scraps. Each time the mulberry trees threaten to outgrow their pots, his silkworms prune them back into submission. Every plant rotates through the enclosure, an ouroboric cycle of consumption and renewal.

Back and forth, boilpot to cool bath. Worm after worm soars over the rail, taking their first and final flight despite being denied their wings when their life cycle came to a roiling halt. The repetitive motion soothes Tracy's mind even as it grinds down his joints. He flexes his hands, cracking each knuckle. For good measure, he stretches each finger until the joints pop, then sighs with instant, aching relief. The pain centers him: all worthwhile creation requires sacrifice.

Tracy would lose himself to his craft for days on end if he weren't limited by the looming specter of money. Silkmaking cannot sustain him, for he is bound by the curse of possessing only two hands. The art of silk, if it can still be called an art, has outpaced him. Industrial-scale production rules the market, driven by soulless automatons. Mindless machines rearing, harvesting, sorting, refining, spinning, repeating. What takes his calloused hands hours is accomplished tenfold in mere minutes. Despite knowing his limitations, Tracy stubbornly clings to tradition. He has no familial link to silkmaking, no heritage to uphold. He has a far better cause for carrying the dying torch: his pride. No one held his hands in theirs to guide him through the process. He taught himself, with his meager two hands and a stack of well-thumbed books pilfered from the textile shop. Through trial and error and countless bandaged fingers, Tracy became a self-made man. Even as he aches with exertion, he finds meaning in the sting. Creation should require sweat and sacrifice, a uniquely human touch. No textile mill slop could compare to handspun silk dyed in its maker's own blood. One day he may weild Transformation magic to make silk into a hot meal and shirk society entirely. Until then, he must work.

Spring may be peak silk season, but it is also peak tourism season. Avalon Arts has been busy. Gloria is the proprietor of the humble textile shop. She is a stout, stern-faced woman with steel-gray eyes and salt-and-pepper curls. She barks orders over shelves heaping with fresh fabric while Tracy manages the ledger. The shop is chronically understaffed on account of Gloria's gruff demeanor. Tracy leverages his status as Gloria's only constant to barter for leftover materials and shelf space to display his wares.

Presently, Gloria rattles off a rush order of fine velvet. The material caught the eye of a foppish gentleman passing through town and he simply must have it delivered tomorrow. Tracy has hardly finished recording the details when she descends on him with more demands.

"Damn fool tried to haggle his way out of paying for shipping, but I secured a nice sum for the rush." She tosses a thick envelope onto the desk, presumably stuffed with paper notes. "Mark that down. Count it thrice to keep him honest. Tell you what, boy: he lives in an awfully wealthy part of the city. If you'll save me the cost of hiring an overnight porter, I'll let you sling some silk along the way."

"Certainly," Tracy agrees without hesitation. Trips to the city are costly. He would never turn down an opportunity to restock his silkmaking necessities on Gloria's dime. Besides, this customer has means. If his art catches the man's eye, perhaps he can spin some silk into gold.

Tracy pulls a spare set of silks, socks, and undergarments from his clothing chest, figuring they will serve him well if he decides to turn in at a roadside inn. More likely, he's overpacking, but he can't risk appearing unkempt in yesterday's clothing if he is waylaid overnight. He represents Avalon, Gloria, and, most importantly, his craft.

Avalon Arts lies sleeping when Tracy arrives on foot. His hired cart arrives just as he reaches for the door. Gloria deemed him worthy of paying a cheap driver, but the bulk of the labor falls solely on Tracy. He signals for the driver to wait while he sets about loading his charge. The doorbell chimes when he lets himself in with his spare key: the ultimate symbol of Gloria's hard-earned trust. Gloria herself is likely still abed, so Tracy must make three separate trips to transfer all seven unwieldy bolts of fabric to the cart by his lonesome. Both driver and horse, Hans and Benny, respectively, are content to watch him struggle. By the time he has the final bundle safely tucked away in the cart's hold, he's worked up a sweat.

The journey is a handful of hours at most, but the stink of hot horse has a way of stretching time. Tracy has just managed to acclimate to the stench when the cart comes to a halt. He perks up, then deflates when he catches Hans poring over the map. Hans must catch his fallen expression because he finally breaks the silence: "I know where we are headed. Just need to make sure this is the right turn. Road gets narrow that way, and I don't fancy trying to turn this rig around in there." He punctuates his point with a gesture to their left.

"Right." Tracy fights to hide his skepticism as he follows Hans' point. A small, unpaved path splits from the main road and winds out of sight into dense woods. The ground appears conspicuously untrodden, speckled with weeds and lacking telltale hoofprints or wheel tracks. "Is this some sort of shortcut?"

"You got it. Shaves off a good half hour." Hans nods after a final confirmatory glance over the map. Tracy keeps his doubts to himself. The driver seems confident enough.

Benny steps unevenly off the pavement, jolting Tracy's nerves along with the cart. Early morning light gives way to dappled twilight once they cross the canopy's threshold. Hans was right about the path narrowing; Tracy would wager he could touch the trees on either side with his fingertips if he spread his arms wide. The horse snorts their distaste for the cramped quarters, nostrils flaring and ears flicking. Tracy silently agrees with their assessment.

Time begins to drift in the way of a dream: minutes blur together when every shadow looks the same. Tracy expects a break in the foliage any moment now, but the sun's relief never comes. Instead, warm damp seeps across his skin, the air thickening around him. His lungs feel heavier, the fog settling deeper with each inhale. If he thinks about it too much, Tracy is certain he will lose his nerve and beg Hans to turn around, narrow path be damned. Distantly, he notices when the soft crunch of the horse's tread gives way to the moist suck of mud.

Even the insects fall under this spell of perpetual twilight. Fireflies begin to wink in and out in Tracy's peripheral vision. Their ephemeral glow forms strange clusters on the ground, reminiscent of paper lanterns fashioned by children during the harvest festival. A series of jolts and whinnied frustrations shake Tracy from his daze. Benny strains against mucky inertia, but their efforts are futile. The cart is stuck.

"Damn it all. Hold on." Hans drops from the cart to inspect the damage. Tracy eyes the moist ground with distrust, but that nagging unease forces him to follow. If there's a threat lurking in the shadows, he needs both feet on the ground.

Tracy disembarks carefully, cringing at the wet squelch beneath his boots. He's not confident that his showy leather footwear will hold up in this terrain. Shuffling unsuccessfully in search of more solid footing, he silently thanks himself for the foresight to pack extra socks. He's less comforted by his choice of silk tunic. Gloria designed the piece with Tracy's handmade materials, making the ensemble an excellent advertisement for their combined talents. The garment hangs perilously low to the ground, draping his curves in the warm hues of an overripe peach. Not that anyone could make out his dye-work in this awful gloom. Tracy takes a moment to wallow in his misfortune as he frees a ribbon from his braids to hitch the fine tunic up his hips. Better wrinkled than soiled.

Hans grunts as he hefts a rusted shovel from under his seat. "Stretch your legs while I dig us out. Should be safe. It's probably too early for weretoads."

"Probably?" Weretoads are rat-sized menaces prone to nip off a toe or two if a passerby treads too close to their burrows. They're most ornery when they emerge from hibernation in summer. It's only spring, but Tracy doesn't take his eyes off his boots as he picks across the soggy ground. One leather-clad toe nudges a flickering firefly cluster, but the insects don't budge. "Strange," he mutters, clutching his tunic tighter about his hips before dropping to a squat for closer inspection.

The fireflies are not frozen; they are trapped. Each tiny life sticks fast to dew-speckled tendrils that curl at the end like young ferns. The insects' dying golden light refracts through the dewdrops, casting a macabre prism across the iridescent wings of snared moths. Just beyond the faint pool of light, another plant emits its own eerie glow. The lights trail away from the main path, gradually coalescing into a misty aura filtering through backlit tree trunks. Tracy is not a superstitious man, but he can't deny the way the sight sends static prickling up his neck. This path is paved with death.

He turns back to ask Hans about the plants, rendered temporarily blind as his eyes readjust to perpetual twilight. His question dies on his tongue as a tense scene takes shape before him. Hans was wrong about the weretoads.

Hans draws his knife, but Tracy doubts it will be much help. The driver stands between the horse and the nastiest weretoad Tracy has ever seen. The beast is a dog-sized, hulking monstrosity. The scene only becomes more grotesque as his eyes accommodate further. Bloody sclerae melt and weave like spun fibers into swampmoss in a revolting, pulsating mess ribboning from twin eye sockets. More mucoid moss oozes from the toad's fanged maw. Tracy stands frozen before an unnatural abomination of plant and beast that should be confined to storybooks.

Benny stamps the ground and the monster locks onto the movement. The weretoad lunges at Hans just as the horse bolts, overturning the cart in their wake. Their expensive cargo spills, forgotten, into the muck. Tracy blinks, and Hans is half-enveloped in the weretoad's fleshy mass. The thing's saliva melts his skin like acid. Each flailing attempt to free himself tears his own viscera. In seconds, Tracy cannot tell where the monster ends and Hans begins. The thing writhes in agony, Hans's cries morphing into grating croaks. "Ben...ny–" the thing rasps in a stricken death rattle. A malformed appendage reaches towards the sound of retreating hoofbeats, then sloughs off the mass with the sickening elastic snap of ruptured sinew. Finally, the last distinguishable bit of Hans is enveloped in the creature. Hans, as Tracy knew him, is gone.

Tracy's mind spirals into blinding white noise. He would be sick, but he has lost all sense of connection with his body. He wants to run, but he has no legs to command. He is reduced to quivering nerves and eyes glued to this impossible horror.

"Fuck," someone croaks. It sounds like Tracy, but he cannot be certain he still has a mouth.

The abomination whirls toward the sound, flinging clumps of moist earth across pristine silk. This desecration yanks Tracy back into his body just as the weretoad surges forward. Hot rage meets icy fear in his gut, sending a thunderclap of adrenaline through his system. He's moving before his mind fully registers the threat, crushing delicate biota beneath his heels in his desperate flight. Slick sludge gives under him and his knees crash to the ground, splattering him in more filth. He throws himself forward, raking his nails through the mud for purchase. He grabs a clump of curling tendrils and, mercifully, the roots hold. Tracy hauls himself up and scrambles toward the glow, driven by animal instinct to seek safety in light. He can no longer hear the monster at his heels through the roaring pulse in his ears.

Each foothold becomes easier even as his adrenaline wanes and his strength begins to flag. The plants are thicker here, their dense roots providing sufficient leverage to propel him onward. Each breath rakes a harsher coal-hot wheeze from his lungs until his body finally fails him. His arms fling out to catch himself but his palms slide across the slick dew, sending him sprawling. With the last of his strength, Tracy rolls himself onto his back. The glow is stronger here, reflecting off the canopy like firelight. Shadows blur and swirl above him as his eyes fight and fail to focus.

Tendrils sway above him like kelp in a gentle tide. A tattered Luna moth perches atop one to sip at glistening nectar. The elegant creature seals its fate the moment pale wings brush cool dew. Sated, the insect attempts to take flight. Fails. It struggles against the plant's deadly grasp, shimmering scales tearing from its soft body. Tracy feels a woozy smile tug across his lips as he watches, drunk on depletion. In this dark place, plants thrive on such humble sacrifice. They can reform a lowly insect into a fragrant, blush-pink inflorescence. Hans, Benny, and the monster are already distant memories. Tracy was mistaken: this is not a place of death. He is witnessing life renewed, transformed. He fans his fingers across soft, wet vegetation. Closing his eyes, he revels in the sensation of cool dew across his skin. A sour tang of envy poisons his exhausted stupor: if only he were a tiny creature, destined to become part of something greater. If he lies here forever, will he be consumed, too? As his mind's hold on consciousness begins to slip, Tracy imagines he can feel the delicious burn of dew dissolving into his skin.

"**H**ello, little moth," a gentle voice, edges course with disuse, nudges Tracy's eyes open.

A figure looms over him, backlit by the soft glow of dying fireflies. Tracy blinks slowly, too drained to startle. His body is leaden, pressed flush to lush foliage. He cannot make out the person's eyes in the wavering shadows, but he feels the heat of their gaze creeping up his thighs and settling on his hips. Too late, he realizes his tunic has ridden up past his hips.

"Oh!" He lurches up to smooth his soaked silks and recover some decency. He must look like a drunken harlot. Face burning with shame, Tracy turns to get a better look at this stranger.

He finds himself knee-to-knee with a god. All other explanations fall short of the glory before him. Eyes of translucent, green-tinged jelly. Skin of pale mint with prominent, verdant veins. Bare except for locks of rose-stained tendrils spilling down their chest and shoulders. Their hair closely resembles the carnivorous flora, frizzing with fine, dew-studded fibers that glisten like jewels in the firefly-light.

"What are you?" Tracy gasps before he thinks better of it.

That earns him an amused huff. "You may call me Drosera, he, or they. What are you?"

"Tracy. He or him," he offers without hesitation, hoping this is real, that there is truth to tales of magic and name-stealing fae. He would surrender the moniker in a heartbeat for the smallest taste of possibility.

"He." Wonder lights Drosera's blank eyes. "We are not so different, then. Well-met." A nearby tendril unfurls to take Tracy's hand, causing him to startle.

"Oh! Is that yours?" Tracy suppresses the impulse to free his hand from the plant's ticklish grasp.

"Yes, I'm—" A horrible croak interrupts Drosera's explanation, striking fear through Tracy's heart. The mutant weretoad heaves itself gracelessly towards them, chasing their voices. Tracy turns to flee but is anchored to the spot by the tendril's deceptive strength. He is a fly caught fast in a predator's web.

"Calm yourself, little moth. He's harmless." Drosera smiles patiently, chiding Tracy as if he were a child.

"He ate Hans." Befuddlement muddies Tracy's terror.

"Ah, friend of yours? Rest assured, Hans hasn't gone anywhere. He's simply been...integrated. Seems we now have a friend in common."

"What did it do to him?" Tracy ceases his attempts to flee to eye the monstrosity. A man died to birth this horror. Drosera's levity should be dissonant to Tracy's ears. Instead, he feels more curiosity than disgust when he meets too-human eyes peering back from its bloody sockets.

"Nothing malicious, just magic: my experiment in accelerated evolution. I fed him a Transformation charm that recycles his prey into new adaptations." Drosera squeezes Tracy's hand, reminding him he remains tethered.

"That is...incredible," Tracy murmurs, awestruck by this revelation: that Transformation magic is real.

"Thank you." Drosera watches the beast with a sad smile. "Too many hate what they do not understand. I worked as an apothecary in a former life, specializing in tinctures made from bog flora. I loved my work and tried to love my neighbors, but they grew to resent my differences despite relying on my labor. One day, a man cornered me and threatened to 'fix' me by force. I called on my Transformation magic and my beloved sundew answered. Did you know that some plants eat meat?" They paused, and Tracy felt their grin mirrored on his own face. "Ironic, how the same people who tried to rob me of my humanity called me a monster when I surrendered it freely. They othered me, so I found euphoria in being 'other.'"

"Euphoria," Tracy breathes. That smoldering hope in his heart roars into a blaze. He is consumed by that familiar, inexplicable draw towards evolution. He cannot deny the way his heart races when he takes in this new possibility.

"I sensed you would understand." Relief washes over Drosera, easing a tension Tracy had not noticed they held in their shoulders.

"Could you do it again? Transform someone else?" Tracy's elation awakens that familiar, bone-deep hunger.

He must hide it poorly, for Drosera's demeanor curdles into distrust. "I'm sorry, no."

"I'll give you anything you want." Tracy reaches for his satchel. "Gold, silk–"

"Such powerful magic is not to be used lightly." Their eyes turn downcast, avoiding his intense gaze.

"You made the frog," Tracy counters, jaw set in a stubborn line.

"A frog is not a man. I will not be accused of corrupting men into monsters." Drosera jerks to their feet, releasing Tracy's hand. Fragile roots snap between their body and the earth.

"Wait," Tracy grasps at the roots in a panic, scarred fingers slippery with dew.

Drosera's lips curl into a derisive snarl. "Perhaps I have not made myself clear: I no longer suffer those who would use me for their own fulfillment." Drosera tries to retreat, but Tracy outflanks them and yanks a fistful of their locks.

"I will tell." Tracy's eyes go hard. "They think you are a monster and know you are a murderer. They will slay you and mount your head as a trophy." Unless Drosera slays him first, a wager he is desperate enough to make. Before him is proof of all he desires: a sinful power he feared would be confined to fables and his own restless dreams. Who is this creature to deny him Transformation?

Drosera stills, verdant flush draining into pallor. "You truly are a man," they bite out. "Willing to seize what you feel entitled to."

A thrill shivers down Tracy's spine: the threats are working. Every instinct screams for him to take it back or run, but some insane fragment of his mind yanks the reins, urging him on.

"Is it not selfish to stand in the way of evolution? To tie the hands of creation? Change me. We can be gods together," Tracy cares not that he sounds mad. This magic is the culmination of years of longing for a future he was told was mere fiction. "Transform me," a whispered demand, all clutching hands and crazed eyes.

Drosera continues to stare wordlessly at him. For a long, agonizing moment, the air hangs empty between them. Slowly, languidly, a cherry-kissed spiral unfurls from their locks, not quite unwound when it reaches Tracy's fingertips. Cool dew brushes his knuckles, the touch so tender he involuntarily releases his grip. Syrupy fibers of dew stretch and break between his fingers and the crushed tendrils.

"You will give anything?" Drosera's tone is a warning. The tendril snakes through Tracy's fingers, leaving a slick trail that sends an unexpected wave of nausea through his belly.

"Yes." Tracy stares unflinchingly into Drosera's eyes, squaring his shoulders in the face of their rage. He will ascend at last. His heady delight lasts but a moment before a sickening *crack* pierces his skull. High-pitched whining drowns out all other senses for three slow heartbeats. He blinks uncomprehendingly, shock-addled brain struggling to reconcile sound and sensation. Slowly, through an adrenaline-laced haze, his gaze drops to where his fingers meet Drosera's appendage. Blood swells between pinkish ridges of bone, smooth and slick, pulsing gently with the roar in his ears. Crimson wicks along fine fibers, swirling through dewdrops like liquid smoke. Tracy can only stare, helpless, at the mangled mess of his left hand. He barely registers Drosera's words. The sweet nectar coating his skin turns against him. The split flesh of his knuckles sloughs off in soft wrinkles where tissue meets enzyme. The gnarled appendage curls into Tracy's chest, curdled flesh smearing his handcrafted silk tunic. From raw, bony fingertip to throbbing forearm, he is nothing but seething anguish. He inhales, exhales "no..." through numb lips.

Drosera scoffs, unceremoniously dropping the limb. "See how your resolve breaks at the first blush of pain." Their expression softens but their words remain firm. "I feel your desperation with my own heart, but I will not allow you to exploit me. Leave with your life and learn from the scars of your hubris."

Unleashed, Tracy stumbles into a run. He nearly reaches the path when the agony in his arm recedes into throbbing numbness, allowing scraps of thought to reform into something coherent. Drosera's pretty words cannot distract him from his destiny. His pain is merely proof of the Witch's power. His lip quirks, something between a grimace and a smirk. "No." His voice is raspy with determination. He recenters himself, focuses on breathing. With slow, controlled steps, he turns back to that glistening, verdant field of death. He is a moth drawn to poisoned nectar. Nothing will stop him from drinking his fill.

When he reaches the trampled vegetation, Drosera is gone. Except Tracy knows that isn't true. These plants are part of them: symbiotic organisms.

"Damn the pain! I will not leave until you change me or kill me." He yanks fistfuls of fragile flora from the earth until, at last, a familiar tendril traps his raw hand. Caustic dew sinks into the scabbing crevices. The burn returns with a vengeance, searing into his shredded flesh and causing ragged edges to melt together. Tracy is being digested inch by inch, but this time he welcomes dissolution.

Drosera resolves from the shadows, eyes blazing with fury. "Very well. You seek transformation? Then know what it means to be unmade." Their anger is music to Tracy's ears. Rosy fibers wilt into Tracy's bones, pooling in vibrant splotches below the rippling surface. "I will unravel you and remake you in my image."

Tracy watches, transfixed, as their bodies meld without seams, twin rivers of cells flowing into one. He releases a pent-up sigh at the same time Drosera grimaces and he knows: they feel it, too. Nerve fibers splicing, intertwining. Threads of green climb Tracy's arm like a trellis, forming lacy, organic patterns in their wake. They arch around his shoulder and dive out of sight beneath his sleeve. He traces their progress as their numb ache delves beneath his sternum and pulses within his breasts. An unseen, icy grip shocks his heart into a stutter along with his resolve. What remains of his left arm twitches with an involuntary instinct to clutch at his chest. For several long seconds the roar in his ears goes quiet, panic stealing the breath from his lungs.

His eyes catch Drosera's cold gaze, pleading for mercy as the edges of his vision go up in smoke. Something has gone very wrong, unless they truly intend to kill him. *Please*, his hypoxic brain screams the word that never makes it past his lips as his world fades to black. Is this what his silkworms feel just before his deft fingers tear their souls apart? Tracy succumbs within his cocoon.

Sensation resumes first. That icy ache pulses with each slow heartbeat as if it never fully abated. Tracy is uncomfortably aware of his blood; it feels thicker, somehow. His heart contracts hard and slow to force the syrup through his arteries. A wave of relief passes over him when he notices that his left arm doesn't hurt anymore, followed by the cold realization that he can't sense his arm at all. He reaches out with his mind and senses his limbs are incorrect. He tries and fails to open his eyes, unsure whether he still has eyes at all.

Sound seeps in next. Distant birdsong comes in a strange, four-dimensional echo that only serves to disorient him further.

Sight returns at last. Tracy's eyelids feel mossy. He grunts with the effort to open them, squinting into a golden glare. The sun has set and the fireflies blaze impossibly bright against the ink-black shadows. How long has he been at Drosera's mercy?

Dread courses through Tracy's sluggish heart. Has he made a mistake? Slowly, he surveys the wreckage of himself. Silk hangs off his frame in pieces, stretched to the point of tearing. The fabric has melted into his skin, painting him with shimmering peach filigree. He takes in his bare chest with a startled gasp: his breasts are gone, leaving only the soft swell of pectoral muscles. Tracy is mesmerized by the rise and fall of his breaths, a confusion of terror and elation surging through him. Nausea follows close on its heels. Just beyond his navel, fuzzy lepidopteran appendages anchor him to the earth. His back bows under unseen dead weight as if a heavy tapestry has been thrown across his shoulders. The weight recedes with each heave of his remade chest. He can feel delicate wings unfurling, expanding beyond his previous boundaries. Novel sensations whispering along the periphery of his consciousness.

"What did you do to me?"

"Since you forced my hand, little moth, I made do with the materials I had available. It required a bit of improvisation, but I think this form is fitting." Dorsera's words are clipped with a hint of regret. "However, since you do not possess arcane abilities, the Transformation is impermanent. High-energy spells degrade without a steady supply of magic."

Tracy tests the bounds of these alien limbs. Insectoid legs reach in sync with his human arms across the darkness separating himself from Drosera, making tentative contact with their chlorophyll-stained skin. Tiny hairs brush across their chest, mapping their form with new neural connections. Elation wins the battle for his heart. Tracy settles into this upheaval of his body, his senses, and his mind. Everything is strange and unsettling and undeniably right. He will not permit devolution. "Then you will use your magic to make it permanent. I will take it, if I must."

"You are insufferable. I ought to let you fall apart." Drosera eyes him with contempt. They try to pull away but yank Tracy with them, stuck fast to him by their own dew.

"Yet you will not." Emboldened, Tracy leans in to test how far he can push them. His lips brush past their cheek as if to steal a kiss when he is possessed by a sudden invertebrate instinct to consume. He clasps his teeth around shimmering locks. Crisp flesh gives under the crush of his jaw, sweet sap turning acrid on his tongue. Drosera cries out, tendrils thrashing against the assault of his embrace. The bite of wet lashes against his fragile new form only stokes his primal desire. He begins to chew. Drosera stills against him, carnivorous tendrils caught in iridescent vellum wings. Tracy swallows down mouthful after mouthful of exquisite vegetation, blurring the line of predator and prey.

Tracy feels a slick jab tendril between his ribs just below his left clavicle. He leans into the sting of melting flesh. In that moment, he no longer needs words to convey his gratitude for their gift of corruption. He will take and be taken. The sentiment pulses through their connected bodies with each sluggish heartbeat.

Drosera slowly presses into him. Tracy closes his eyes as his flesh parts for them, the wound oozing bitter hemolymph. The pain is exquisite, all-consuming, far more sensual than anything he felt between his legs in his former body. Driven by lust and loathing, Dosera heeds his unspoken invitation. A second tendril laps along his intercostal muscles, sending electricity twitching through each sanguine fiber. Tracy involuntarily curls and spasms around them even as his mind begs them for more. They eagerly assent, more tendrils working their way under his skin. They work his tense muscles open even as his body fights against this welcome violation. Soft whimpers escape Tracy's lips as Drosera thrusts deeper. The wet squelch of blood and dew and dissolving flesh threatens to send him over the edge of ecstasy.

Just when Tracy assumes Drosera is fully seated within him, they surge forward with unexpected force. He feels more than hears them rip through fascia and pierce into a rubbery sac in his very core. His breath stutters as they press on, emboldened by the way his body finally goes slack around them. Tracy coughs iron and salt, feeling Drosera's grip tighten with each weak convulsion of his lungs. His last shred of sanity begs them to stop but his heart urges them to take more. They begin to pull. Gentle traction turns firm, wrenching something hot and quivering and vital from Tracy's body. The muscle pulses and stretches against the dripping orifice of his chest before pulling free with a wet sucking sound. The sound stirs an unexpected heat between his legs. Either his nerve endings have been rearranged, or his brain is too dizzy with endorphins to register any real pain.

Tracy is boneless, supported only by Drosera's strong arms. Between them, cradled in a viridian bed of dew-kissed tendrils, a mauve muscle twitches in sickening synchronicity with his heartbeat. He watches as the dew works its way into the organ. The flesh dissolves into a pool of deep crimson, seeping into the slick tendrils like water to a taproot. Fueled by Tracy's life force, new sprouts begin to grow from the wounds he inflicted upon Drosera's flesh.

"Did you just– My heart–?"

"Do not fret, little moth, I am only complying with your demands. Your human heart was vestigial to your new body." They punctuate their words with a slow stroke along his sternum. "However, if you were to betray my trust, if I were to rescind my magic and force your body to revert…How long do you wager a man can live with stagnant blood in his veins?"

Tracy inhales to protest that he would never renounce this gift, humid air whistling through the hole in his chest. Drosera silences him with a bloodstained tendril pressed to Tracy's lips.

"You seek to bind me, and I seek reciprocity. Use me, and I will use you. Consume me, and I will consume you. I bind you to me in symbiosis."

The promise reignites that bone-deep desire within Tracy's new body. His lips part and his tongue ventures forth to taste Drosera's divinity. Their nectar coats his mouth like honey made sweeter with the salt of his own blood. He welcomes them deeper, shudders as they probe past his teeth to caress his palate with downy fibers. Insect urges bid him to close the vice of his jaw and take sustenance from their offering. Still more primal hunger pries him open wider, pleading for him to take and be taken in transnatural communion. Tracy's wanton gags muffle around the press of foliage past his uvula, sending his throat into involuntary spasms against the intrusion. He can only submit to Drosera's hungry gaze as they delve deeper, spreading his vocal cords to silence his plaintive whines. He raises shaking fingers to his abdomen when something curls within his belly. Tracy has starved his entire life. At last, he knows satiety. His insides soften under Drosera's caustic touch, their body remaking his anew.

He willingly settles into their embrace, fragile wings caught in the sundew's trap. Their bodies meld into a cycle of destruction and creation, each iteration closer to perfection.

You Know What Happens After Dark

By Aaron Romano

I

The voice in the closet came back the night after Eddie called to tell her he was sick. It was a relief at first to hear his voice, before he told her. She hadn't heard from Eddie in nearly two months and was worried he'd gotten hurt or arrested. Eddie, her blonde muscle stud, nearly ten years her junior in his early thirties and still radiating youthful strength. She couldn't reconcile the image with the withered specter she associated with the disease. She'd seen so many people she loved go like that – shriveled away, their flesh brittle and prone to sores.

"Where are you?" She asked, "Why haven't you called sooner?"

"I'm in Chippewa Falls." He sounded so tired.

"Is that upstate? I can rent a car, Eddie, just tell me where–"

"Wisconsin. I ran home to my fucking mother. Don't come here, Sylvia." Then he hung up.

He never said goodbye.

Perhaps that was too close to acknowledging that it was for the last time, not in their relationship but in his life. Sylvia sat on her couch staring down at the pink cordless phone she still held in her hand. On the television, turned down low, the news reported an increased danger of civil war in Iraq.

Eventually the sun went down and the room grew dark and she drifted into bed. She lay awake, staring at the ceiling, listening to the strange music of sirens and car horns and the cries of all-night hotdog vendors. The voice showed up around two in the morning from behind the white, slatted folding door of her closet.

"He gave it to you, you know."

It startled her so intensely that she sat up in bed. The voice hadn't said so much as peep in seven years. Not since she threw out Jorge back in '99 because she couldn't deal with his particular brand of crazy anymore. She stared at the closed closet door, waiting for the voice behind it to say something else. Beneath her oversized sleep shirt, she felt a cold drop of sweat trickle down her spine.

"You're gonna go like all the rest, wasting away. By the end you'll make a holocaust victim look like a beauty queen."

"Fuck you," she whispered harshly. "Just fuck you. You don't know shit."

"Ok," the voice responded. She could hear the smirk around the words. "Ok, Miss Twist, we'll see."

II

Sylvia attended her first ball at the Harlem Elks Lodge when she was seventeen. That was back in '83 and she was still living as Lenny Rivera then. It wasn't exactly that she saw herself as a man so much as she wasn't yet aware she was a woman. What she saw that night amazed her. It wasn't the kind of ball she imagined like with white people in a BBC production late at night on PBS – though some people were dressed in similar attire. It was more like a Carnivale, overflowing with sequins and rhinestones and plumes of colored ostrich feathers. The house was packed way beyond the fire code, filled with men dressed as women and women dressed as men and those who tread the tightrope somewhere in between. There were people dressed in evening attire and in all black leather, in military uniforms and latex body suits. There was a young man wearing full riding clothes with a horsewhip in his hand and beside him a waifish teen dressed like a horse.

Each person in costume had a chance to flaunt and pose before the crowd, to receive their approval or their judgement. Many of the performers belonged together in cliques that the MC called "Houses." House LaBeija. House Pendavis. House Dupree. House Xtravaganza. To Sylvia it was almost like hearing her junior history teacher list off the combatants in the Wars of the Roses. When a trophy and a cash prize was bestowed upon the best dressed queen, Sylvia envisioned a future for herself that she'd never imagined.

It was that same night, filing out of the Elks Hall, that she first met Joe Giordano. Their bodies collided and their eyes met, and Joe grinned down at her. He shouted, "This is fucking nuts!" before he wrapped his arm around Sylvia's waist, flung the elbow of his free arm square in the back of a teenage boy dressed as Walt Disney's Cinderella and forced their way out to the street together.

"Thanks," Sylvia said. "I'd have been trampled."

"My pleasure," he clapped Sylvia on the back. "My name's Joe, well Joseph, but you can call me Joe if you want to."

"Well, thanks, Joe." Sylvia waved awkwardly.

"You got a name, boy? I mean your real name, not some fairy shit."

"I–I'm Lenny Rivera."

Joe's eyes narrowed. "Mexican? You ain't got an accent."

"Puerto Rico. My family moved to the States when I was two."

"My parents are from Sicily." Joe said as if that were remotely the same part of the world. "You wanna go get something to eat with me, Lenny?"

She liked the thick Brooklynn honk of his voice and his broad, muscular chest and shoulders. He was actually quite handsome, she decided, with thick, black hair and moody, dark eyes. She realized as she appraised him that she'd never slept with an Italian—or any kind of white boy for that matter—and had heard conflicting rumors. In part to satisfy her own curiosity, she took his hand and said, "Sure, Joe, I could use a bite to eat."

III

The morning after Eddie called Sylvia woke up, opened her bedroom window and leaned out on her fire escape. She wondered if the four story fall would kill her. It was a damp, gray day. In the distance towards midtown she could see the tower of Rockefeller Center vanish into a low hanging cloud. She supposed she had to go to the health center.

At Mount Sinai there was the usual disheartening combination of suspicion, judgement and a plethora of documentation written only for men born as men and women born as women. There were no boxes to check for anyone like her. When it was finally sorted out and she was sent to an examination room, she was visited by two doctors, a man and a woman. They both talked and stumbled over each other, neither entirely sure who was acting as chaperone for whom. Though they knew why they were there, both doctors' stunned silence after they asked her to remove her clothes belied their unfamiliarity with trans bodies.

"Are those implants?" The male doctor pointed to her chest, forgetting himself.

"No," Sylvia unconsciously crossed her arms over her breasts. "It was all hormones."

"Hell of a thing," he said, before suddenly recollecting where he was. He looked down in real embarrassment only to realize he was staring at her penis. Then he planted his eyes firmly on his shoes and allowed his colleague to take the reins.

The other doctor, the woman, poked and prodded and swabbed her. She drew Sylvia's blood, asked about the function of her genitals and palpated her breasts for lumps. When Sylvia was mercifully allowed to redress, they asked Sylvia if she regularly had homosexual sex while they ticked off a list of questions.

"I have sex with men," she said. "How they identify is their own business."

The male doctor blinked. "What does that mean?"

"Well, some are straight and some aren't."

They didn't ask her any more questions after that, just told her the HIV blood work would be back in a week and sent her on her way. When she got back to her apartment, she flung her bag on the couch and retreated to her bedroom where she plopped down heavily on the cushioned stool at the vanity across from her bed. She poured over her reflection for any hint of sickness in her features but only managed to find a few new grays in her long, black hair. She looked no more or less healthy than usual. Then her eye caught the closet door reflected behind her and she went cold all over while she waited for the voice's opinion. There was a soft chuckle and a sound like weight shifting in the dark. The door faintly shuddered in its frame.

II

By '85 Sylvia was a rising queen in the House of Twist. Lemon Twist, who by day was Marcus Campbell and at night took the stage as six and a half feet of yellow clad Female Black Excellence, became her mother in all things drag. Lemon taught Sylvia how to paint her face, how to style a wig, how to sew, walk in heels, design a look. Publicly she left the name Lenny Rivera behind forever. She took up the Twist family moniker and chose the name

Sylvia after her paternal grandmother. At home, in private, Joe still called her Lenny but the name seemed increasingly foreign to her, more and more detached from who she felt herself to be.

She performed well, won prizes at the balls and made her drag mother proud.

"That's my fucking daughter!" She'd hear Lemon screaming in the audience from beneath an enormous, banana-yellow updo.

Increasingly, she felt herself becoming Sylvia. What she experienced on stage decked in velveteen and rhinestones felt correct – and impossible to ignore. No matter how tired or uncomfortable she was during a performance, she found herself unwilling to get out of drag when it was over and did so only reluctantly. Outside of drag she began to grow out her hair and in a matter of time it spilled over her shoulders in glossy black curls. For a time, it eased the sense of a widening fissure between the two halves of herself and Joe seemed to enjoy it at first. In bed, as she lowered herself on her hands and knees beneath him, Joe would seize a fistful of her hair and pull back her head to kiss her from behind while forcing her spine into a more perfect arch. It cheered her that her longer hair pleased him, and she relished the tender approval in the squeeze of his blunt, strong hands.

But when she eventually asked him to start calling her Sylvia outside of work, he expressed discomfort and ultimately refused.

I

She cancelled all her gigs for the week she'd spend waiting on her test results and told everyone she had a summer flu. Then she stocked up on trash food and instant meals from the bodega around the corner and sealed herself in the apartment. Unable to bring herself to do anything, not even read or watch TV, she paced the apartment and drove her downstairs neighbors crazy.

It wasn't her first HIV scare. She'd had one in '92, the same year Lemon died right after Easter. Her behavior then hadn't been much different. She'd been alone then, too, wouldn't meet Jorge for another three years. The voice had come for her then as well, sniggering from the bedroom closet.

When she wasn't pacing, she spent her days in bed waiting for the call from Mount Sinai. But the phone remained maddeningly silent.

"How do you think it will happen?" The voice jeered, "Pneumonia? Hepatitis? Maybe tuberculosis?"

"Shut up," Sylvia hissed at the faintly quivering door.

"You'll probably just get cancer like your drag momma."

"I said shut up!" Sylvia shouted, flinging her alarm clock towards the closet door, the unbidden image of the husk that Lemon Twist became flashing in her mind. The clock struck the closet door, shattering its glass face.

II

In '87 she trained her first drag daughter, a five foot tall, eighteen year old Panamanian chica who she dubbed Cha-Cha Twist. She hosted a coming out party for Cha-

Cha at the Elks Lodge and the entirety of the House of Twist was present. Lemon, with one to many 7 and 7s in her, threw her arms around Cha-Cha and screamed, "My Grandbaby!"

Now that was a hell of a night. There was music and good food and dancing. Colored lights hung from the ceiling and flowers were everywhere. The reigning queens of the other Houses attended and, though Sylvia was not house mother to the House of Twist, for that night alone everyone deferred to her as if she were. A couple of famous queens had picked up chatter of the party and poked their noses in as well. She saw Divine that night, enormous and sweating under a white wig like a dollop of cool whip, her staccato laughter hacking through the dense, smoke-filled air. Holly Woodlawn was also there, her face wide and aloof, eyebrows painted in high Dietrich arches. By the end of the night, when it was time for Cha-Cha to perform for all her guests, they finished off the number by dropping seven hundred pink and gold balloons onto the crowd.

Joe was there all night as well, though he spent most of his time floating around the bar. Sylvia hardly had any time to speak with him, so busy was she with the court politics of her world—greeting everyone, trading reads, introducing as many people as possible to Cha-Cha—but every time she swung by to ensure that the bar was well stocked, she stopped to plant a kiss on his cheek.

They made a nice profit off charging guests at the door and, when they finally shut down at four in the morning, Sylvia gave Cha-Cha her cut and sent her off to celebrate with her boyfriend, Hector. It was a damp night, still a few hours before dawn, and the walk home was dreary. Joe looked ill, but when she asked if anything was the matter, he was uncommunicative and sullen. When they got home that night, he punched her in the face so hard he gave her a black eye. She had to cancel gigs for days until the swelling went down. That was the first time he ever hit her. Everything changed after that.

VII

"You deserved it, you know."

"Stop it."

"It's gonna hurt so fucking much."

"Please," she whispered, staring up at the ceiling. "Please stop."

"It'll take forever and by the end every day you'll pray to God to die. You remember how Lemon was."

"I'm begging you. I'm really begging you."

"Do you still pray, Lenny?"

"Fuck you!" There was a dull ache high in her sinuses as tears gathered in the corners of her eyes.

"You better pray, you better start fucking praying right now, Lennymylove—though God never shed tears for any spics and faggots I ever heard of. Did He have any sympathy for Lemon when all her teeth fell out and her skin erupted in sores?" The voice rose steadily in pitch and in volume. "Why should He give a damn about you? You – a shift tranny faggot who stole your abuela's jewelry to buy your way to New York and live like a freak?"

"Stop it!" She screamed. "Stop it! Stop it! Stop it!"

She clasped her hands over her mouth and silence filled up the room. There was a rustle of fabric behind the closet door. The voice affected a dry little laugh.

"Sure, lady, no problem."

VIII

She told Cha-Cha and Lemon first, sat down with them over hot toddies at the round, green table in Lemon's apartment and announced,

"I am a woman."

She said she'd started talking to doctors about hormones and would soon see about changing her name. They both hugged her and laughed joyously as they congratulated her on her epiphany.

"I always knew, girl," Lemon actually wept. "I saw the woman in you the day we met."

Joe didn't see things the same way. Though she wore her hair long and dressed exclusively in women's clothing, he still persisted in calling her Lenny.

"What the fuck do you mean you're a woman?" Joe asked as if he were blind. He stood in his boxers by the fridge, pulling the tab off a can of PBR, his body a stack of corded muscle.

"Goddammit, look at me, do I look like a man?"

Joe lowered the can from his lips and sneered, "Yeah."

She knew he'd say it the moment she asked but it hurt to hear anyway. "I'm going to see a doctor, Joe. I might even have an operation. I'm gonna be me for real."

His beer flew at her so fast she didn't even realize he'd thrown it until after it hit her. The can was still mostly full when it struck her in the face, mashing her nose and forcing two hot squirts of blood from her nostrils. It sprayed cold beer on her as it fell to the kitchen floor where it rolled under the counter, vomiting foam.

She stood before him, wet and bleeding. "And I'm gonna leave you, Joe, I'm gonna leave you."

Then he came at her.

Their bodies collided in the center of the kitchen and immediately they slipped and fell in the spilled beer. The fall stunned Joe and Sylvia used the second it bought her to roll away from him. She swung her arm up and caught hold of the handle of the top-most kitchen drawer to pull herself to her feet, but as she rose to her knees Joe seized hold of her hair and yanked her back. It happened so quickly she had no chance to release the handle and pulled the drawer out of the cabinetting as she fell, scattering silverware across the room.

Joe threw her on her back and sat on her chest. "You stupid fucking faggot." He pulled back a fist and punched her hard in the side of the head, blinding her for an instant. "You really think I'll let you fucking walk out on me?" Then he wrapped both of his hands around her throat.

Sylvia knew his strength and knew there was no point in trying to pry his hands away. She reached out with both arms into the pell-mell of silverware that surrounded them, feeling for anything that could save her. He slammed her head against the floor and for a moment she forgot what she was doing, so stunned was she by the pain. Then her fingers brushed the handle of the paring knife and, almost with an agency of their own, snatched it up and fed the three-inch blade into the soft flesh under Joe's chin.

His eyes grew wide and a distant part of her realized it was the first time she'd ever seen Joe well and truly shocked. He released her immediately and fell away as she came up, choking and gasping for air. There was a dull thud as he slumped back against the fridge, gagging around the unyielding strip of metal lodged in his throat. He looked like he was trying to say something but, instead of words, a glut of crimson burst from his mouth and spilled down his naked chest. Piss darkened the crotch of his boxers and formed a puddle around him. She stood and slumped against the counter and quietly watched him die. She never imagined she could do such a thing. It took three minutes. That was in 1989.

IX

For two days she'd been in constant conversation with the voice. Never before had it been so garrulous; it gave her no peace. It talked through the night and, if she was lucky enough to fall asleep, it was there to wish her good morning when she woke up. She could not get away from it. If she went to the bathroom it would yell, "Better check your urine for blood, huh? You know how it eats the kidneys." She tried escaping it by going out for a walk but the moment she returned it shouted, "Welcome home, Lennyboy!" She wondered if the neighbors heard when it shouted, if they thought she was shacked up with somebody.

"Why?" She asked, lying in the shag rug in her bedroom, "Why won't you stop tormenting me? Why won't you just go away?"

"Don't be childish. I'll always be yours to carry with you everywhere you go and, honey, I am heavy."

"You're not real. You made me crazy with all the shit you put me through and now I'm stuck hearing your voice."

"Baby," the voice said implacably. "I'm as real as the cock in your panties."

"You're not," Sylvia said lamely, sounding as unsure of herself as she felt.

"I can prove it. Look upon me, Leonardo Rivera. Come and See, baby."

She sprang to her feet, suddenly energized by the voice's goading, and flung open the closet door. Yards of brightly colored tulle and satin fell out on her, but she swatted the fabric aside. She pushed past the costumes and evening gowns and capes and feather boas and towers of wig boxes until she found what she was looking for buried in the back right corner of the closet. A trunk of darkly stained walnut held shut with two heavy metal clasps. She bought it at an antique shop back in '89. It took all her strength to drag it from the closet. She paused, panting, waiting for some comment from the voice before she continued but it remained stubbornly silent. When she'd finally caught her breath, she undid both of the latches and opened the trunk.

There was a large object inside sealed within an army green garment bag. There was no way to open it because she'd deliberately snapped off the tongue of the zipper to keep it closed for good. She retrieved a pair of meat scissors from the kitchen and methodically began to cut the bag open. The stench that filled the room once the seal was broken was immediate and powerful. She gagged but she persevered, peeling away the vinyl to reveal a form packed in baking soda and cocooned in layer after layer of cellophane. She tore into the plastic wrap with her bare hands, tearing it away until clumps of the baking soda – discolored an unsavory shade of brown from years of absorbing the unspeakable—spilled out into the chest to expose a mummified head and torso.

It didn't look so much like Joe anymore. It was so withered and frail; the once muscular chest nothing but a husk, the strong arms reduced to little more than twigs. It was the hair that stunned her, still as black and glossy as the day she killed him.

"You can prove it huh?" She hissed, "Not so talkative now."

The desiccated thing that was once Joseph Giordano opened its eyes. They were milky and sightless, but they saw her. The skin of its face cracked and peeled away into a ghastly smile. Its head lolled on its narrow shoulders as one withered arm rose out from the crumbles of befouled baking soda and a skeletal hand encircled her wrist.

"Lenny," it said. "Darling."

The Trade (Hymn to a Crossroads Angel)

By Sera Quim

YOU DON'T KNOW HOW SHE FOUND YOU—
or at least, that's what you say.
In truth, you called her crying,
begged her "Please, take me away.

I cannot live this lying life
of frail obedience;
my body must be built anew,
with blood of Theseus."

She told you what you had to do,
an' you took her words to heart.
Tears soaked through your cotton dress
as you walked into the bar.

The old man looked you over
and deemed you womankind
so you took his shiny pistol
and shot him right between his eyes.

His body weighed you down that night
as God reclaimed his son;
your hands, bloodstained, baptismal red
proved what you had done.

The pilgrimage felt long and tough
under the raging moon,
each step became a mantra:
you'd meet your maker soon.

Buried in the crossroads
between the city lights n' home,
his bones went in the dirt:
a roadside catacomb.

Still bathed in red, you saw her
the woman clad in white—
a life for her, and one for you,
"You're gonna be alright."

Between your legs split up your chest
and underneath your chin,

a chasm open *just* enough
to let the woman in.

She wore your skin, a velvet coat,
a guise to call her own,
her every inch held all of you,
and quivered with each moan.

Her cock, her chest, her rotten kiss
felt more like you than her—
confidence took up your chest;
your selves began to blur.

An orgasm, a little death,
a vibrant, pleasing sin;
she ate your heart and cunt in turn—
"You taste of blood and gin."

A dance, a fight, a hot duet
a vicious tit for tat;
each moment twined you further in
to her midnight sabbat.

When long at last her pincers slowed
and laid your body down
you felt along your breasts and knew
she'd taken off your crown.

"A man at last," you whispered there
into her collarbone.
She shook her head and touched your chest,
traced where she had sewn,

"You've always been the man you are,
I only made it known."

THE LIGHT BEHIND THE BLACK CHRYSALIS

By Carlos Ruiz Santiago

She is perfection made flesh. She is sinuous curves beneath red velvet, eyes of fire in a night drowned in its lack of stars. She is a flame when everything else is extinguished, the comforting closeness, the delicious tension of burning.

She is perfect, and Ethan hates her. Entwined in a flesh-bound embrace, they enter his apartment. They kiss, they touch, though not in the same way. She grabs him, kneads him with hunger. She's drunk, and this was not the ending she expected for the night—horny in the house of a stranger.

Ethan feels her, brushes against her, touches her with the dexterity of a sculptor, the care of an artist. Six hours ago, he didn't know her, and now he is inviting her into his home. He doesn't know why he does it. Out of inertia, out of fear, out of insecurity. To admire her. The truth is closer to fascination than to hatred.

The girl peels off that blue dress with a sweaty kiss, and her bronzed skin gleams with a sour sheen. Curves and flesh—hips, breasts, and lips. It is physical, but also mental. She has lived in that body since she was born, breathes it, and her blood beats to the rhythm the world has set for her. And she smiles now, ignorant and innocent of her sins. She lives without asking for anything in return.

Ethan suppresses a gag as best he can. He hates her—she has always had it so easy. He thinks about grabbing the old bronze pheasant statue he inherited from his grandmother and driving its base into the back of her skull until all that remains of her head is a swirl of blood-matted hair. The mere thought of it disgusts him, not just because of death itself but because of the idea of breaking something so beautiful. Revulsion is a mirror, after all.

The girl gives him a dazed smile and moves closer, oblivious to it all. They lie down on the bed. She rubs against him, and he touches her, feeling her heat, her wetness coating his fingers. Ethan can't get hard—not that it's unusual. The woman barely notices what's happening, and he is grateful when she falls asleep quickly, sparing him from having to go through with it all.

Despite everything, a ravenous fear grips his throat. He worries she'll tell someone from work, a friend, people who ask too many questions. He opens the window and lights a cigarette to calm his anxiety. He looks at the stars and the moon, blue as the macabre hollow in a perfect smile. A void in his heart.

Ethan casts one last glance at the woman sleeping in his bed. He doesn't hate her—he knows that now. He is not like that—he knows that too. It gnaws at him like a tangle of worms.

He.

He smokes a little more, blowing smoke over the city that never stops murmuring, no matter the hour. He closes the window, though he can still hear it.

He.

He.

He already knows what comes next.

Normalcy rises with the sun, moving forward like a splintered wheel. He walks through streets full of eyes. The disguise Ethan has woven over the years is meticulous, a diamond-threaded web that reflects every light that touches it. Tall, strong, well-groomed, wearing long jeans and a shirt that leaves his muscular arms and sculpted torso exposed—the product of years at the gym. A sly gaze and a charming smile.

He.

He crosses the street and looks at the people around him. Them. They always avert their eyes, but he knows that when he isn't looking, they *do* watch him.

And they judge.

They whisper. They analyze.

They speculate.

He enters work and smiles broadly, an exaggerated grin. During his break, he grabs a coffee while chatting with his coworkers about his nighttime exploits. They are all a *he*. They drift away, dogmatic. Ethan recounts what happened, altering the details to suit his disguise, and they all laugh, nudging him with their elbows. A pack of shattered lights—that's how they sound, their faces warping like torn tapestries in an undeveloped negative.

Around him, the office burns. Ethan smiles. He isn't thinking clearly; the chorus overwhelms him. Soon, he must return to work, but those figures with distorted faces—those he (he) calls coworkers—don't disappear. They grin with rigid, paper-thin expressions every time their eyes meet his.

The workday ends, and he returns home to his daily tasks before the sun sets. The faces have merged into a legion of gleaming shadows, a dense storm cloud trailing behind him. A constant presence that only grows as the hours pass, reveling in his mask while scrutinizing what lies beneath. They never succeed, but Ethan always feels like they are close.

And the truth terrifies him.

Only under the layer of unreality that the night bestows does Ethan sit alone, and in the darkness of his room, he allows the disguise to slip slightly from his skin. Then, as usual, he opens a private chat—one of those anonymous corners of the internet where people unleash their perversions. There, he types his name as *Emily*, and for mere moments, he feels free. A power, an ease in being and speaking. Reduced to a mere piece of flesh, crude and emotionless, a fetish to be used and discarded—but alive, real. It's a pale substitute, but for a while, Ethan ceases to be *him*, his brain forgetting everything beyond the cathode glow of his screen.

The change comes when, in the middle of that routine, something intrudes—a pop-up. Ads are always closed out of habit, but this time, the mouse lags, the computer seems to freeze for just a fraction of a second.

A purchase ad. A strange object with poorly formatted text. Ethan reads it and feels a dry chill crawl up his nape—a pause that nails him to the text, to the photo. And to the blue of the purchase link. The messages start coming in, buzzing in his ears.

He clicks the ad.

His head spins.

For the next two and a half weeks, Ethan spends his time thinking he's a foolish idiot.

The sheer stupidity of clicking on a pop-up ad, of entering his details. The darkness of the night and the heat within had clouded his judgment. A fancy way of saying he had fucked up.

Every time he locks his door, he stares at the bolt for a few seconds, his anxiety mounting. He compulsively checks his bank statements, expecting at any moment to see a charge of hundreds of euros. A threat lurking in the shadows—refreshing, in a way. At least it doesn't strike the same wound as the others.

The weeks trickle by like a river of molasses, and his ignorance is shattered one night when he takes out the trash.

Right outside his door sits a cardboard box. It's small, barely a hand and a half across each side, well-sealed, and without a sender or recipient written on any of its six faces.

And yet, there is no doubt in his mind that the box is for him. A pulse throbs at its heart—an echo with a plastic dimension, more akin to what one might hear inside a ribcage than within a massive metal locker, more biological than mechanical.

It wasn't there when he got home from work, and no one had knocked on his door since. There's no way to know how long it has been sitting there, waiting for him in the hallway of his apartment building, within reach of anyone. And yet, Ethan isn't surprised that no one has stolen it, just as he instinctively knows it belongs to him— etched in stone like an undeniable truth. That heartbeat, invisible yet palpable, is an atmosphere Ethan is sure no one could ignore.

He grabs the box and brings it inside. He turns it over, searching for answers in its smooth surfaces. A pungent stench settles in the room, and he isn't sure if it's from the bag of trash he left beside him or something else.

Using a kitchen knife, he opens the box.

White. A mountain of packing pellets shielding a delicate object. He rummages through the filler and finds a single item. The recognition is immediate. Ethan has seen it before—only now, it's free from the low-quality filter of an internet photograph. It's the object he ordered from that pop-up, from that poorly designed website he could never access again. One of those countless dropshipping sites that are born, rot, and die at a breakneck pace.

In his hands, Ethan holds an old-chained pendant bearing a rough stone medallion. It's half the size of his palm and scarcely a finger's width across, yet he feels his arm wanting to give under its weight. A simple, crudely carved circle, depicting a face emerging from another face, which in turn births another—forming a loop, like an ouroboros drawn by a child who never had a childhood. At its center lies a concavity where a small red gem rests, pierced and held in place by a tiny metal cylinder.

That mysterious mineral is as roughly hewn as the rest of the medallion, riddled with pits, imperfections, and sharp burrs, as if its nature were more metallic than crystalline.

Ethan stares, mesmerized, his earlier sense of foolishness consumed by something inexplicable and magnetic.

He (he) feels the medallion watching him as much as he watches it.

Sometimes, things attract one another, foreign feelings meet in conversation, and the pull becomes inevitable.

As unquestionable as his impulse to visit that dubious website was, so too is his urge to place the pendant around his neck.

Its incomprehensible weight digs into the vertebrae in his nape. He feels the somber metal scrape his skin, leaving behind a raw, irritated red.

He runs his fingers over the stone, letting its sinuous curves guide him. Without even looking, with his eyes shut, the electrifying texture seems to move his fingers by its own will. Like rats behind the piper, his fingertips unconsciously follow the carved path—until they reach the crimson gem.

A gentle touch, and it begins to spin around the metal cylinder.

Ethan feels a sharp pull from his fingertips, a sudden yank at his wrist. His hand jerks away on reflex, pain-driven.

The gem does not stop turning. Faster, and faster, as if defying all logic.

A metallic scent floods the room, eclipsing everything else.

Then, the pain.

An indescribable sensation consumes Ethan. Something twists inside him.

Not something. Everything.

His ribs spiral. His blood turns thick and turbulent, like a stormy sea. His muscles unravel and slither like snakes.

Ethan tries to scream, but his throat contorts, amorphous, refusing to let air pass.

He collapses, writhing. His limbs twist one way, his torso another. Every fiber of his being is drawn taut. The pull is immense, the tearing grotesque. Blood rains from every pore, every orifice bursting into jagged splinters of bone laced in scarlet.

No air. His skin darkens to a bruised purple.

Something carves space inside him. He feels it growing, throbbing. Wet and viscous at first, then assured, solid.

His flesh tears in its wake. Blackened nails claw their way outward. His bones yellow, his muscles blacken. Everything falls away with the scent of rot. Ethan is devoured, consumed. Only his eyes remain intact, pupils blown wide, staring without agency.

The bubbling within him ceases. Slowly, the gem slows its spin—until it halts. The tension vanishes. Air rushes in. Ethan lies on the floor for minutes, catatonic.

When he finally decides to stand, he is startled by how light he feels. He takes a few steps, and they feel graceful, sure. From the corner of his eye, he catches the shape of his own hands. His heart hammers.

He runs to the bathroom. Flicks on the yellowed light. Looks in the mirror. It takes a moment to focus—his vision blurs, adjusts. Then, a nervous laugh. He touches his face, needing to confirm it's real. That the reflection doesn't lie.

The only proof he has that he's still *him* is the stone medallion hanging from his neck—and those disbelieving eyes. Perhaps his soul still lingers within these walls of flesh, but he can no longer be called Ethan.

Nor *he*.

Not anymore.

As a child, a boy named Ethan had a very specific obsession. He was mesmerized by the performances of a horror movie actress with skin like snow and eyes a vibrant cosmos. Her name was Dawn. The memory of that old actress became a link between Ethan and his new self, so the woman decided that would be her new name: Dawn. It repeats in her mouth like honey, which makes her like it even more.

Dawn buys new clothes that fit her new curves, her sinuous shape, enhancing her lips, her cheekbones, her hips, and waist. She gazes at herself for hours in mirrors as if her flesh were marble from a Bernini sculpture. She is perfect, mind made flesh, soul revealed. She is a she.

She.

The word on her lips dissolves like shredded, hot flesh. She puts on her clothes and leaves. She walks under the sun and feels the caress of the rays and the furtive glances. The lightness of her steps intoxicates her. Dawn is free, she is finally herself.

Night falls, and she enjoys its cold and vibrant caress as well. The strobe lights of the bars and nightclubs. She dances. She sways like a possessed doll. She lets herself be and be done to. Beams of light wander between the sweaty flesh. Hands brush her shoulders. They slide down her waist. Dawn only enjoys. She turns and smiles. She leans and reclines. She kisses, bites, and touches. She enjoys. She fills herself with herself and with others. She feels alive.

Everything vibrates. Everything resonates. The necklace sways to her rhythm, tightened by the fabric of her dress. The stone is not cold, it pulses with her. She almost doesn't distinguish it as something external.

She approaches the bar to drink something. A drink that mixes greens with yellows and orange embers. She takes a good sip without asking its name, and a warmth with fruity tones runs down her body. She taps her heels a little more on the blue floor, and the golden light from the bar frames her silhouette like a goddess.

Her knee trembles, and the woman stumbles. She regains her balance. Dawn isn't surprised to have tripped over something; the place is packed. Her smile returns, reddish, and she advances with her eyes framed in blue and cheeks in pink. Then she trips again. This time it's worse, and she falls flat on her face.

She looks back. Confirms her feelings. Grayish fingers have torn a shadow and gripped her ankle. Her heart gallops up to her throat. The woman frees herself. She stands up as best as she can. She looks around. The world detaches. The corners melt.

Red eyes watch her. They move, slimy. Shapes begin to be distinguished. They look like people, but they're not. Neither him nor her. Nothing in between, alien things hard as ash and ice.

The specters advance through the crowd. No one makes an effort to see or feel them. They look like people, anthropomorphic chrysalids. Fragile, torn. They point at her. They surround her. Dawn turns, frantic, from side to side. They get closer.

Everyone dances except them. Chrysalids of death. They smell her. They are drawn to her. She doesn't know why. Or maybe she does. They don't take their eyes off her.

Her.

Her she.

Maybe they envy her. They hate her, for sure.

Dawn runs. She tries to escape, but the beings block her way. She tries to slip through the fire exit, but shadows accumulate in it, and monsters emerge. Long fingers with gaps at the tips like black suns.

Dawn flees, seeking refuge in the bathrooms. She breathes something. Through the repetitive thudding of the music, she hears their footsteps. They sound like stones hitting the surface of water, trash bags filled with gelatin.

The bathroom door creaks open. Dawn hugs her legs. She cries. She freezes. Smoldering bone claws scrape the door. They corner her. They are there.

Dawn presses her hands together. A silent prayer to someone she doesn't believe in, nor hears anyone else's pleas. Her door trembles. The metal of the latch weakens. They see her through the wood. Through the flesh.

The fingers touch the necklace. Dawn exhales in a whistle. She pulls out the necklace. The shadows gather. She spins the gem. Dawn feels something fast, an ongoing vomit reduced to a fraction of a second, the tearing of fabric and pulling of hair in a dry snap.

The bathroom door opens.

Silence.

Before Ethan, now just Ethan, there is only a smear of dark blood with a rotten stench. No trace of monsters. No one is watching him anymore.

He breathes with difficulty, lying on the bathroom floor. He cries silently.

A girl enters. She calls him perverted and screams. Ethan tries to run, but the dress won't let him move fast enough. Some men catch him and beat him, hard knuckles and cold soles.

No one looks at him.

The cotton separates with a caustic kiss from Ethan's skin (him, him again). It leaves microfibers in the remnants of dried blood, threatening infection. The boy grits his teeth and holds on. Trembling, he touches the softened gap where his rib pieces dwell. A storm of bruises degrades his skin from purple to black, passing through various shades of yellow. His lip trembles, his eyes itch. Nevertheless, the worst blows come to his mind.

The image of the red eyes watching him, of the twisted, withered hands rising towards him. Towards her, actually. They smelled her, like hounds. They looked like burned paper, but they conveyed much more, a dense atmosphere of pure horror. Inexplicable, inextricable. They chased her, like hounds, with clear intentions and blunt methods.

Ethan sits on the toilet and gazes at the pendant whose arcane medallion rests on the basin. The cluster of shapeless faces watches him, stained with water, iodine, and blood. He will never wear it again. Ethan repeats this over and over. No more pleasure, not even happiness. Never again.

God had decided that his life must be one too bitter to swallow without breathing. The sweet aftertaste on his palate was something he would have to learn to live with, to ignore. He couldn't risk living that again. That blessing that came hand in hand with a macabre curse, for the world is cruel, and his happiness attracted hatred. And the monsters always lurk.

Always.

Dawn eats sushi in a small restaurant on a street parallel to the main avenue in the downtown area. Her body lives, she feels it vibrate.

She existed.

She had kept it inside her like a pile of vomit, but containing it was sulfuric for the heart. She saw no need to justify her existence, to resort to that other self, that him. She hated him, and once she had tasted the sweetness of being herself, returning to Ethan felt repulsive. An old, rubbery skin that mimicked life and happiness. No, that was nothing worth revisiting.

A thick clot stains what's left of her tempura vegetables. Black like septic blood, bubbling like a cauldron. Two heavy drops accompany the first. Dawn looks up to find herself face to face with the dissolving ceiling, and one of those Mephistophelean figures emerges from it. A body, a gray chrysalis with red eyes that watches her, furious at her mere existence. It extends a single arm towards her, famished.

Dawn runs. She slips through the early night, between straight streets and spirals. The creatures separate from the shadows. In an instant, they don't exist, and in the next, they spring up like weeds. They surround her and chase her, hunting dogs imitating human form.

The creatures don't run, though they always shorten the distance. Each corner tighter, each street shorter. The entities make no noise beyond the cracking of their joints with every movement. Their intense gaze follows her.

Dawn squeezes through the alleys. No exit, a stone wall, a broken sign. The creatures crowd at the entrance. Specters with the shape of pressed ash. Red eyes that judge, that pursue.

The woman screams and demands they leave her alone. The specters advance, unperturbed. They extend their claws, twisted with blind hatred. The woman raises the medallion. The creatures drool dark venom. They want to take the only thing that makes her be herself.

The only thing that keeps her away from him. They brush against her. Their touch is cold, just like the stone against her back. Something grabs her tightly.

Dawn spins the gem, and with a jet of blood, the creatures disappear. Their memory dissolves in the humid air as if they had never been there. Ethan watches those shadows and their vague reflection in her. His mind clears. He had promised never to wear the damned necklace again, never to go through all that again. He feels pathetic, miserable, and slimy. He feels betrayed by himself and slams his head against the stone.

He screams something mushy and unintelligible. A dizziness shakes him and throws him to the floor. Blood covers his eyes, and the tears clear his face.

Ethan is alone, in communion with the shadows.

It smells like blood. It's acidic, acrid, metallic. Dawn wipes her nose. She grips the bat she's armed herself with more tightly and swings it in front of her. The creatures don't retreat, their bodies bend and crack under her strikes, but they return to their original shape instantly.

After the last incident, Dawn had returned with the intention of being, above all. She had barricaded herself in her apartment, armed and prepared for battle.

The woman steps back. Her logic has led her to fight, to rebel, to try to be. However, those specters are stronger than her. Their strength, their hatred, corroding bone and flesh, tendon and muscle. She tries to fight back, but all she can do is retreat. The monsters flood her floor, crawling like vermin and howling like wolves. They drool black slime and cover the ground.

Dawn grabs the medallion, and a sharp rage burns in her eyes. She doesn't understand why, doesn't reason what has led her to all this. Not even miracles allow her to be happy, and luck brings her no good news. For her, only torment.

She grips the gem tightly and rips it from the metal cylinder. She squeezes it between her fingers and screams. The creatures crackle, mute. The stone breaks, and streams of scorched blood cover her hand. Then, her body bubbles and cracks. A tense pull of dry skin, thick blood. A shattered scream trapped in crystal.

The shapes retreat. Dawn cannot kill them because their existence is tied to the gem. Ethan cannot see them because he lives in another plane, distant from the medallion and its magic. However, one is more than the sum of its parts. Flesh, blood, and bone separate with a bloody groan. A thunderclap lights the distance.

Dawn opens her eyes and gazes at Ethan. Face to face, they looked at each other. Disgusted and hated, desired and feared. The multitone reflection of their lives, each one the longing and repulsion of the other at the same time. The broken curse.

They both embraced. Then they kissed. They touched. Ethan contemplates her. She is perfection made flesh. She is curving lines beneath red velvet, eyes of fire in the night choked of stars. She is a flame when everything goes out, the comforting closeness, the delicious tension of burning.

She is perfect, and Ethan loves her.

They kiss, they touch, equally. She grabs him and molds him with hunger. He admires her, he wants her. He no longer envies her, he understands her and accepts her. She no longer hates him, she feels pity for him and regrets not having been able to communicate with him. They lick, they undress. They penetrate, they hold each other. They moan, they sweat.

Their fire boils the black tar. The monsters scream this time, they twist. She cannot kill them, and he cannot see them, but the two of them are something different. Something more powerful.

Ethan eagerly grabs her hips. The pace quickens. Dawn screams. It's a moan that breaks all barriers and concessions, it's freedom and happiness. She grabs him, scratches his back, holds him with her thighs. The pace increases. The creatures retreat.

Dawn pulls him toward her. The rhythm doesn't stop. It grows frantic. In longing, they unite, their flesh burns. With the orgasm, the shadows dissolve.

No one watches as Ethan and Dawn sigh, at peace.

A hug. From the ashes and flames, it's all that remains: a simple hug.

Ethan leaves. Dawn doesn't know where to, nor does she care too much. She doesn't wish him ill. She will never deny him a kiss or a bed, but that man is now behind her. It's ideal. The medallion has shattered into black ash and no longer holds power over anyone.

The woman inhales and exhales, free from curses, both her own and others'. She looks out the window. The world stirs and vibrates, watching and judging her. She smiles, knowing that, beyond the shadows, no enemies remain. She fills her chest with air and pride and steps out of her house with determination.

Outside, the sun shines.

THE GODDESS' CREATION

By A.W.

LITTLE GHOSTS OF PAIN AND PLEASURE DOWN MY NECK,
The moon beams to illuminate each scratch, bruise or
bite.
The hand of a goddess, traces the bones of her creation
Solliquizing:
"Your veins run with rivers of heated, perfect maroon,
and your heart beats for me."
I come face to face

With my creator.
An ever changing, imperfectly perfect
Being
Immortal, glimmering fingers find every beautiful divit;
They trace the valleys and river of
Scars and stretch marks.
Her esoteric touch brings me to tears.
I call out her name in ecstasy,
My body is divine for a single moment.

As she leaves me, heaving in the sheets,
She whispers:
"You are made of bits of stars galaxies, an ethereal being-
You are perfectly made."

THE ANGEL OUT OF SPACE

By Lindsey Betty

Jackie Woodfall sat in the back, David Roberts in the front, and even though she couldn't hear the congregation over her headphones, she could tell from the look on David's face that something was wrong. He stared at the pulpit, frowning, sweat shining on his forehead. A million miles away.

Jackie's mother tugged at her pant leg. "Pastor's about to speak."

Jackie slipped the headphones around her neck and found herself immersed in the chatter of the crowd.

"Did you see his face?" An old woman's voice rose from the hum.

"Why, no," said another.

"What was the matter?"

"All beat up."

Jackie leaned over and whispered. "Is something wrong?"

"I don't know, dear." Ms. Woodfall answered in her most proper voice, back stick-straight against the pew. She tried to fold her hands casually on her lap but wound up wringing her skirt between her fingers.

The back of the pastor's head rose from the crowd, and a hush fell over the room. His footsteps, slow and jilted, cut through the uneasy silence as he made his way up to the pulpit. He turned around, revealing a battered face of purple, yellow, and red. One of his eyes was swollen shut, and his top lip was puffy and dripping with blood.

"Oh my…" Ms. Woodfall whispered, then put her hand to her mouth. The crowd began to murmur.

"Ladies and gentlemen," he bellowed, and the crowd fell silent once again. "I have a confession to make."

He surveyed the rows of pews with his good eye, his expression unreadable. Jackie shuddered when his eye landed on her and rested there for just a second too long. He moved on, settled his gaze on David for a moment, then looked up into the middle distance. He spoke. "I have deceived you all, and in my deceit, I led you, my flock, astray. I soiled my divine union with my wife and damned the soul of my one and only son. It brings me no joy to admit this, but it must be done. To save my flock and to preserve the sanctity of God's will, I must say this to you all today."

He paused, clasped his hands together, and took a long, wheezing breath. "I have been a homosexual."

A murmur started in the crowd. Ms. Woodfall gasped and looked over at Jackie. Jackie felt her stomach knot up and her cheeks turn red. She looked at David, who now had his face in his hands.

Pastor Roberts continued. "Yes, I have been a homosexual, and I have done heinous things without count or measure. It was on account of these acts that last night I found myself standing on the cliffs overlooking the river, and I sought the coward's way out. I believed that no just God could ever see redemption in a soul as wretched and deceitful as my own. So, I cast myself down into the waters, consigned to my fate, the only hope left in my heart a foolish notion that the river's icy depths might soothe my skin from the eternal hellfire that awaited it."

"That's right!" Someone shouted from the crowd.

"Sinners will burn!"

The pastor's voice rose over the commotion. "As I plunged towards my fate, I saw the reflected starlight dancing in the rushing water, and I thought of God. I thought of David. I thought of my wife. I thought of you, my flock. Then there was a terrible pain, and all thought ceased. My will was replaced by a rushing torrent of agony, agony beyond measure or reason. Dreamlike. Divine. I know not how long I spent in that state, swept up by the current, dragged along the rocks, at the mercy of the fates and of God above. All I know is that I came to rest on the banks of the river. The pain lessened a little, and my conscious mind returned piece by piece. My first thought was that I had arrived in hell. I was just beginning to come to the realization that all was not hellfire and brimstone, that I had by some miracle survived, when a brilliant light shone through my eyelids."

A few in the audience began to murmur and babble. Above them, only a few coherent words could be made out.

"Hallelujah!"

"Praise the lord!"

"I opened what I could of my eyes, and I saw it, a heavenly streak of light blazing across the night sky. Suddenly, all was clear. I felt no pain, no sorrow, no bitterness. I felt only a certainty that I had been saved, sent back to the mortal realm to enact God's will. God had sent me one of his angels and all there was to do now was rise and meet it. I stood up, felt my weight bear down on my bruised and broken legs. There was a glow in the trees, maybe a mile upstream, at a spot I recognized as the very place I had attempted to leave the earth. A test, I knew. A test of faith. My broken legs must carry me back to the spot where I had chosen to forsake myself, forsake God. Then I would be forgiven. Then I would be given my divine mission. I suppose I don't need to tell you whether or not I made it."

The passion of the crowd grew, and their babbles intensified. A few hallelujahs rang out, but most of it was incoherent. Jackie realized with familiar unease that they had begun to speak in tongues.

The pastor turned his eye back on David. "Now, my son, I ask you to rise and come to the front."

"Dad, no." David's voice was teary, his face strained.

"Go!" shouted the crowd.

"Respect the Father!"

"David," he said casually, but firmly, as if coaxing his son into finishing all the peas on his plate. "You must."

"Please..."

"David." The pastor's tone turned grave, and Jackie thought she could see his good eye glow yellow.

David stood and moved slowly to the pulpit. His hair drooped over his face, and a white flannel shirt hung like a pall over his thin, slouching frame. Jackie, acting on instinct, moved forward. Her mom grabbed her by the shirt tail and pulled her back.

The pastor received his wincing son with open arms, hugged him firmly, then turned him to the crowd. "This is my son, my one and only. Isn't he beautiful?"

The crowd roared.

"He is!" Ms. Woodfall shouted, eager to be a part of things. Jackie shot her a betrayed, hateful look.

The pastor grinned. "I knew you'd think so, Ms. Woodfall. I suppose no apple falls too far from the tree."

Ms. Woodfall's eager expression disappeared into confusion. She turned to Jackie. "What does he mean?"

"Just shut up." Jackie replied and looked toward the door. She wanted nothing more than to leave, but she couldn't abandon David.

The pastor turned his attention to his son and continued. "David, would you say that I've been a good father to you?"

David nodded his head.

"Speak."

"Yes," he said meekly.

"Tell the truth."

"What?"

"Tell the people what I did to you."

The tears returned to David's eyes. "Dad, no. I can't. I...."

"Tell us!" the crowd screamed.

"The truth will set you free!"

"Amen, amen, amen."

"David Roberts," the pastor bellowed and grabbed his son by the back of his collar. The yellow glow flashed again in his eyes; this time undeniable. The crowd began to screech and moan, and the pastor shouted over them. "Tell the people, I command you. Tell them how I hurt you."

David squirmed, writhed, wretched, and finally he wailed. "Fine, okay! You... you... touched me! You know what you did. Please, just stop this."

The crowd fell silent.

The pastor dropped him, and he fell to the floor weeping. The pastor's voice was calm again. "Of course. I touched you. I hurt you, David. I know that. I would apologize, but I know that God has forgiven me. The question, dear boy, is whether God has forgiven you."

"You're crazy!" David shouted from the floor. "Fucking batshit! I wish you had died. I wish I could kill you...I wish...I wish..."

The crowd screamed and jeered, all risen from their pews. Their tuneless, meaningless vocalizations brought the atmosphere of the room to the brink of total chaos.

David returned to a puddle of sobs, and the Pastor shouted over the crowd. "Now, that's no way to talk to your father." He looked out at his riotous flock. "You see, when I found my way to the top of that cliff, I *did* find an angel. Genuine, in the flesh. The angel touched me, gave me power, told me things. David-" He looked to his son, quivering on the ground. His voice quieted. "What do you think the angel told me?"

"I don't know."

"I think you do."

"Fuck you."

This set the crowd over the edge, and they began to move toward the stage in a singular, teeming mass,

The yellow glow returned, this time not only in the pastor's eye, but emanating from his entire body. The crowd hesitated. He grabbed David by his long hair and lifted him off the ground. The yellow glow spread over David's body, causing him to scream and convulse in horrible agony. Jackie began to cry. Ms. Woodfall only watched in shock, along with the rest of the congregation.

"Tell them what you did!" The pastor shouted. "Tell God what you did! If your soul is judged to be repentant, then you will be spared as I was. If you do not allow into your heart the divine energy that flows from my fingertips, then you have only eternal hellfire to await you! So, speak, now, boy. Repent!"

"I fucked her, fuck!" David screamed. "I loved her. I'm sorry."

"Who?"

The crowd was now completely silent.

"Jackie..." David's sobs were now weak, hollow.

"I'm sorry," said the Pastor. "I don't believe I know a Jackie. Speak again. Use his real name. The name God gave him."

"Jack," he sobbed. "I'm sorry, Jackie. I'm sorry."

"Young Mr. Woodfall is not who you should be apologizing to," said the pastor. The yellow glow surged, and David gave one final, soul-splitting scream, then fell to the floor.

"Now," the pastor turned his yellow eye on Jackie. The crowd's attention followed suit. "Mr. Woodfall. Would you please come to the front?"

Jackie sprang up from her seat and moved for the door. Her mother grabbed at her shirt tail, begged her to stay, but Jackie broke loose and tore out into the street. She made it halfway down the block before she looked back, and saw the church door still closed, nobody in pursuit. She ducked into an empty yard and made a run for the forest beyond. When she hit the river, she waded through to the far bank, collapsed against the rocks, and began to sob. David's screams were still in her ears, the image of his body crumpled on the shabby orange carpet still in her head. She didn't know what she had just seen, didn't know how to even begin to accept it.

She was closing her eyes and fighting back tears when her phone buzzed in her front pocket. It was David's number.

"Hello?" she answered quietly, cautiously.

"Hello, Jack," the pastor's voice came in reply.

"Leave me alone." Jackie tried to sound strong, but her voice trembled. "Leave me alone or I swear to God I'll..."

"Let us not take the Lord's name in vain, Mr. Woodfall. It will only make matters worse for you."

She sniffled. "What do you want?"

"I want to administer your judgement, Jack, you know that. If you open up your heart and accept my grace, then you won't be harmed. You'll be left standing on the other side, clean of your sins and free to live the life God meant for you. Doesn't that sound nice?"

"Is that what happened to David?"

"David got what he deserved. He was blind. He refused to cleanse his soul, and so God sent him where he belonged. He burns now in the flames of eternity. I advise you not to resign yourself to the same fate. You're so young, Jack, so innocent. There's still time for you to heal from whatever caused you this affliction."

"Fuck you." Jackie spit, her anger rising to cast out her fear. "I don't take spiritual advice from pedophiles."

He laughed. "We're all sick in some way, aren't we? That's why I need you to believe me. If I, of all people, could accept God into my heart and become one of his chosen, then just think about what God could have planned for you. You are part of my flock, Jackson. I care for you, and it is my job to shepherd you to the promised land. You could still have a happy ending, a happy eternity. All I need is for you to trust me."

"I don't trust you, and I don't trust a God who would do his work through somebody like you."

All the warmth left his voice. Now he spoke in a low, slithering tone. "Oh, Jack. You have so much to learn, and I fear you never will. Still, you must be judged, and I'm in no state to chase you through the woods. You may not care for your own soul, but I know you care for your mother's. So, it may interest you to know I have her here at the church, bound up, at my mercy. If you don't render yourself unto me before midnight, I'll consider her complicit in your heathenry, and I will judge her in your place. I happen to recall you were born of sin, a bastard child without a father. Your mother is to blame for that. I suspect God will not like what he sees."

"You're..." Jackie struggled, then the word came to her, pure and simple. "You're evil."

He laughed again. "Oh, am I? Then I suppose God is too. I'll be waiting for you, Jack, and so will your mother."

The line went dead. Jackie looked up at the first few twinkles of light popping through the reddish haze of the evening sky, and had a thought. She began to walk upstream, towards the bluffs out east of town.

Soon the sun's red glow disappeared behind the western horizon, and another glow rose to replace it in the east. It was yellow, like the light that coursed through the pastor, but fringed in iridescence. At first sight, something shifted inside Jackie. She was no longer confused or afraid, she was only certain. Certain that the pastor had been right, there was an angel up in the cliffs. Certain that all she needed to do was rise to meet it.

As she came closer the glow seemed to drift through the trees like a fog, shimmering with alien color against the velvety dark of the woods. Finally, she reached the cliff, standing some two hundred feet above a curve in the river, adorned at its top with a shining beacon. Jackie thought this must be what the stars looked like up close. Without hesitation, she began to pick her way up the hillside.

When she reached the top, she slowed, not out of fear, but out of awe.

The light spoke. "Jackie."

Its voice was low and sonorous, neither masculine nor feminine, but powerful enough to send vibrations through the ground.

"At your service," she replied, unsurprised that it knew her name, her *chosen* name.

The light said nothing.

"And...what might that service be?"

Again, there was no response. Jackie eased herself forward. The space between her and the angel stretched on forever, growing wider with every step rather than shortening. Still, the gap closed somehow. She fell to her knees.

"What do you want?"

No response.

She decided to try a different tactic. "I want…" She thought for a moment. "To save my mother, I guess."

Nothing happened.

"And stop Pastor Jacobs."

Still nothing.

"And…" She hesitated, realizing with some amusement that she felt embarrassed. "I guess I want to be a girl. Is that possible? Can you do that?"

The light, still totally silent, began to pulse and swirl. At first, Jackie recoiled. Then she gathered herself, reached out, and the light filled her vision. She was falling, the water rising, the whole world visible and all of it rushing toward her. She heard the pastor screaming as he plummeted into the river. She heard David wailing and writhing on the floor of the church. Her own weeping. Her mother pleading. The sky alight with color.

Then, an all-encompassing pain. Soon, nothing.

She found herself standing alone on the cliff's edge, her body unchanged. The woods were dark and silent. The river ran sure and steady. She walked down the slope of the hill and made her way back towards town.

The church doors were open and unsteady organ music filled the streets. The closer Jackie drew, the more she could hear another sound underneath it; moaning, mumbling, droning voices with an almost hallucinatory quality. She felt no fear. She walked up to the double doors.

A room full of eyes turned to her. The voices stopped. The music stopped. The old man on the organ was red in the face, drenched in sweat. He looked either very afraid or deranged with anger. It was hard to tell the difference. On the stage, Jackie's mother was tied to the cross in a horrible imitation of crucifixion. Her eyes were scrunched shut with pain, and her face glistened with tears. Pastor

Roberts stood facing her. When the noise stopped, he turned around.

"Well, if it isn't the man of the hour!" Pastor Roberts roared magnanimously as he stepped down from the stage and into the center aisle. "Mr. Jackson Woodfall, how kind of you to join us."

She took a step forward. "It's Jackie."

"Call yourself whatever name you please." The glow came into his eye. His voice grew sharper, angrier. A few in the crowd started again to hum and babble. "You may fool some, but you won't fool God. He will always know you for what you really are - a man. More than that, *Jackie,* you're a corrupter, a sinner, unrepentant and undeserving of God's grace. If you had any shame, any remorse at all, you'd have followed my path. But I can see that you didn't, you believe yourself above judgement. And so, the job of submitting you to God's will falls on me."

"God's will, or yours?"

"What's the difference?" The pastor grinned, his broken face contorting into something unnatural and inhuman, and the yellow glow creeped over his body. The man at the organ resumed his play with something low and funereal. The crowd's low hum quickly elevated to screams and wails. Their eyes bulged, their faces were ghastly white and drenched in sweat. Some fell to their knees; some raised their arms up in exaltation. Jackie only stood her ground.

"Jackie!" Ms. Woodfall's strained voice was barely audible amidst the cacophony. "Get out of here! Go! Let him take me, please! I'm so sorry, this is all my fault! Go!"

The pastor moved down the center aisle towards Jackie. Jackie stared back at him with as much hate as she could muster.

"Jack, my boy," Pastor Roberts said as he came closer. "Prepare to meet your maker."

The pastor reached out his hand and placed it on Jackie's forehead.

"I already have," Jackie said in a voice quiet enough that only the pastor could hear.

The pastor's mangled face distorted into something like confusion, and the yellow glow climbed from his body onto Jackie's. The music stopped. The crowd fell silent.

Now it was Jackie's turn to advance on the Pastor. He stumbled backwards, his injured legs failed him, and he fell onto his back.

"What do you say?" Jackie commanded as she towered over his crumpled frame.

"Devil! Heathen! Black magic!" the pastor cried, writhing on the floor.

"No, no, no," she said, and crouched down over his face. "I believe the words you're looking for are 'I'm sorry.'"

The pastor looked away, refusing to meet Jackie's yellow gaze. "I'm sorry," he choked out, almost inaudibly.

"Louder."

The pastor turned to look at her, at first with anger, but quickly turning to fear. "I'm sorry," he said clearly.

"That's better." Jackie rose, and the yellow light dissipated from her body.

As she walked up the center aisle to free her mother, she noticed the man on the organ staring at her. With awe, she thought, not with fear. She made eye contact with him, he looked a little flustered, then began to play again. This time the music wasn't funereal, it was celebratory. The crowd began once again to moan and babble.

When she reached the pulpit, she turned around. "Maybe I can find it in my heart to forgive you," she called out to the pastor. "But your 'flock', the people you've taught nothing but fear and hate, well, I expect that to be a different story."

Jackie didn't watch as the congregation fell upon the pastor, paid no mind to their jibberings as they carried him screaming into the street. She only untied her mother, eased her to the floor, and hugged her as hard as she could.

"I'm sorry, Jackie," she sobbed into Jackie's chest. "I'm sorry for everything."

"It's okay, Mom." Jackie said. "I forgive you."

MARGARET

By Freddie A. Clark

There was something liberating about climbing. Conquering the peak of a snowy mountain had always given me the freedom I hadn't experienced since I was twenty.

Climbing allowed me to escape. It allowed me to free myself from hands touching me against my will. Free me from the overwhelming memory that would haunt me forever. Therapy and meds didn't help as much as hitting the frozen rock with my ice axe, grabbing small outcrops with my gloved hand, and pushing myself up.

Climbing set me free.

When I reached the top, I took off my ski goggles and enjoyed the view. The cold air blew uncomfortably against my face, but I didn't mind. A magnificent, endless panorama of snow-capped peaks spread before my eyes. Dense clouds loomed over the stunning scenery, spoiling an otherwise unblemished sky. I took a deep breath, my lungs filling with the clean, frozen air I couldn't breathe in my polluted city.

As I stood at the top of that mountain, I felt invincible. Margaret, Queen of the World.

"We did it, Maggie," I heard. I was startled when another gloved hand patted my shoulder. A relieved sigh escaped my throat when I turned to my friend Joey, and I saw his full lips curving into a smile. Only the lower half of his dark umber face was visible under his goggles and the hood of his hardshell jacket – turquoise like mine.

My whole group joined him not long after. I wasn't alone anymore. That mountain and that view weren't only mine, and that intense joy faded.

"We did it," I whispered. We did it, yes.

I hadn't climbed for eight months. *It* had started a month after my last climb.

Churches were packed with people begging God for mercy and hospitals overflowed with people mutating. As a nurse, I had to perform my duty.

There was no way to stop this horror from spreading. The doctors who were still alive only provided euthanasia, aided by the military. The end of time had come, and I was living through it. I was scared and I wondered when my time would come.

The first patient that day was Anthony, a middle-aged man. His open ribcage had calcified before our eyes as his guts turned into worm-like creatures covered in spikes. One of the creatures leapt into a doctor's mouth and slid inside, devouring him, butchering him, making his body its new home. Three soldiers shot before the doctor could mutate. It was a matter of time, since the doctor had become a bloody, shaking mess whose skin was melting.

The shotguns deafened me. I burst into tears, hugging my sobbing colleague, Sarah, in a corner of the operating room. The area itself was a nightmare come true: the walls covered in fleshy, pumping veins; a disgusting fluid flowed inside them; the veins sighed as they breathed. The first time I'd heard that sound, I puked.

I was used to it by now.

The soldiers instructed me and Sarah to leave as they put the corpses in two body bags. The bodies couldn't remain, or *The Collectors* would retrieve their parts to use as building material.

Sarah and I crossed the operating room's doors and ran to the corridor. I stopped as I heard screams and pleads inside a room. "Sarah, wait!"

Sarah didn't care. She kept running.

I cared. Someone was in pain and I wanted to help. I *had to* help them.

My hands shook, but I opened the door and gasped. A flayed man was welded to a calcified structure coating the wall, a complex bone-like pattern covered in more pumping veins. He begged for help, skinless, suffering. He stopped and exhaled his last breath as a creature approached him.

A Collector.

Collectors' bodies were flayed too, although some bony parts – a textured organic armour – made them appear inhuman. Their heads were white and smooth, with no eyes nor noses, their red lips always closed. Their bodies were naked, muscular, wide-shouldered, flat-chested, with their genitals on display. This Collector had a vulva like me.

"*Help me, Margaret.*"

Collectors spoke through telepathy.

"Why should I help you?" I asked, my voice trembling.

The Collector's arms opened, and the flayed body detached from the wall.

"*Because you entered this room to help a man. That's what you're going to do. You'll help me collect this subject's parts.*"

"This is not a *subject*; it's a man and you killed him!"

"*I did not. The* Chrysalis *did.*"

"The…Chrysalis?" I asked, confused. My heart beat so fast my chest hurt.

The Collector climbed down the bed with strange grace, holding the flayed corpse in his arms. He was way taller than me, which was strangely reassuring despite his appearance. The longer I watched him, the calmer I felt. I realised he meant me no harm.

I took some slow, careful steps towards him as he laid the body down. The motion was gentle, as a doctor or a fellow nurse would do.

"*The Chrysalis is the stage preceding the* Metamorphosis. *Earth has reached the point of no return, and it's time for it to evolve in order to survive. Humans aren't accepting the transformation and they're slowly dying, one by one.*"

"What about you?" I asked, "Are you a human who accepted the transformation?"

"*No. I'm an instrument of evolution and I was born the way you see me. I was generated by flesh to serve flesh. The time of humans and their toxic invasion is over. It's not a threat, but a matter of fact."*

I gulped and kneeled on the floor, observed the flayed corpse still seeping blood. I stared as the Collector pulled bony blades from his armour; they vaguely resembled surgical instruments. "Why do you collect human parts? What are you doing with them?"

"I take them to the Builders. They'll recycle them to shape the world, give it the appearance it craves. Earth is choosing its new face and we're helping it achieve it."

Builders were massive humanoids with eight arms and a bizarre biomechanical appearance. The military tried to fight them, without success, and the Builders didn't even fight back. The sudden realisation that none of these creatures had ever fought back or attacked uninfected humans made me feel dizzy.

Earth was getting rid of humans. We were the problem. We were the enemy.

"What's your name?" I asked as the Collector stared with his eyeless face, waiting for me to pick an instrument.

"I have no name."

"Would you like one?"

"We'll see. Help me, now."

I sighed and picked a blade resembling a bone saw.

Three months had passed since I started helping the Collector. We worked together endlessly, collecting the body parts of those who didn't accept transformation. Nothing had happened to me yet, and I didn't understand why. Neither did the Collector.

He didn't like any name I suggested. At first, I had suggested Max, my first boyfriend's name, but he had said no. I then suggested Paul, my father's name, but he had refused again. I wanted to suggest Christopher, but I hesitated.

Christopher was the chosen name of the man I never stopped loving. A man with a body similar to mine, but a masculine identity. Christopher died in a car accident and I never recovered from the loss. He'd been the man who made me feel loved and made me enjoy intimacy again. I was lost without Christopher, alone, with no purpose.

But I had a purpose now. I aided the Collector with his task and I felt complete, useful, helpful. My job as a nurse wasn't comparable to what I was doing to further evolution. The world was changing, and I had accepted my role in it.

Collecting body parts wasn't hard for me. I was used to death, to corpses, to surgeries. I did my part and the Collector enjoyed my company as much as I enjoyed his. I had no idea how long it would last, but I would help him for as long as needed. There wasn't anything left in this world for me, except this role, except the Collector. *My* Collector.

Five years passed since I met my Collector and we never had a break. The Collector made sure I rested, that I ate something my body wouldn't reject, that I took care of myself.

I turned thirty-five. It was my birthday, and the Collector remembered. In my now-transformed city, a triumph of biomechanical breathing flesh, he found something for me: mountaineering gear.

Some mountains remained untouched, so he found gear for both of us. We travelled to the nearest mountain, walking for days only stopping to allow me to rest.

It wasn't comparable to some peaks I conquered in the past, but it was perfect with him. We climbed together. I taught him and we climbed and felt free together, enjoying the vast panorama while holding hands.

The world around me was ending, but with my Collector by my side, I was happy.

Ten more years passed. I was forty-five when I was the last human in the world. My Collector still had no name, but we were inseparable.

I loved him, deeply, and I hoped the same was for him. I woke up from my rest in the fleshy wasteland the world became, with my Collector sitting and enjoying the view. We were at the top of a mountain, but no snow had fallen in at least three years. The weather was too hot to wear clothes.

I was undressed now, in my pale and skinny nudity. My hair was still blond, straight and the longest I've ever worn it. There was no time to cut my hair, shave, or take care of my hygiene. My Collector didn't care. He didn't care about my body hair, something I'd been insecure about except with Christopher. I rose and sat next to my Collector. Despite his eyeless head, he could apparently see.

"I have a last suggestion," I said, "if you don't like this name either, you can stay nameless forever. I'll give up."

"Say it, Margaret. I'm curious."

I sighed and closed my eyes shut. I hadn't pronounced that name in years, but I was finally ready. "Christopher."

The Collector remained silent for long. We both did, until I heard his thoughts.

"I like it."

Tears ran down my cheeks. I lay down and cried, sobbed. I cried until my Collector lay on top of me and dried the tears off my face with his hand. I truly loved him: my Collector, my Christopher.

His lips couldn't utter a word, but they could kiss. I found out when I pressed my lips to his for the first time in fifteen years. He let me and I kissed him as fervently as I could. He had no tongue, but I didn't care. Feeling his lips against mine was enough and I kissed him, loved him as much as he deserved.

I moaned when Christopher moved his lips away from mine. A shiver ran through my spine, so pleasant I wrapped my arms around his shoulders. He sat on his knees and observed me with his eyeless face. He tilted his head as my body reacted to my desire, my legs spread, my hips moving.

He touched the spot between my legs, felt my wet flesh, and I moaned. He touched me more, more insistently, rubbed my clit with his fingers. I abandoned myself to him. I was his. I belonged to him.

Thin flesh tendrils grew from his fingers and started wrapping my thighs, my hips, my chest. Christopher took good care of me. As his fingers found their way inside me, the tendrils reached my nipples and caressed them, squeezed them, rubbed them. They didn't leave them alone for a moment. I kept moaning and followed the rhythm of his fingers with my hips.

More flesh tendrils sprouted and wrapped my neck gently, while others found their way inside my mouth.

I closed my eyes and instead of seeing the Christopher I had lost, I saw him. My Collector. My healing.

I abandoned myself to that pleasure. The most intense I'd ever felt, the pleasure I craved for years. It was a pleasure free from any pain, free from any harmful memories. I felt as free as when I climbed mountains. I felt loved and full of love. I was happy.

Nobody was around so I screamed when I orgasmed; loudly, freely, excitedly. My scream echoed off the mountainside.

When I was in control of myself again, the tendrils retracted, and my Christopher still stared at me. I heard no thoughts, but I could tell that he was as happy and free as me. He bent down to hug me and I hugged back, cuddled him. I loved him and I was sure he loved me too.

I had to wait until the end of the world to feel happy and loved again, to feel healed. I was whole again. I was free, with my Christopher with me.

Twenty years passed since I met Christopher. I was fifty when the world finished its evolution.

"I'm ready," I said.

"Ready for what, Margaret?"

"I'm ready to become a Collector."

Christopher held my hands and caressed them as I stared at him.

"Collectors are not needed anymore. I'm part of the new Earth, just like you."

"I'll age and die, Christopher, unlike you. I'm ready to live with you forever. I want to become like you. I accept the transformation. I've done it for years, now."

"I don't want you to change."

"Twenty years ago, you asked me to help you," I said, "I did. It's your turn now. Can you make me like you?"

Christopher looked uncertain. He kept caressing my hands for a while until he nodded. As I helped him in his role years ago, he had to help me join this new world. He owed it to me, the last human standing. He owed it to me, the one he loved.

The last memories I had as a human were him: anaesthetizing my nape with a long, weird needle; shaving my head fully with one of his surgical instruments; removing part of my scalp; attaching organic cables to my nape.

When I woke up, I was like him.

Literally like him.

We looked alike and it felt right. We were the same as it was meant to be, as *I* was meant to be.

The new world was an ensemble of bony textures, blood, and flesh, and I was part of it. I was part of it and I would be forever.

The old Margaret was gone, but a new one had taken her place. She was happy and free. She was with her Christopher, her eternal love, and she would live forever. Part of the world, part of the future. Part of the Metamorphosis.

Margaret was safe. Margaret was loved.

Margaret.

My name is Margaret and this is my story. A story of trauma, pain, transformation, and love. A story of acceptance, a story of healing.

Margaret.

Dana was a good mother. She knew that she was. It wasn't the accolades from the church based on the perfect attendance, the dedication to charity work, or the donations to the church camp that assured her. It wasn't the home cooked meals, or the regimen of vitamins, or the clean and tidy house. Dana knew deep down in her soul that she was a good mother. It was one of those gut feelings and Dana had learned early on to always lean into and trust that feeling that curdled in her stomach like vinegar and milk.

Sure, things had been hard when Dana's husband of thirteen years decided one day that he didn't want her anymore. There had been no warning. No disruption in Taco Tuesdays and Wednesday night bible study. In the middle of a prime potato casserole on a Thursday evening, Dana's husband Harvey had announced that he didn't love her anymore—that he hadn't loved her in a while. No, there was no one else. He had just grown tired of regimens and scheduled birthday sex and...well, Dana. He'd packed his bags and left without ceremony and certainly without any regrets. Dana didn't cry when he left, even though she had wanted to. Instead, she drove herself to the community dinner her church hosted every Sunday. She stood in line, scooping congealed gravy onto lumpy potatoes for the poor and homeless and with each thump she convinced herself she had no right to be sad. So many others had it worse.

That had always been Dana's approach to life. Raised in the faith and the kitchen, she knew where her place was. She had married young, as she was supposed to and did her best to keep a clean house and a happy husband. She had been challenged in the child department—losing one after another until the doctor recommended they stop trying. But she knew better, she knew God was challenging them. Her faith was rewarded by the conception of their first and only child. The pregnancy was long and difficult, but Dana managed each symptom with a prayer and a smile. When their daughter was born, Dana immediately took her to the church to be consecrated. She and Harvey began their new life as parents, with Dana taking her child's spirituality as a life-or-death situation. Dana had done the bulk of parenting herself, so she wasn't worried much about that when Harvey made his announcement. After her husband left, she gathered up any mention or picture of him and locked him away in a closet. She cleaned the house, bought new sheets, and poured herself into her church and her teenage daughter who looked like Dana but acted like Harvey. Rachel had always been a daddy's girl, preferring baseball caps and t-shirts to Princess crowns and dresses. It had irritated Dana to no end.

While Dana had run things virtually on her own, Harvey had at least been good for one thing: reasoning with Rachel. He would bargain game time and jeans for Wednesday and Sunday dresses. Rachel complied, begrudgingly. Dana was never completely satisfied with the outcomes, but she took what she could get and reasoned that Rachel would grow out of it. *It's just a phase,* she would tell herself.

When Harvey left, the reasoning left with him and Rachel could not be convinced or bargained into dresses anymore. For a while, Dana let it slide. After all, she had lost her husband, but Rachel had lost her father and even though Harvey called, it wasn't the same. She tolerated Rachel's baggy tees and cargo pants, swapping jeans out for church service, her beautiful hair stuffed under caps. She tried to ignore the comments she received that Rachel "looked like a boy". Dana prayed over her wayward child, pasted Bible verses over Rachel's bed, and installed a tracking app on her phone. That was how she found Rachel at the salon, shearing off her long golden hair. Dana had been heartbroken, screaming at the stylist and at Rachel, dragging her home and locking her in her bedroom.

"I'm not Rachel anymore, why can't you see me?!"

The desperate cries from the other side of the door did not move Dana. She knew the devil when the devil was nigh. She'd grown up under the shadow of a belt or a wooden spoon if the devil came too close. While she'd never been one to inflict that on her own child, she began to wonder if that had been a mistake. Dana slunk to the floor, missing Harvey for the first time in a very long time. She wondered briefly if she should call him. The calls had come further and further apart as time went by and three years down the line, they were virtually nonexistent. It was for the best, Dana reasoned. Rachel had changed. She didn't need the added influence of her heathen father. He had encouraged this ghoulish behavior far too much. It was ultimately his fault. Dana couldn't give him a real son, so he had tried to take away her daughter. It all made sense. Dana couldn't turn to the church, either. They had already wavered in their opinions of Dana's faith and resolution. Dana's salvation was reflected in the actions of her offspring and Rachel had done nothing but condemn them both.

But Dana was a good mother. She resolved to do this on her own, if she must. The locked door had just been the first step.

Dana was reflecting on her situation when she was disturbed by a thump upstairs. She smiled happily, realizing her beloved child was up and awake. Breakfast was nearly done, a farm fresh egg sizzling sunny side up in the cast iron skillet. Pancakes, bacon, and fresh fruit waited on a paper plate. Dana had learned not to waste the porcelain. Plastic cups of orange juice and apple juice were placed on a tray, along with the full breakfast and goopy eggs. Rachel preferred her eggs a little less cooked.

Dana picked up the tray and made her way upstairs, the keys to the house and Rachel's bedroom jangling on her waist. She softly hummed *Jesus Paid It All* as she unlocked Rachel's door and opened it.

The smell hit her first, but then it always did. It took a few moments for Dana to adjust. The room itself was mostly dark, the windows having been papered over long ago. The floor rustled as she walked, and she tripped over a fleshy mass as she neared the bed. She made a mental note that it was time to change the tarp on the floor.

"Rachel?" she softly called.

The shape on the bed moved, chains rattling against the bedframe. A sickening squelch filled the room as the form shifted and rolled over. A low, guttural moan escaped from the dark and it pricked Dana's skin and burned around her gold cross necklace.

Dana reached down and clicked the light on. "Good morning, Rachel, shall we say our prayers?"

Dana bowed her head over the tray, whispering pleading prayers to an empty ceiling, bestowing blessings on her daughter.

"Bless this house and we that dwell here. We pray for your hedge of protection, that we may know who we are in the sacrifice of Christ. Amen."

Ignoring a waft of putrid decay, Dana opened her eyes and set the tray down on the bed.

A mottled gray hand reached for the mostly raw eggs. Bones peaked through rotting skin, tendons and nerves exposed and pulsing. The other hand joined, this one missing fingers, the skin grown black and green. The hands dragged the food to a dislocated jaw, barely hanging on by scraps of skin. A purple tongue lapped at the dripping food, a loud pervasive slurping filling the silent room. There was a struggle to reach the rest of the food due to the chains and Dana nudged the tray closer.

The chains had been a necessary evil when Rachel had become ill. It had started as a head cold and Dana had dutifully nursed her sick child. The illness had soon turned violent, with Rachel clawing and snapping at her mother. Dana knew something had taken over her daughter and that it was her duty to drive it out.

"The devil has a hold on you," she had said, subduing Rachel and forcing her to swallow water laced with dissolved sleeping pills. "I will not let him take you."

Dana was a good mother, after all. Of course she would do whatever it took to save her child. Even if it meant chaining her daughter's wrists and ankles. Even if it meant watching the devil leave her daughter's body part by part, flesh by flesh.

Dana raised her eyes over her child and quickly realized what the fleshy mass was she had tripped on earlier. Rachel's chest had fallen off, stringy bits of muscle framing a barely beating heart. The rib cage was also disintegrating, with bits of bone and blood pooling onto the bed between macerated legs. The chains around the ankles had rubbed into the bone, bits of skin growing over while pus and gangrene oozed through the loops of galvanized silver. Dana swallowed the nausea and leaned forward trying to make contact with the milky eyes that were once a clear and vibrant blue. There was no recognition there. No awareness.

The hunger for connection was disrupted as the jawbone finally gave way, falling onto the tray and releasing with it a river of black blood and other foul-smelling liquids. Dana jumped backwards, her heart beating rapidly and filled with horror. For the first time in months, Dana looked at the creature before her in clarity. What had happened to her beloved daughter? Dana's eyes filled with tears; her hands clasped to her mouth as she stifled silent screams. She backed away from the putrid creature and realized she missed Rachel's shorn hair over the few sprigs remaining on a cracked and bleeding scalp. She missed Rachel's sass and combative nature over the silence and squelching. She missed the jeans and ball caps and tees over the naked, decaying body staining the mattress and filling the floor.

Rachel, or whatever was left of them leaned back, the milky eyes cast to heaven and heaved as blood continued to pour from their jaw. The heaving was replaced by gurgling and choking, the whole body shaking limply.

Dana could do nothing but watch in horror. Her prayers died on her lips, as even her faith abandoned her.

"You're not Rachel anymore, are you?" she finally whispered.

The body that once belonged to Rachel did not respond. It stilled, the last bubble of breath leaving an already empty vessel.

Dana's tears spilled onto the floor as she looked wildly about the room, her eyes landing on her child's favorite ball cap.

"You never were Rachel, were you?" She cried, lamentations and despair undoing her resolve.

"I am a good mother!" she screamed.

Silence.

"I am a good mother!"

Silence.

Dana wiped her eyes, straightened her apron and smoothed her hair.

"This is no way to treat your mother. We will see how you feel tomorrow. I will pray for you."

Stepping over the decayed flesh on the floor, Dana exited and locked the door behind her. She closed her eyes and prayed away the visions she had just witnessed. She knew none of it was real. It was the work of the devil, and she would not be sidetracked or seduced by this darkness that came to claim her child.

After all, Dana was a good mother.

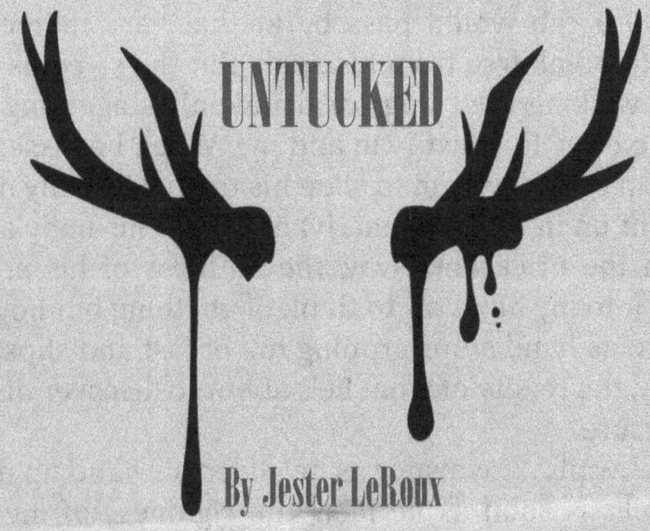

By the third date, I worry I look like a prude kissing goodbye on the step of Ivan's brownstone. His fingers linger, delicately bringing my hand up to his mouth to kiss each of my knuckles goodbye. His blue eyes declare: *I would kiss every inch of you, if you just allowed me to bring you upstairs.*

"I should get going," I say, squeezing his hand adieu.

But his fingers do not slacken, his voice serious as he says, "Did I do something to offend you, Emma?"

Beneath the warm glow of the nearby streetlight, he appears impishly handsome, stubble covering his jawline and the coppery curls of his hair shimmering in the light. I should go, yet I remain drawn to him, saying, "You want me to stay?"

"Of course, I want a beautiful woman like you to stay," He says, pulling my hips towards his own. I resist just enough that we aren't quite touching.

I wish a cab would pass by at that very moment, an excuse to break free from his spell. But the street is silent. No one walking their dogs or drunkenly staggering home from the bars. It is just Ivan and me. When he kisses me, I can't help but allow him to slide his tongue into my mouth.

Caught up in the moment, Ivan presses his body against mine in the brick entryway, the stiffness of his erection digging into my hip. I try to think of anything but how sexy he is. As his hand stops groping my breast and slips down my body, the reality of what he's about to discover disrupts my pleasure.

"Ivan…wait…" I whisper as he slides his hand up my leg. He recoils as soon as he feels the rigidness of my penis throbbing against his palm. Red-faced, he paces across the stoop. I try to comfort him, saying, "I told you I was trans, Ivan."

He sucks air through his teeth, spitting out venom upon exhaling, "I know you did, Emma. I just…I just assumed you had it taken care."

"Taken care of?" I reel back, the hurt audible as I reply, "I was upfront about this, Ivan. It's not that big of a deal."

"Not that big of a deal? How am I supposed to look past something that noticeable? It's bigger than mine for Christ's sake." Ivan pushes past me, digging in his pocket for his keys. I know then that I should leave and never talk to him again, but there is the matter of my penis, no longer confined in a way that he finds palatable. He hisses, "You know how much of a turn-off a girl with a dick is?"

So, my penis becomes undeniable, snaking its way free from my underwear despite the finesse of my tuck. It slithers down my leg, curling like a viper beneath the fabric of my skirt. My penis isn't like other penises. It's bizarrely muscular, thick blue veins siphoning blood from my body to enable the cursed thing to move on its own volition. Before I know what's happening, my vision blurs from the lack of blood in my brain. The wretched organ stretches beyond its perceived capabilities, a noose of veiny, corded flesh that catches Ivan around the throat. As it constricts about his throat, I desperately try to ease it back into my body, but every movement applies more pressure to his windpipe till Ivan collapses against the stoop. My mutated cock goes flaccid as I look at his body, a necktie of bruises around his throat, busted capillaries turning the whites around his eyes a bloody red.

When I arrive back at my apartment, the first thing I do is grab the pint of frost-dusted cookie dough ice cream, chipping away at it as I delete every dating app off my phone. But before I can finish the task, I find myself once again swiping and imagining a white-picket fence and two-and-a-half kids based on four photos and a shitty bio that reads *I never know what to write for these things*. I can't help but be a sucker for love.

"This can't happen again, Emma," I mumble, then create a Google search for extra sturdy chastity belts.

The world I stumble upon is one that both fascinates and frightens me. Evangelical purity culture overlaps with painful, pleasure-inducing BDSM. Searching for the perfect device, I ponder the benefit of leather or steel, of padlocks or combination dials. But by deciding to cage my penis, I am acknowledging its undeniability. The dysphoria is nauseating.

I refine my search for belts specifically for trans women. The results are much narrower, but eventually I come across a website covered in pink frills and boutique graphic design that draws my eye to an assortment of gender affirming BDSM toys. Their signature chastity belt is a piece of art made of curved steel that both tucks and shapes the penis, creating a look reminiscent of a woman's external sex organs. But I freeze when I look at the price tag. $900 for the thing that would solve my problems. Almost the price of a month's rent. A rent that I already struggle to pay.

Settling for a cheap leather substitute, the image of Ivan's corpse is seared into my eyelids each time I blink away tears. I pay $20 for rush shipping as I shovel the melted ice cream down my throat.

When I'm good and sick, I pull down my underwear in front of the mirror, recreating the moment in high school where I realized my penis wasn't like everyone else's. Carefully, I fold my anatomy backwards, squeezing my thighs shut to create a silhouette that is smooth and recognizably female. But then I part my legs, my penis appearing massive as it falls back into place. Then I repeat the process. Concealing my wretched anatomy between my legs, letting it fall, and with each repetition, it becomes until it's touching the floor, snaking around my body as I sob. Just the sight of it is enough to cause me to vomit onto the floor.

It's impossible to style a chastity belt. What was once form-fitting and pleasing to the eye suddenly appears bulgy, the device concealed beneath my skirts bulky like a soiled diaper. Even the loudest pattern can't hide the fact that beneath my clothing is a device of medieval proportions. My phone dings, a groan escaping my lips as my friends ponder what bar we'll be drinking and dancing in till the early hours. I type quickly before anyone has a chance to protest: *It doesn't matter, as long as it's dark and crowded.* I slip on a loose black dress that won't draw the eye and order a Lyft.

As soon as the driver stops outside the club, a line of spiky-haired Jersey Shore wannabees greet me with catcalls and wolf-whistles. The bouncer motions me into the club with a beckoning wave like he's backing in a truck full of fresh meat.

Inside, I'm comforted by the darkness. The flashing lights concealing patrons in momentary blackness, leaving one's dance partner to focus on the sway of their hips not the bulk concealed beneath their cocktail dress. I'm greeted by my friends with a vodka tonic shoved into my hand.

Sobriety smothered beneath the weight of well liquor, I ask, "Shall we dance, ladies?"

But my cis friends are hypnotized by handsome men with open tabs. There is no suitor asking what I'm drinking. As a kid, I was a sissie without a leg who was chosen last for kickball. As an adult, the heterosexual male clocks me as the unideal mate, my femininity not quite to their taste. But two drinks are enough to give me the confidence to dance alone.

I love the anonymity of dance floors. The undulating, grinding bodies not quite separate. An arm belongs to no one, a swaying pair of hips part of the collective. Bad remix after remix blasts from the overhead speakers, so when a familiar song comes on, everybody belts out the words, wild as we dance beneath the flashing lights.

Then I see a pair of hazel eyes and a strong jawline that makes me bite my lip. A total Fuck Me, Daddy staring right back at me. He walks towards me with a shoulder thrown out, the crowd parting at the sight of his tatted beefcake arms. He wraps his arm around me and commands, "Dance with me, baby."

I agree, but I do so with caution, hyperaware of the distance between us. But the way his big hands seem to support every vertebra of my spine as they run down my body is dangerous when mixed with alcohol. I let him pull me close against my better judgement.

The music smothers any chance of him hearing me as I say, "Let's take things slow."

The daddy's hand tightens around my inner thigh, pushing up my skirt as he holds me firm. I try to playfully push him away, but the higher his hand climbs, the more desperate I become. The chastity belt feels tighter the more we drunkenly struggle.

I'm disgusted with myself, my body unable to differentiate his forcefulness from consensual masculine domination. Genuine discomfort indistinguishable from fantastical bliss.

My penis goes rigid as his fingers skim the leather chastity belt, his eyebrows rising with curiosity. The belt digs into my waist, the seams aching as my body no longer obeys my will. I try to push the man away, to shout over the sound of the speakers, to create a scene that will draw me into the safety of a group of pissed-off women ready to beat down another creep hunting the dance floor. Before he has a chance to grope what lies beneath the belt, I feel the sudden absence of it around my waist, the sound of leather being shredded audible even against the music.

The creep stumbles backwards. Shock registering on his face as blood gushes from his eviscerated fingers. He screams, "You cut me."

I bolt from the dance floor, retreating to the sanctity of the dark hallway of the club's restrooms as blood spills down my leg. A line snakes out of the women's, ladies applying lipstick and wiping away mascara tears without putting down their drinks. Any other woman would simply ask for a tampon or a pad, the shared urgency of unexpected leakage being enough to bypass the queue. But the women stare at me, clocking me much too fast and turning their backs to whisper even as blood drips down my leg.

Dysphoric nausea wells in my belly as I rush into one of the empty stalls in the men's room, which smells of vomit and sex. I hike my skirt up and sit down on the toilet seat, some man's piss soaking into my thighs.

What lies between my legs isn't a penis, it's a monstrosity. A weapon whose only purpose is to maim and ruin. But I suppose that is what a penis is in the first place. I take my phallus between my forefinger and thumb to pull it free from my blood-slicked thighs. A jolt of pain stops me. Blood isn't the only thing holding the organ stationary. Along the underside of the organ protrudes a half dozen chitinous spines like the quills covering a porcupine's back.

The more I fret, the more blood spills onto the floor. My thigh aches as I push into the tender skin, forcing one of the sharp barbs free from the meat of my leg. I can't help but to sob as I look at this new feature of my anatomy in the dim light. "Oh fuck, oh god."

The more agitated I become, the further the spines extend. I take a deep breath in, then try to force one back into my body; however, the barb is sharp to touch, unwilling to retreat beneath the skin. Looking at my unique adaptations, I am reminded of how an animal, when frightened, will do anything in its power to defend itself, expressing violent and desperate manners of self-defense. As disturbed as I am, I can recognize that this transformation is a defense mechanism itself. My penis may be something I wish I could be rid of, but while I'm stuck with it, it itself is a way for deterring men whose allyship only goes as far as the bedroom. The thought relaxes me, the row of spines retreating into my body.

I pull my dress down, throwing the stall door open as I wipe the smeared mascara from my eyes. But in the process, I run smack dab into a body that doesn't budge. The shock of it cracks my composition, the tears spilling down my cheeks as I look up a face that is much too pretty to be seeing me crying. The man's chiseled features immediately soften as he sees the mess of my face, stuttering out, "I'm so sorry, miss."

He reaches out to touch my shoulder on instinct. While his touch is tender, his hand immediately retreats upon realizing that he's touching a stranger. I push by him as he shouts, "Are you sure you're okay, miss?"

I stop in the doorway, unable to stammer out a response, yet unable to leave. Again, he speaks, his voice so soft and level that I am comforted by the calmness of it, "That creep out there started screaming that some girl cut him, but if he made you cry, that'll be the least of his worries...because,

because I'll make him learn what his fucking teeth taste like."

I sniffle, turning back to him and saying, "You're sweet for a stranger in a disgusting club bathroom. But I should run before the police are called."

"They're already here. They sent me to check the bathroom before my shift is over."

"Fuck."

"There's another exit," he murmurs, "I could show you."

"I need a fucking drink."

"I think I have an answer to that problem too," the stranger says, beckoning me to follow.

We retreat to a hole-in-the-wall where the lights are dim and the glasses are dirty, but the drinks are cheap. When I sit at the bar, all I can mutter is, "A couple shots of vodka"

The bartender lays out three shot glasses, sloshing liquor over the bar mat as he overfills them. I down them without worrying about the liquor dripping down my wrists. All I want is to reach a point where I'll forget what happened.

"What's your name?" I ask before I throw back the final shot.

"Looks like you won't remember it anyway."

"Looks like you don't know how to be memorable," I reply, smiling so my joke isn't lost to him.

"Billy," he says, taking a swig of a beer.

"Really?" I shouldn't laugh, but I do.

"What? Never met a grown man named Billy?"

"Never met one so handsome. I'm Emma." And with that his hand reaches across the bar, fingers gently circling about my wrist to lift it from the counter. I stare up at him, my heart fluttering with the question: *is this fate, or is the booze just turning this stranger into a dream boat?*

"You just put your hand in someone else's beer." Billy lets go off my hand as a blush warms my cheeks. I turn away, trying to hide this embarrassing admission of my attraction by tucking a lock of my hair behind my ear. But beer still dripping down my hand, he bridges the space between us to push the strand out of my line of sight.

Now I can see him unfettered. His eyes are the amber color of honey, his voice just as slick and sweet. His touch is tender, his expression curious, leaning in ever so slightly to ask me more and more about myself. It's that sort of instant connection that I always thought was just something that happened in movies. The longer we talk, the more I can feel the bartender's eyes on us, neither of us nervous enough to wave a hand for another drink.

"Think he's getting ready to kick us out?" Billy says, his thumb tracing loops around my knuckles.

A line now snakes out from the bar's front door, bodies squeezing closer and closer to us as the bouncer waves them in.

"Guess I was paying too much attention to you to notice it got busy," I say.

"Talking to a beautiful woman like you really makes this shitty bar less shitty, but it's getting late," Billy says, his hand lingering atop mine.

"I don't want to say goodbye."

"Maybe we don't have to?" A sheepish grin on his face, his eyes say only one thing: *what about my place?*

"There's something you should know about me first—" I protest, the uncomfortable truth resting between my thighs.

"—Nothing you could say would make me change my mind about wanting to spend more time with you." Billy says, throwing down a couple tens as he tries to shepherd me to the door.

Billy leads me through the crowd with his shoulder parting the bodies around us, his mannerisms gentle as he guides me onto the sidewalk. His kindness is arousing, his company exactly what I needed, but I know I should do anything to stop this before it begins. I picture him as dead as Ivan, his body bleeding like the creep's in the club, but I let him hold my hand and lead me into the night anyway.

His apartment is impressive, not a wall without a painting nor a cushion without a throw blanket in sight. But I avoid soft surfaces, tiptoeing from corner to corner as Billy pops open a bottle of wine. I guess what I'm looking for are red flags, but considering how well-decorated his apartment is, my bet is Billy knows that you shouldn't include such noisy displays.

I wish I knew how to bring up my transness, but there's never a right way to go about it. A text message creates a buffer that can serve as a wall behind which one's opponent can hide and slug vitriol. A reveal over dinner can leave you with the bill as your lover slips out of the bathroom window. But to present one's most precious secrets aloud in the moments before a hot, sweaty tryst, that's like pinning a sign to your chest that reads MURDER ME.

"I spent too much money on that couch to have my guests stand on their feet," Billy says as he gives me glass of wine before flopping onto the sofa.

I stare at his slumped form, my eyes unable to glance away from the inch or so of hairy belly peeking out from beneath his too tight shirt. Finally, I sit down a foot or so away from him, just close enough not to raise concern.

"You weren't this quiet at the bar," Billy mumbles, looking away after a long, silent beat, "Is everything okay?"

I take a deep breath, fingers crossed that I won't regret this as I say, "You seem like a really nice guy, and I would love to go to bed with you. Hell, I'd love to go to bed with you, then take you to breakfast. But the thing is...well, I'm not exactly like the average girl you bring home from the bar. If I unzip my dress, it's not going to fall to the floor and reveal all smooth curves. Billy, I'm trans."

"I mean I didn't want to assume, but I had my suspicions," Billy says, reaching out to cradle my chin in the palm of his hand. "I enjoy you for you, Emma. Whatever you're scared of me seeing, it isn't going to make me change my mind about that."

I want to protest that he's speaking too soon, but he's looking at me with those honey-slick eyes. I'm a fly drawn in by the sweetness, trapped beneath the syrupy weight of his presence as he presses his lips against mine. I kiss him back hard, as if the ferocity of it will force the memory of my confession from his mind. But then he's on top of me, his thighs pressing up against mine, his hand groping at my breast as his mouth explores the perfumed skin of my neck. Everything is happening too fast, but before I can ease him off, I hear the tearing of fabric.

"Fuck, I'm so sorry. I'll pay for the dress," Billy apologizes, inspecting the impromptu slit running up the length of my dress.

But the tear is the least of my problems, the barbed protrusions of my penis carefully concealed by the crossing of my legs. *He isn't going to hurt you, Emma. There is no need for this reaction.* I take a few deep breaths, the most dangerous parts of my anatomy easing back into my body as I motion for him to come back and kiss me.

Everything Billy does is right, his body responding to mine in just the right ways. Hands move slowly down my spine, flirting with the prospect of my legs. Kissing me with just the right amount of tongue. I undo the button of his jeans, his face showing no sign of embarrassment as I look upon his erect penis. Billy pushes up my skirt, gently kissing around the curve of my knee, his lips inching their way up my thigh.

The closer he gets to my penis, the more in my head I become. I picture the beige couch we sit upon stained with blood; his moans replaced by the sound of desperate screaming. Billy eases up, looking up from beneath my skirt. "Do you want me to stop?"

"No...it's just that I've had men be disgusted by my penis. They promise me I'm a beautiful woman, but as soon as they discover it, they seem to change their mind. They look at it like it's monstrous."

Billy peels back my skirt, his eyebrows raising in an exaggerated manner, but quickly fall back to a neutral expression. We both laugh at this as he says, "Looks like a penis to me. A sizeable one, but that's never stopped me before."

Billy kisses me, then disappears beneath my skirt. I flinch as he touches it, the organ growing more and more noticeable as his fingertips ease it into his mouth. I watch as he slips off his boxers, clearly enjoying pleasing me as he masturbates. When I close my eyes, succumbing to the bliss of Billy's actions, all I can picture is Ivan dead on his stoop, the daddy and his bleeding fingers screaming.

Billy suddenly reels back, my eyes fluttering open to see my penis curling up the length of his arm. Before I can say anything, Billy relaxes himself, easing his arm free, but continuing to embrace my anatomy as he takes it both hands. He falls back onto the couch, his muscular legs pulling me on top of him. He kisses me before he whispers in my ear, "I want you to fuck me, Emma."

"I don't want to hurt you, love," I mutter as he grabs for a bottle of lube hidden in the coffee table drawer.

"Give it to me. I can take it."

So, I do what he says, and his moans are a choir proclaiming again and again: you are not your anatomy.

JUICE

By v.f. thompson

*"Design in nature is but a
concatenation of accidents, culled
by natural selection until the result
is so beautiful or effective as to
seem a miracle of purpose."*
— Michael Pollan, *The Botany of Desire*

Nature is cruel.
The words echoed in Jamie's mind, mingling with the staticky warble of NPR's *Folk Alley* on the radio. A half-smoked menthol dangled from the ends of the spindly fingers which dangled from the end of her spindly arm out of the window and into the fall air. She watched the water

through the windshield, gently burbling down the bank, and thought of cold things killing each other underneath the surface.

"Nature is cruel," she said, tasting the consonants. They were bittersweet, like the too-ripe mulberries she had plucked that summer in the woods on their house camping trip. She looked at her reflection in the rearview mirror, ran her thumb along the stubble that was already blooming even though she had shaved before the show, felt her Adam's apple bob, and closed her eyes.

Whatever she had told the enchantrex, nature *was* cruel, and she didn't need to be told that.

She fiddled with the dial, skimmed past a country station and an ad for car insurance, and settled on a Tom Petty song that made her think about the first boy she'd ever dated. Somewhere outside, back towards the street, a stray cat screamed. For the thousand-and-first time she wished her CD player wasn't busted.

Biting her lip, she turned the stereo off entirely. She rummaged through her backpack, sifted past lighters and frayed patches until she found the lacy little bag with the bottle inside. Dropping her unfinished dart in the cupholder, she undid the ribbons and plucked forth the treasure within.

It shimmered in the darkness, recognizable even in the shadows as a vibrant orange. She turned it over, watching the liquid move inside. It felt alive. The smell of ripe peaches wafted through the car, unconstrained by the cork; it smelled hyperreal, more fruity than fruit, like the concentrates at her work tasted. She pressed the glass to her lips, kissing it. It came away with the faintest purple stain. Most of her lipstick had been shed hours before.

She held it up to the trickling moonlight, considering her possible emancipation from her own cells. Smelling that sweetness, Jamie wished that she had some flower to smoke, imagining how good it would taste in the perfumed air.

Fuck it. She would do it tomorrow. Call into Smooth Moves, tell them she was sick. She hadn't missed a day in months. They would cope.

She returned the bottle to its *(her)* bag, pausing to pull out the other goodies inside. There was a sticker of a cartoon bat, a button with a constellation on it, and a business card with silver lettering on black stock. *Lysistrata Woodrose,* it read. *Storyteller, Artist, & Apothecary.*

Nervously biting the corner of the card, she added the sticker to the smattering across the dashboard, next to a Bellsprout planted in a Halloween pumpkin, and pinned the button to the seat belt.

Again, she fiddled with the radio knob. *Folk Alley* was over, and NPR was playing classical, and she turned it off again before turning the key in the ignition and pulling back onto the street. She fished her menthol from the cupholder.

On her way home she saw a dead raccoon on the side of Willow Street, her guts busted open and spilling out of her ribcage.

Nature's not cruel, she had said. *It's full of beautiful things.*

A tinkle of laughter like heady wine.

Darling, the beautiful things are the cruelest. The beautiful things die.

How Jamie had ended up with her legs spread open on a stranger's twin size mattress in the back of a camper she wasn't entirely sure, but that was how the evening had unfurled. The air was tinted blackberry indigo by the string lights above, and the heavy incense was making her head spin. She closed her eyes, breath caught in her throat, and then she remembered that her body existed, and she put a hand up against the stranger's chest.

"Wait," she said, breathing. "Wait, I think we need to stop."

She winced as she felt the rubber cock slip out, looking up at the face above her. Xer pierced eyebrows crinkled in concern, xer eyes almost black in the colored light. "You okay?"

Jamie bit her lip, nodding and pulling a pillow over her A-cup tits. The bed was covered with a selection of stuffed animals, and a snowy owl peered at her with big amber eyes. "Yeah, I'm fine. I just. Need a second."

The stranger, Lysistrata , rolled off of the bed, going over to the sink to wash the strap. "You need some tea or anything?"

She shook her head and then nodded. "Actually yeah, that sounds nice." Jamie watched as xe worked, washing the toy and leaving it in the drying rack, setting the kettle on the stove, rummaging in the cupboard. Xe was so confident in xer nakedness, xer tattooed body a complex instrument of tensing muscles and falling curves. There was something primal, almost animal, in xer physicality, but also a kind of sophistication. Watching xem, Jamie felt even further from her own body, and she reached for the silk sheets to cover herself.

"You can shower if you need a minute," xe said. "Besides, you might be a lil sticky. Throw that towel on the bed in the hamper when you go, would you please?"

"Yeah, thanks," Jamie said, bending to grab her balled up clothes from the floor and straightening up only to be hit in the face with a t-shirt.

Lys laughed, xer voice a little too rough for it to be a giggle. "Sorry, bad thrower. But that's yours. Assuming you want a reminder of tonight, of course."

Jamie blushed, stammering a little. "Oh God, no, it's not like that. It was me. I just—"

"Sweets, you don't have to explain anything." Xe rattled two tins at her. "Raspberry rose clove or honey cinnamon vanilla?"

"Uh, raspberry," she said, heading for the bathroom.

"Shampoo is the pink bottle, conditioner is the purple!" xe said as the door closed, trapping Jamie in a little box. Though the yellow light was dingy, it still seemed very bright compared to the darkness in the rest of the camper, and she felt even more exposed.

She looked at her body through the sheen of soap scum, a little gasp crawling out of her gullet, not quite a cry but not quite not. Her thumb ran across her hairline, down her forehead to the tip of her nose, and then her hand over her breasts, wrapping her arms around herself and hugging tight as she stared at the thing in the mirror.

Stupid. Stupid. Fucking stupid. She should have known this would happen, shouldn't have pressed her luck and pushed herself too far.

She cranked the water as hot as it would go and forced herself to bear it, as if she could burn away her skin and reveal something better beneath. Reaching for the shampoo, she felt immediately calmer as soon as she touched the bottle. She smelled plums and pears, with just a hint of coconut, and as she ran it through her curly black hair she felt as if her anxiety was slipping away and down the drain along with the water. By the time she had moved on to the conditioner and then washed it all out, her breathing was again normal. She dried off, slipping into her jeans and examining the new shirt. It was screen-printed with the image of a tarot card, recognizably the Magician, but with the artist's name below. *Lysistrata Woodrose.* Jamie tasted the name on her tongue, sank her teeth into it and felt it burst in her mouth. If it wasn't for her body playing Judas, kissing her with dysphoria, it might have been the best fuck of her life.

When she emerged, Lys was sitting at the little table, wearing a silky black robe. "Take your pick," xe said, pointing their clove cigarette at the two mugs steaming on the tablecloth.

"Well, I do hate Mondays," Jamie said, taking the Garfield mug and leaving Kermit the Frog for xem. "Wow, this is good," she said, taking a sip.

"Thanks. It's one of my best blends. Tins are six dollars, if you want one. You already got the shirt and the action, you're not getting any more freebies."

"I would, but I have so much tea at home I never drink," she said sheepishly. "I know I should, but I just keep buying Mountain Dew like the animal I am."

"Nectar of the gods," xe teased, clasping a sugar cube between two dangerously long black nails. "No shame, I've been known to Blast some Baja from time to time."

Jamie smiled and shrugged. "I dunno, you're into all this hippy, witchy shit, I figured you might think soda was, unnatural or something. You know, it's all chemicals or whatever."

Xe rolled xer eyes. "One, not a hippy. Two, also not a witch. Three, *everything* is made of chemicals."

A purring noise materialized, and a sphynx cat hopped up onto the table and rubbed against Jamie's hand. "I've never actually met a hairless cat," she said, scratching him behind the ears.

"Well, you still might not have," xe said. "Suppose it depends on your take on the Ship of Theseus."

"What do you mean?"

"I mean that the cat you're petting used to be Daniel Braithwaite, lead singer of Flannel Leg and serial fan molester. Now he's just Deedee, and isn't he *scrumptious*."

Jamie cocked her head to the side. "Once again, what?"

"I told you back in the kitchen, after the show. I'm an enchantrex. I enchant things. Like this little guy here," xe said, cooing and scratching the cat under the chin. "Look, don't worry too much about the ethics. Believe me, he's much more likable this way."

Peering at xem from across the table, Jamie tried to tell whether xe was joking or whether xe was off xer rocker, and then, remembering what she thought she had seen during xer performance, simply decided to roll with it. "Okay."

Xe raised an eyebrow. "Okay?"

"I believe you."

"Cool, I didn't ask. I don't need the validation. I know what I am." Xe paused, and then it was xer turn to shrug. "Then again, I don't usually let people who disparage my work eat me out. So touche."

"You weren't actually playing," she said. "During your set. You weren't playing. It looked like you were. But your fingers never moved." Thinking back to that moment, she tried to remember exactly what she had seen and felt in that space. She could clearly recall the image of Lys's fingers dancing up and down xer guitar, of xer voice filling the room, but something about the memory was off, hazy, dreamlike.

Lys grinned. "Caught red handed. Can't play guitar for shit. I can craft a song and turn it into a candle, though, and make people hear it when it burns."

"So, the whole lighting display at the top wasn't just for show, huh?"

"No, but you have to admit, it does add to the ambience."

She sipped her tea, running her fingers down Deedee's spine and down his tail. "He really used to be a person?"

"Yeah," xe said, fingers skittering along his skin. "He came to me after the allegations came out, in total breakdown mode. He asked if I could fix things. I told him I don't fix things, but that I can change them. He needed my help, and I try to give people what they ask for. He asked for a fresh start, so he got it."

She wondered, briefly, why she was swallowing all of this so easily, and then discarded the thought. She had always suspected magic was real, always known reality was thinner and weirder and stranger and more complicated than it appeared, and now, as this person told her that all of those things were true, she saw no reason to refute xem. The simple fact was that a world with magic made more sense than a world without it, and the enchantrex was offering her reason and sanity in opposition to the random absurdity that had always defined the boundaries of her life.

Besides, she thought. She was bored, she was depressed, she was sad and bummed out and burned out all the fucking time, and the enchantrex was offering her the possibility of something more interesting. She'd be crazy not to believe it.

"I know you said I don't have to explain anything," she said, taking another sip. "But can I explain?"

Lys nodded, palms up and open. "Be my guest." Deedee crossed the table, and Jamie scratched him behind the ears. He was softer than she expected, almost like velvet, and she relished the sensation.

She sighed, searching for the words, trying to explain the intense dysphoria of spirit that sometimes pounced and pinned her and made her choke and bleed. "It's like my own body is constantly hunting itself with a knife, and every so often, it catches up with me and slits my goddamned throat," she said, sipping her tea. "Usually during sex, like tonight, but fuck. Sometimes I'll just be at the grocery store, or doing the dishes, and I'll remember that I have a body, that I have skin and kidneys and lips and fingernails and a cock, and I'll lose my goddam mind. It's like I was born a diamond when I should have been a spade."

The enchantrex listened carefully, smoking xer clove and nodding. "Have you considered that you might be transgender?" xe asked, face serious.

"The thought's crossed my mind," she replied, smiling lightly.

"I sympathize," xe said. "I won't lie and say I understand, but I sympathize. I won the lottery with my body myself." Suddenly, xe looked embarrassed. "Sorry, that totally sounded like bragging, didn't it? I just meant I got lucky."

Her slight smile turned into a rueful grin. "Christ, I feel like I won the lottery with your body tonight too." She paused and then shot for the moon. "So. You said you can't fix things, but that you can change them. Can you change me?"

Xe looked at her for a long time, silent, crushing out the butt of xer clove in the ashtray on the table. When xe spoke, xer voice was sorrowful. "No."

She nodded, bitter, not disappointed exactly because she hadn't had much hope to begin with. Still, she had to know, needed a reason for why transformation was allowed but not allowed for her. "Why?"

Xe sighed a long sigh. "It's not an easy answer."

"It's not an easy question."

"Fair enough," xe said. "Okay. So, here's the way it works. Gender affirming magic is something I've been working on trying to get right for a long time, but there are... complicating factors."

"Like what?"

"Reality has a lot of old-fashioned ideas about itself," xe said. "And magic is about negotiating with reality, getting a better deal than you had before. The problem is that means pleading your case with all kinds of gods and monsters, even if you're not playing the game with them directly, because they set the terms of engagement. And all of those gods and monsters, they're just different faces for the same essential force, that being, well, *reality*. Some are on your side, the ones who savor chaos, usually, but there's a lot more who fetishize order, and see any kind of serious transition or movement as a threat to that. There's rules, strictures, restrictions, all sorts of red tape that have been put in place and make things difficult if you don't have the clout to swing big demands. And me, I'm small time."

"You're saying Mother Nature's a TERF?" said Jamie, giving a bitter laugh.

"Her politics aren't that petty. I'm saying that she's a brutal cunt of a dealer, and that she generally expects you to be happy with the role she's given you because she's proud of her work. She doesn't have time to go back and fix mistakes; she's too busy crafting the next new thing."

"Sounds petty to me," Jamie said, again relishing her tea. "So, you can turn a man into a pussy, but not a cock."

Lys smiled. "It's a lot easier to negotiate punishment than it is pleasure."

Jamie smiled back, mirthless and hollow. "Typical."

"I'm working on it," xe said. "But it's a hard swim upstream. The fact is, nature, gods, the whole kit and caboodle—they're just as bureaucratic in their way as we are. It's primal, it's brutal, but it's also basically just paperwork and requisition forms and work orders in the form of genetic code and fractals."

"So, you're not a magician. You're a lawyer."

"Fuck you," xe said, still smiling. "But you could say that and I wouldn't call you a liar."

Jamie gave a long sigh, leaning her head back and closing her eyes. "Fuck."

"I'm sorry," said Lys.

"Why?"

"For your pain," xe said. "I don't like to see people hurting."

"No," she said, shaking her head. "I mean why the fuck is it like this?"

"That way lies madness," xe said, voice measured. "Tread carefully."

"I'm sick of being careful," she spat. "I'm sick of being nice and pliant and pretending to be soft even though my body is all hard ridges."

"Alright," xe said. "I'll tell you why, then. It's because nature is cruel."

"Nature's not cruel," said Jamie, surprising herself. Why the fuck was she defending the world and its hunger after everything Lys had just told her? Why the fuck was she going to bat for her own abuser?

She looked at the enchantrex, aching with envy and lust and admiration, tasted the afterglow of xer cunt in the back of her throat like the memory of New Year's champagne. "Nature's not cruel," she said again, as if trying to convince herself. "It's full of beautiful things."

"Darling," xe said, still wearing that sad little smile. "The beautiful things are the cruelest. The beautiful things die."

They were silent for a moment. "More tea?" xe asked.

"Yeah," she said. "And I'll take the honey vanilla whatever this time."

Xe rose silently, returned the kettle to the hotplate, letting Jamie's thoughts germinate. What the fuck was she doing? She should be at home with her own fully-clothed cat, not here, chasing dreams with a total stranger, learning the hard truths she had always known about the world were indeed true. Why was she worth this person's time, xer sympathy, xer plain answers and explanations? She wasn't special, was just another rotting stone fruit littering the ground beneath the World Tree.

Xe returned to the table, handing her her refilled mug. "For what it's worth," xe said, the first hint of timidity she had yet noticed nipping at xer voice. "I think you're one of those beautiful things. I think you're absolutely goddamned drop-dead gorgeous, head to toes, and I'm honored to have touched and tasted you tonight. You're exquisite."

Tears welled up in Jamie's eyes as she sampled the tea. She remembered reading that despite its reputation, vanilla was actually an incredibly complex flavor, full of volatile aroma compounds and subtle tricks.

"Thank you," she said, her voice soft, her voice raw, her voice tart and sweet. "But it doesn't help. My beauty is alien to me. If I'm exquisite, I'm an exquisite corpse. There's only the utility of its pain, its confusion at being itself. I know that's selfish, I know it's narcissistic. I know I should learn to be grateful, since it's the only skin I'll ever have. But I can't be, not now, not as a kid, not ever. If I can't be anything other than what I am, then I at least deserve the reality of my grief."

Again, xe was silent, again xe looked at her for a long time. When xe eventually spoke, xer voice had gone beyond timidity and into full anxiety, xer air of careful confidence washed away like a glamour.

"Jamie," xe asked, clearly debating whether to continue. "Jamie, how badly do you want it?"

"Want what?" she asked, no sweetness left, only cyanide.

"To change."

They looked at each other in the wine dark light, two punk ass kids with no respect for authority on two intersecting journeys through the Wildwood. Together they sat at the heart of a clearing, legs crossed, playing cards, considering their fates and fortunes and fantasies.

"I'd give anything," she said, finally.

"Even your life?"

A much shorter pause. "What are you playing at?"

Just as xer timidness had blossomed into anxiety, that anxiety now took on the look of plain old fear. "I shouldn't," xe said, petting Deedee. He purred softly, their human foibles as alien to him as Jamie's beauty was to her. "It might not be safe. It probably isn't."

"What," said Jamie, needling, pressing, cutting through the brush. "You brought it up, so fucking tell me, please."

"I can maybe help you," xe said. "Maybe. But it's dangerous as fuck. It's completely untested."

"What is?" Her voice was harder than she meant for it to be, almost angry, and she flinched.

"I have a potion," xe said, standing up, going to the cupboards above the sink. "Like I said earlier, I've been toying with this for a long time, trying to get it right. But I had sort of a breakthrough about a year ago."

"What kind of breakthrough?"

Xe pulled a mason jar from its dozens of brethren, full of a shimmering orange liquid. Even through the glass, Jamie could suddenly smell the neon scent of ripe peaches, bursting in the heat of a summer sun.

"So, uh. Well. You've heard how they used to make estrogen for hormone treatments out of horse urine, right?"

Jamie nodded. "Yeah?"

"Okay, so. Last year I was playing at a Rainbow Gathering, and I met this dryad. We hooked up, and, well. She left a mess, and I was about to wash the sheets, when I started thinking about phytoestrogens, and about how they're not usually feminizing."

Jamie remembered a YouTube video she had watched on the subject. "Yeah, that's just a conspiracy theory. *Soy makes you gay*, all that shit."

"Right," xe said. Xe was obviously still on edge, but seemed calmer now that xe was discussing xer craft. "But I started envisioning the chemical structure, and I started thinking about what if you *could* force the pieces to fit together? This wasn't ordinary plant matter; it was seeped in magic. And magic's a wild card. It makes things do what they don't naturally want to do."

Jamie looked at the liquid in the jar, sitting on the table, basking in the scent. There, the kitchen full of the fragrance, she could almost believe the things Lys had told her about her body.

"So let me get this straight," she said. "You're telling me what's in that jar is the piss of a tree spirit?"

Now xer smile returned, thought subtler than before. "No, I'm telling you that it's *synthesized* from the piss of a tree spirit." Xe blushed. "And the squirt."

And then they were laughing, the both of them, high and loud and oh so sweet, as if it were the most natural thing in the world. They laughed until they were both crying, tears ruining their makeup and leaving black streaks down their cheeks.

"This is crazy," Jamie said.

"Bonkers," xe agreed. "So anyway, if you want to try it, you can. But you shouldn't."

"If I shouldn't, why are you offering?"

"Because I believe in informed consent. It's your body, your choice, and if you want to take the risks, I'm not going to stop you because I think I know what's best for you. I might know you Biblically, Jamie, but I don't even know your last name."

She paused, no longer laughing, but no longer afraid, no longer angry. Her whole world was rich with that wonderful smell. "So then," she asked. "What are the risks?"

"Well," xe said. "There's a chance that the parts of the dryad's soul that are in this solution won't like what you're asking it to do for you and will punish you for daring to ask."

"Punish me how?" Jamie thought of Actaeon, seeing Diana bathing in the woods, of his metamorphosis into venison, torn apart by his own hunting dogs.

"However she sees fit," xe said. "So. You told me earlier that I'm a lawyer. What's the verdict, your honor?"

The answer came easily, as easily as the laughter—as if it were the most natural thing in the world.

She watched as xe produced a little glass bottle nearly identical to the ones which held her estradiol, watched as xe used a pipette to draw the solution out and transfer it from vessel to vessel. Xe corked it and dropped it into a mesh bag, added a few other goodies and xer card, and handed it to Jamie.

"Do you have needles?" asked Lys.

"Yeah, I do injections," she said.

"Okay then. Just like normal."

"I think I can handle that."

"I really hope you can, Jamie," xe said, stroking her hand. "I had a lovely time with you tonight. I'd hate to know that I signed your death warrant."

"What happened to informed consent?"

Xe nodded, leading her to the door, leading her to the lips of the waiting world. "Thank you again," xe said. "Can I kiss you one more time before you go? For posterity's sake?"

Jamie closed the distance, pressing her lips against xers, relishing the last kiss that she would ever feel inhabiting this particular form. For better or for worse, tomorrow, she would no longer be a walking corpse, would be something else, something fresh.

"Goodnight, Jamie," xe said, opening the door for her. "Goodnight, and good luck."

She had slept with the bottle on the nightstand, shimmering and scintillating, her whole room filled with that delectable smell. Despite the anticipation of the liberation to come, the aroma almost seemed to mock her as she felt horribly trapped in the jagged angles and razor-burned skin of her body. Again, as she had during that last kiss, as she had on the drive home after, she wished that she had had the courage to ask the stranger if she could stay the night, sleep in xer bed, press against xer skin and wake up and drink more of xer tea in the morning.

Instead, she slept alone, and slept fitfully, but she did sleep, and when her eyes opened, it was time.

She did not make breakfast, though she did pour herself a glass of orange juice, no pulp, and took it back upstairs with her. She agonized over what music to play for a long while, and then, looking down at the T-shirt she was still wearing, remembered an LP by the band who had played the first house show she had ever attended, a concept album called *The Fool & the Magician* by The Hills and the Rivers.

As the music began, she lit a rose candle, turned off the lights, and began the ritual. She started as she always did, rubbing her thigh with an alcohol swab, then screwing the draw needle into the syringe. Taking the bottle in her fingers, she breathed deeply and steadily as she slid the tip through the cork, drawing the solution into the device. She pushed the plunger just a little bit to remove any air bubbles, exchanged the needles, and took one last breath. In this moment, for better or worse, she was inviting the world to change her. With a sharp twinge, the world accepted her invitation as she forced the potion into her muscle.

She didn't know what she expected, if she was anticipating an immediate transformation, like she was a spinning magical girl. Instead, she only felt like herself, exactly as she always had, and as she dropped the syringe into the empty Arizona can where she kept her sharps, she tried not to feel stupid.

Give it time, she told herself.

So she gave it time. She whiled away hours on her Asobu Twitch, picking fruit and fishing and doing all sorts of silly tasks in *Critter Village*. When that got tiring, she finally decided to throw on the newest season of an anime had been meaning to get around to for a while.

As she sat there and watched the images flicker across the screen, a torrid romance unfurling between a deer, a wolf, and a rabbit, she realized that she had forgotten to call work. She swore loudly, fumbling for her phone, grateful that it was Loren on duty, who easily bought her excuse about a family emergency.

"Of course, Jamie," they said, and she winced at their sympathy. "It's been pretty dead today anyway. Will you be in tomorrow?"

"Yeah," she said, her voice bitter, finally letting herself feel as stupid as she felt. "Nothing going on tomorrow."

"Great," said Loren, "I'll see you then."

As they hung up, Jamie began to cry, letting out a loud, tangled sob. "Fuck!" she said, slamming her fist against the mattress. "Goddam it!"

She cried for a long while, hating the enchantrex, hating herself, hating the world that had made them both and had braided together their paths. She didn't believe that Lys had lied, didn't believe xe was crazy, still believed there was magic in the world—just not for her.

As miserable as she felt, she was relieved that she seemed to be truly exhausted, and as the show continued to flash on her TV, she fell into a deep sleep.

At first, she noticed nothing. At first, she operated on the damnable assumption that everything was normal and everything was awful.

Then she noticed the heat between her legs, the strange glow centered around her genitals. Half-asleep, her fingers went to probe at her cock, only to discover that it simply was not there. Instead, the fingers landed on a swollen clitoris, nestled between velvety petals, and unconsciously began to rub gently. Waves of unfamiliar pleasure pulsed through her body. Fuck, it felt good, this dream, this pleasant little fantasy—

Her eyes shot open, throwing off the blanket, looking down at her new skin. It was a rich blushing pink, almost orange, and where hair had been the night before there was now only a light dusting of peach fuzz. Her fingers moved down her stomach, experimentally hovering over her new glans, her new labia, her new self, brushing the soft downy thicket that surrounded it, hardly daring to touch the thing itself—and then she did, fingers testing, teasing, plunging, circling, dancing, and when orgasm came it was like nothing she had ever experienced, a quake through her whole body that seemed to make her very foundations shudder. Juice, hot and sticky, gushed out of her, staining the sheets.

"Fuck," she said, and again she was crying, sobbing. "Fuck, God. Thank you. Thank you. Thank you."

Dimly, absurdly, she remembered that she needed to go to work, and she sat up, trembling, and walked to the mirror. With no time to shower, she wiped herself off with a t-shirt from the hamper, examining the particulars of her new form. She was still recognizably herself, but her skeletal body was now plumper, rounder, silkier. Her curly black hair now had a pinkish tinge to it in the light, and it too was softer.

"Holy shit," she breathed. It had worked. It had really worked.

She thought of Lys, and her heart ached with gratitude.

"Okay," she said, knowing that further exploration would have to wait until later. "Alright."

She discovered that her new breasts did not fit into any of her bras, and her work polos were all tight against the curves of her stomach. She dug around, knowing she had a large shirt with the Smooth Moves logo that she had gotten at a work event to sleep in, pulled it on, finishing with one of her stretchier skirts. Even with the elastic band it was a little tight, but it fit.

She said a quick good morning to Harrow and Petra in the kitchen, not giving them time to remark on her change in appearance, seeing them exchange a baffled glance as she bounded out the door and got behind the wheel.

"Jamie, hey," said Loren, looking at her in a way that clearly said they were trying not to stare and failing. "You, uh. Look great. Did you get a tan?"

"Something like that," she said, clocking in.

"And is that perfume? You smell wonderful."

The morning passed uneventfully, and there was only an hour left in her shift when it happened. She was preparing a Mango Banana Boost, dumping in chia seeds and chunks of plant matter and fruit concentrate, when she leaned over and vomited, a perfect stream of bright orange liquid that landed in the blender along with everything else and splattered the counter around it.

"Oh, hey, whoah!" said Loren, running over. "Jamie, hey, what the hell, are you okay?"

She nodded, wiping her mouth on her wrist, smiling weakly. "Sorry," she said. "I don't know what happened."

There was none of the vile acidity that usually came with that particular maneuver. Whatever she had thrown up had emerged tasting sweet and tart and pleasant.

"Jamie, I—" they paused, a glazed look coming over their eyes. The customer who had ordered was watching the whole scene, a look of placid repulsion on their face. "Jamie, that smells really good," they said. Then they shook their head, stirring their senses and said "Hey, you've gotta go home. Take the rest of the day off, get some rest, call and let us know how you feel tomorrow. Okay?"

She nodded, stumbling outside, her belly seeming fuller, her skirt tighter, her thighs bigger, wondering why she didn't feel more upset, wondering why she didn't feel sicker, wondering why she felt so goddamned good—and then, as she got behind the wheel, she stopped wondering and just decided to enjoy the ride. People honked at her several times as she went, weaving a little from side to side, feeling a little buzzed, a little fucked in the head, and wanting nothing more than to get home, climb into bed, and worship her new body.

By the time she fumbled open the door, she was nearly bursting out of her clothes, her plump belly sagging, her skirt cutting into the skin, legs jiggling. Now she felt full on drunk, giggling, laughter bubbling out of her belly, and she leaned against the doorframe as it opened, relishing life, relishing *her* life.

"Jesus, Jamie," said Harrow, looking up from the couch, setting her sketchbook aside. "Jesus, what the fuck—"

"It's fine," she said, smiling serenely. "I'm fine. I'm good. I'm so fine. I'm great."

"Dude, you don't look great," said Harrow, standing up, coming over to her, helping her towards the couch. "You look fucking..." She paused, her eyes seeming to glaze over, her look of worry turning to serene hunger. "... beautiful," she finished. "You smell beautiful."

As Jamie fell onto the couch, she looked at her housemate, who had always seemed so effortlessly gorgeous, so flawlessly, naturally confident, and who had always hated her body as much as Jamie hated her own. Harrow looked at her in dizzy confusion, looming over her like a tree. When she spoke, she was almost breathless, almost timid. "Jamie," she asked, nearly panted. "Can I kiss you?"

Jamie desperately wanted to be touched, desperately needed to be tasted, but had enough of her wits about her to ask "What about Petra?"

"I don't care," Harrow said, and then she was on top of Jamie, grabbing her shoulders, grinding against her, kissing her deeply, biting her lips. Jamie closed her eyes, head swimming, losing herself in her housemate's touch, not thinking about all of the times she had wondered what it would be like to kiss her, barely thinking at all—

Rough, eager hands were ripping the clothes from her body, revealing the breasts that were now the size of melons, trembling under the touch. Harrow squeezed them gently, rubbing, kneading, kissing each engorged nipple, and then kissing down her stomach, biting the edge of her skirt, using teeth to pull it down. It was discarded, and her underwear soon followed, revealing the pert and perky petals of the perfect vulva she had dreamed of having so long.

"Can I?" Harrow asked, and without waiting for an answer began to kiss her stomach, kiss her thighs, and then to press her lips to her clit. Her mouth was hot and wet and hungry, and every tender fiber of Jamie's body ached to be eaten, to be tasted, to be hungered after. There were no coherent thoughts left in Jamie's head, only pleasure pure in purpose. She was flowering, blooming, still transforming, ripening with each new wave of delight.

"You taste..." Harrow moaned, sucking, biting, "... you taste so fucking..." And then her words were lost as she used a little more teeth, bit a little harder, and then her mouth opened wide and bit down. Her teeth sank easily through Jamie's flesh, separating her glans clitoris from the nervous tissue inside, leaving a mangled crater between her mons pubis and vulva. Juice and ejaculate poured out of the wound and over Harrow's face, and when she had swallowed the tissue, she began to drink greedily, ravenously, deliriously.

"Oh, yes!" screamed Jamie. "Oh, God, yes, yes, God!" Her eyes opened, her hands in Harrow's hair, pulling up and towards her. Again they kissed, and Jamie tasted herself as Harrow spit a juice and pulp between her waiting lips.

Harrow moaned, slipping down, stumbling backwards onto the floor. "Fuck," she said, and some of Jamie's wits returned as she watched this new transformation. She had heard that there could be differences between oral and injected hormone therapy, but never imagined anything this drastic. Where Jamie's transition had been agonizingly slow, she watched as Harrow's thin body grew plumper, fuller, breasts and stomach swelling, blonde hair turning pinkish-orange as her skin erupted in blush. "Oh, it feels so good."

The door slammed open, and both of them looked to see both Petra and their other housemate, Ash, standing there and looking stunned. At first Petra's face was a mask of rage, but it soon turned to horror as they took in the scene before them. "What the fuck—" they began.

Ash looked dazed, peaceful, and they smiled. "It smells so good in here," they said. "It smells like—"

"Taste her," said Harrow, breathless. "You have to taste her, she tastes so good."

"What the fuck," Petra said again, but now they sounded far off, dreamy, voice swimming in the heady perfumed air.

Ash was already coming towards them, stripping down, taking off their shirt and their binder, kneeling in front of the couch. Harrow grabbed Petra's hand, helped them out of their shirt, kissed them tenderly. Jamie was still leaking juices everywhere, and her hands eagerly guided Ash between her legs. They drank deeply, savoring, and then they were fingering, penetrating the mutilated flesh. Petra and Harrow were on the floor now, wrapped around each other, all of them naked or nearly so.

"Take a bite," said Harrow in between kissing her partner. "It won't hurt her, she likes it."

Again, Jamie felt teeth slipping through her body, severing herself from herself, and again she came, ecstatic and shaking and shuddering, her fingers digging into Ash's shoulders. "Petra, taste," Harrow said, grabbing Ash's hair, guiding their mouth to theirs, the juice and meat running out from between their lips and dribbling between Petra's.

Soon Ash and Petra's transitions began just as Harrow's had, and soon they were all soft, all swelling, all full of fluid and liquid pleasure. They all kissed, all caressed, moaning, tasting, touching, fucking, licking, rubbing, cumming, cumming, cumming, drinking, eating, swallowing, swelling, swelling, swelling. Their bodies rubbed against each other, their flesh of each other's flesh, lost in a communion of fermentation and holy fear.

As Petra kissed her stomach and fisted her ruined hole, as Ash ripped the skin from her arms and chewed, Jamie's mind managed a coherent thought. There had been nothing to worry about, Lysistrata's fears unfounded. Everything had turned out wonderfully, perfectly, better than she ever could have imagined.

Nature was not cruel.

Nature was full of beautiful things.

Still they kissed, still they feasted, still they fucked, tonguing and tearing, until they had exhausted themselves and each other. They lay there together as the sunset filtered through the windows and turned to night, a pile of stoned fruits, lost in themselves and in each other, not dreaming but being. They lay there in perfect pleasure, bleeding together, leaking together, rotting together, another senseless casualty of the natural world.

FALL INTO ME

By Andromeda Ruins

It's an odd thing to wake up tangled in the power lines. The electric buzzing of the wires should be frying his body, but he supposes God planned for this when He gave Angels hollow bones.

They do have their advantages, though. He is lighter than he looks, something that helped when he fell. His wings were just barely strong enough to slow his descent, though he couldn't control what direction they sent him in. It's how he ended up tangled in the wires with no way out.

His wings are pinned to his back at an awkward angle. He can't get them free, the more he tries the more ensnared he becomes. The ridges of the wire catch on his feathers, painfully pulling them out. Blood smears across his back and he begins to panic.

He needs to get out of there. His wings, his beautiful wings, they're going to be damaged. The clothes he is wearing tear apart as he thrashes, the rip of fabric mixes with his screams as the sickening crack of feathers breaking fills the air.

The sun has set by the time he stops fighting. The stars above mock him in his struggle. They taunt him, tell him that he is no longer a part of them. That he is no longer in His graces and that is why he is stuck.

I can't get out on my own, I need someone to help me. His eyes adjust to the lack of light, pupils dilating to take in as much light as they can. The street below him is mostly empty, there are two kids down the way. Humans, or else they would have heard him scream. But there's another figure, someone much closer looking directly up at him.

They're the reason he fell, the demon that he hasn't been able to stop thinking about—stop craving—for millennia. He groans, of course they had to be here. He shouldn't be surprised; they always seem to pop up wherever he goes.

It's a good thing, he supposes. Because that means there is someone that can help him down. He can't see what they are doing, the lit candle they are holding burns his eyes.

The only thing he can see is their red eyes, they nearly glow with the reflection of the dancing flame.

Those damned eyes, the ones that he can feel as they rake over his body every time he steps foot out of heaven. The eyes that follow his every movement, take up his every thought. They have even invaded his dreams, where they tempt him into sin.

They are far away, a blurred speck on the ground below him. But their voice carries itself on the wind as if it were a part of the heavens itself.

"You look a bit stuck; do you need help?"

Before he can answer, they set the candle in their hands down and spread their wings. It takes just a moment before they are set on the wires next to him. He lets them work on disentangling his limbs while he takes in every detail of their scraggly wings.

His arms are freed first and the first thing he does with them is reach out for them. He wants to touch them, wants to know how they feel. Do their wings feel like his? That's not possible, they can't be as soft. His wings were a gift from God himself.

His fingertips just barely graze the edge of the softest feather he has ever felt when he plummets to the ground. He lands hard; the air leaves his lungs. His wings crack and break below him, the pain floods his every nerve.

Tears flood his vision as he heaves. He tries to roll over, but the attempted movement makes the pain worse. It's not long before he feels himself being picked up, the demon's strong arms hook underneath his knees and back.

He cries out as he is cradled to their chest. The now useless wings drag like a dead weight below his body and it hurts, *it hurts,* **it hurts, it HURTS.**

The world fades to black around him, and when he comes to again he is being laid down on a soft mattress. He buries his face in a pillow and his wings splay out across the bed. The pain has dulled, this new position takes the weight and pressure off the broken appendages.

That doesn't mean they're any less sensitive, though. Something he finds out as clawed fingers trail down the skin between the broken wings. They bring pain, yes, but this pain is different. This pain is one that feels so good in a way that he never knew was possible. He moans as he wonders what else he has missed out on in his millennia of holiness.

"You're so pretty like this, covered in blood and lying in my bed," the demon whispers, their warm body pressed against his back. A shiver runs down his spine at the words, an unfamiliar warmth collects in the pits of his stomach.

Their hand is hot, it burns his skin as it traces a path down his side and over the swell of his ass. They don't stop even as they reach the warmth between his legs—the one area of his body that not even God dared to touch.

"Look how wet you are for me. I thought you couldn't sin but here you are, dripping for me."

He presses his hips back into their hand. This is what God wanted the Angels to abstain from? This bliss, this is something he could have had at any point in the past millennia? Oh, how misguided he was.

He whines as they pull their hand away from him, sitting back onto his legs so that they are no longer pressed up to him.

"Are you sure this is something you want?" The tone of their voice is serious as they speak. "This is something that you will not be able to recover from. By crossing this line, you will fall."

"If I shall fall, then I shall fall into you," he grits out. They don't know he's already been cast out. There is no returning for him, he might as well indulge.

He looks up at the demon over his shoulder, his eyes burning in a way they never have before. "Take everything of me and make it yours."

There is a gleam of hunger in their eyes, and it excites him. Nearly as much as the hard press of their excitement against his legs. But it's his next words that set everything in motion.

"Make me worthy of you."

The demon's breath hitches, their eyes shine with something unreadable before lust swallows them. Any hesitation they had evaporates as they begin moving against him. Their hardness haunts him, teases him.

"How did I get so lucky," they lean down to growl in his ear. They nip at his earlobe and *oh God* does it feel good.

Every tease of their sharp teeth against his neck makes him more excited, he wishes they would bite. He follows his instinct and stretches his neck as much as he can, giving them easier access to the area.

He lets out a shaky breath as their arm wraps around him, as their hand enters his warmth. They rub lazy circles there and he's gone. He rocks his hips back into them, begging for more. His muscles spasm as he pleads, "Please, oh God. Please!"

As soon as the words leave his mouth, his pleasure is ripped away as they pull their hand back. He whimpers at the loss.

"Don't say His name," the demon growls. "Tonight, I am your God."

He peaks over his shoulder as he hears them adjusting their clothes. They remove their belt and use it to bind his arms behind his back. The leather holds his biceps secure, providing a slight lift to his limp wings.

The movement causes him to moan, but that moan quickly morphs into a scream as they dig their clawed fingers into the skin at the base of his wing. His back arches as he desperately tries to get away, but he can barely move with his arms bound and their weight on his back.

Tears stream down his face, why are they hurting him?

"Now let me hear you say it. Who is your God?" His mind is foggy and his vision is blurred. He can't feel anything but their fingers in his skin and their hardness against his ass.

"You," he gasps. "You are my God."

The demon above him gives him no reprieve as they twist their hand into his broken feathers. It's less pain this way and a coil of pleasure joins the pain as they card their fingers through the soft plumage.

He feels a rumble deep in his chest at the motion, the release of pain is almost dizzying. He's breathless, he's never felt like this. Never felt like he was flying even when he was firmly planted on the ground, never felt so Holy.

The last of his breath is squeezed out of his lungs as the demon presses him further into the mattress, leaning their full weight on his back as they grab a lit candle off the nightstand.

"Now, we're going to have a little fun. If, at any point, you want me to stop you need to tell me. Understood?"

He nods, though he doesn't think he would ever want them to stop. They could ruin him, tear him limb from limb, and he would thank them for it.

"Good boy," they purr. "Now let's warm you up."

The words are punctuated by drips of hot wax hitting his skin. It burns for just a moment before his skin pulls taut and it dries. It's an uncomfortable feeling, but oddly pleasant. That is, until the wax drips on his broken wings.

The pain is delicious. It's as if his purity is being burned away by the wax and replaced by their sin. He gladly accepts that. They are taking him apart and remaking him with every drop of wax that splashes on his wings.

He's never wanted before, but now he wants to scream. Wants to let the universe know who he is and who he belongs to. He wants to worship the demon, revere them for recreating him. He wants, he wants, he wants.

Just when he thought it couldn't get any better, he feels them rut against his heat. Their jeans are gone, leaving them bare as they move against him. There are ridges along their shaft that pique his curiosity.

When he looks over his shoulder once more, he is met with metal decorating their member. He salivates at the sight, what are those? Why would they alter the form that was given to them by Him?

But then he knows. He knows what they are for as the demon enters him. Each piece of metal hooks against him as they thrust in. It causes him to see stars. He wants to cry out, wants to tell them that it hurts.

They don't slow; their thrusts brutally push him further into the mattress. Tears stream down his face and mix with the spit already polling on the pillow.

There's so much happening, so many stimuli he has never experienced before. The metal he can feel as it moves within him, the punishing force of their hips into his, the burning of the wax on his wings, their fingers digging into his hip and pulling him back into them.

He doesn't know how much more he can take; uncomfortable warmth is pooling deep within him. This isn't enough for them, though, as they blow out the candle and toss it to the side. They use their now free hand to reach below him, wrapping their large claws around his throat and pulling his body off the mattress.

His wings are pinned between their bodies, his hands flatten against their lower stomach. There is just enough room for him to spear his hands, grabbing their hips and pulling them in.

The hand around his throat tightens, constricting his airways. He throws his head back against their shoulder, an invitation which they do not hesitate to accept as they press their mouth to the soft expanse of skin.

He gasps, struggling to take in air. His vision is spotty and *oh God I'm close.*

As if they can hear his thoughts, they bite down hard. Their teeth draw blood as his world explodes into light. He screams, his legs trembling as he comes.

They don't stop their ministrations. They keep pounding into him and they chase their own pleasure. It's too much, the stars in his vision turn to pin pricks of pain.

Just as he opens his mouth to demand they stop they release their grip on his throat, shoving two fingers into his mouth. Then, they utter a command that he has no choice but to obey.

"Bite."

If my God wills it, then I shall give it to Them.

He clamps down around their fingers and his mouth fills with the tang of blood. Their hips stutter as they moan, a warmth filling his insides.

They let go of him and he falls back onto the mattress. The movement rips them from within him. He whimpers at the sudden feeling of emptiness.

Something warm drips out of him, but he's too tired to try and figure out what it is.

The last thing he remembers before falling asleep is the demon removing the belt from around his arms and leaning in to whisper in his ear.

"You have always been worthy of me, I was just waiting for you to see that you deserved more than what He could give you."

HOW TO CHEAT: FOR DUMMIES

By Enoli Lee

The first time Robbie cheated on his boyfriend hadn't been planned. He had felt like such a cliche. It was the usual story of someone's partner being away on a business trip, so then they get lonely, and one thing leads to another. He had felt a gnawing guilt in his stomach the moment after it ended. After the man, the one he had picked up at the local queer bar's trans pride night, kissed him goodbye with his own slick still coating his lips. He had watched the man walk away and immediately started planning on how to make it up to his boyfriend, without him ever knowing, of course.

But the thing was, more than the guilt, he had felt an overwhelming thrill. He had ridden his cisgender boyfriend harder than ever the night he got back, thinking of another man's mouth on his t-dick and wondering if, when his boyfriend went down on him, he could taste the difference. If he could feel the other man's touch branded into his skin. If he would smell his cologne.

The second time, and every other one after it, was intentional and calculated. He had gravitated toward Grindr at first but quickly deleted it after the location services almost outed his activities to a friend. Robbie was instead forced to get creative, learning the subtle art of cruising and hankie codes and becoming familiar with every queer bar within an hour's radius that he knew his boyfriend would never set foot in. The dingy, held together by duct tape and a dream, bars.

His favorite thing about cheating, other than the amazing and anonymous sex he was now having on the regular, was the way his stomach clenched in excitement each time he got away with it. He loved the adrenaline rush he got in those few days after a hookup, where he felt as if he could be discovered at any moment. Just the slightest mistake in putting concealer on a hickey or his pants slipping low enough to reveal hand-shaped bruises and the ruse would be up. It was terrifying, and at the same time, it was the most fun he'd had in years.

He spent each hookup, the ones he had solely with other trans men, thinking about his boyfriend. Robbie would think about kissing him when he got home before he brushed the taste of another man's slick out of his mouth. He would think about what lingerie he would wear for his boyfriend, intricate and lacey things to cover up the bright red handprints on his ass and bite marks inside of his thighs. He would think about the betrayal and sorrow that would cross his boyfriend's face if he found out and come so hard his vision would black out for a moment.

He felt like an addict getting hit after hit, and there was no way he was going to stop anytime soon.

Robbie shimmied into his tightest pair of jeans, the denim causing his lace underwear to ride up into his ass like a thong. He gave himself a moment to admire his outfit in the mirror before heading out of their house, his heartbeat jumping in his skin like it was sending a signal in Morse code of his intentions for the night.

He stepped through the door of the club, smirking and nodding at the bouncer as he was let in. The flashing lights, pounding bass, and smells hit him square in the face as he made his way to the bar, cheap alcohol and sweat mingling together into his favorite perfume. He couldn't suppress the wide smile on his face, feeling a little manic as he waved to get the bartender's attention. Tonight was special like no other, and he slid his gaze around the room to find someone to celebrate it with.

He felt a hand slide into his back pocket and turned around. It was Caleb, the short, burly man he had hooked up a few months ago. Robbie had enjoyed their time together, the man was good with his tongue and made him see stars, even though he himself had spent almost five minutes picking Caleb's pubes from his teeth. Testosterone had made the man into the dictionary definition of a bear, which also meant each time Robbie had kissed across his body, he ended up with stray hairs on his tongue and in his teeth.

"Hello, stranger," Caleb said, breaking him out of his thoughts. He moved his hand deeper into his pocket, cupping his ass and tracing his panty line through his jeans with slow swipes of his finger.

Robbie turned and leaned in close, "Hey there, handsome," He purred, "You here with anyone tonight?"

Caleb was shaking his head with a sly smile before he could finish his question, squeezing his ass sharply. Robbie gasped at the feeling, a shiver working its way through his body.

He watched as the man caught the bartender's attention, taking charge and ordering them a few tequila shots.

Caleb turned back to him as the bartender poured their shots, "I haven't seen you around in a bit. You been busy?" He asked, his mouth so close to his ear he could feel his lips brushing against it with each word.

Robbie carefully shook his head, "I've been trying out new places, seeing what else is out there." He said with a smile as he watched the other man's eyes darken with hunger, imagining just what sort of things he had been doing at different bars.

They worked through their shots quickly, their eyes getting more and more glazed as they tossed them back. He could feel Caleb watching his every movement. His gaze was heavy on him as they continued to drink, and soon all that was left were empty glasses. The moment their last shot was emptied, Caleb grabbed his hips, pushing him onto the dance floor, through the crowd, and back toward the bathrooms.

Robbie was shoved into an empty stall, his back against the sticky, graffiti-covered wall as the other man kissed him hungrily. He clenched his fingers onto the man's shoulders, gripping at his shirt with desperation as Caleb claimed his mouth. His fingers worked their way down his front, unbuttoning his shirt with thick, deft fingers.

Caleb broke apart their kiss to mouth at his neck, leaving marks as he nipped and sucked down his front before folding gracefully to his knees. He watched with hunger, feeling his pupils blow wide, as Caleb unbuttoned his jeans with his teeth, a practiced movement he was sure the man had done dozens upon dozens of times before.

His last thought, as the man pushed his jeans down past his knees and mouthed at his throbbing t-dick, was of the hidden engagement ring he had found in his boyfriend's sock drawer.

The first time Robbie thought of killing his fiancé, it had just been a passing moment, a fleeting thought that he brushed away. But once it was there, the idea kept knocking at his brain like woodpecker, or a Jehovah's Witness. He would fuck another man in yet another dirty bathroom stall or the backseat of his car and think about what his fiancé's face would look like in that moment, the betrayal, the shock, and the anger that would spread across his features like an oil spill. He wanted nothing more than to tell him of his countless moments of infidelity, and he spent most of his hookups getting off to the idea of his fiancé's heartbroken face.

But the thing was, if he told him, if he broke his heart so thoroughly, then his fiancé would tell others. His social standing would be utterly ruined. He knew all of his friends and even his family would take his side instead of Robbie's. They all adored his fiancé and thought he hung the sun itself in the sky, they would turn their backs on him, and he would be left with no one. He wondered if he would even lose his job because of it.

And that was why he had to kill him. He needed, more than anything, to watch the tears fall from his eyes at the revelation that Robbie had been fucking other men on the regular. He wanted to break his heart, to shove a metaphorical knife in it and then a real one in his gut. Robbie wanted to watch his eyes go wide at the pain of his betrayal and then again as he realized that he was killing him, that he was stabbing him over and over.

It became an obsession to imagine murdering him, to fantasize about fucking a knife in and out of his stomach as his fiancé pleaded for his life. He wanted the man to beg him for mercy, even after he revealed his infidelity, he wanted to watch his fiancé get on his knees and beg for Robbie to spare him. He became so obsessed with the idea that he didn't even care what happened to him afterward, if he went to jail or not. The idea of his fiancé dying at his hands was more thrilling than anything else.

He could take the public hate and scrutiny, he just needed to kill him, to look into his eyes as he did it. It would sustain him for a lifetime, it would fuel his fantasies every night.

Robbie heard the soft snick of the front door as he pushed it open, stepping deftly around every creaky floorboard as he walked to their shared bedroom. He could still taste the come of the two men he had eaten out in the alleyway behind the club, and he licked his lips as he thought about kissing his fiancé with the taste still on his mouth.

Every time he came home from another hookup, barely remembering whatever flimsy excuse he had given his fiancé as his reason for going out for the night, he thought "This could be it. I could kill him right now". He would kiss and hug him, sometimes even fucking him once he got home, and then lay in bed next to the man and think of the knife under the mattress.

He thought of it as he changed into his pajamas beside the sleeping form of his fiancé. He watched his body shift with each breath he took, hearing his soft snores with a sneer spreading across his face. He hated him. He hated everything about the man and more than anything, he wanted to watch the light leave his eyes as he crushed him body and soul. He wanted to ruin him completely.

He knelt on the hardwood floor, gently lifting the side of the mattress to curl his fingers around the smooth, cold handle of the knife. He took it out and held it in his palm, testing the weight while sliding the fingers of his other hand along the sharp edge of the blade. He took a shaky inhale as the knife nicked at his fingers.

Suddenly, Robbie clenched his fist hard, rising from his knees and bringing the knife over his head as he loomed over his fiancé. He watched him sleep, thinking of how easy it would be to bring the knife down right then. He thought of how easy it would be to wake him with the pain and then tell him of what he had been doing that night, and every night he had spent away from him.

The man below him shifted, a soft hum escaping his lips, "Robbie? Did you have fun?" He smiled; eyes still closed as he mumbled against his pillow.

Robbie brought the knife down with a whoosh, deftly hiding it behind his back as he leaned further over him. "Shh, go back to sleep," he said as he gave him a gentle kiss on the lips, smothering a smirk at the thought of him tasting the other men he had been with.

In a swift movement he pushed the knife back under the mattress and climbed slowly under the covers. His fiancé scootched closer, wrapping his arms around Robbie and pressing a kiss to the back of his neck. Robbie closed his eyes, thinking of how close he had come to killing him tonight.

"Another time." He thought, and drifted off in his arms.

T4T Text Messages

By Blue Sunshine

GIVE ME
to the Repo man
when he comes,
cut from me the parts
you cannot live without,
change me irrevocably,
violently.

Melt me
into one piece again,
make me whole

if you must rearrange
my molecular structure,
softening my body, anew.

Stretch me
flexible, thin, laid
out on the counter, taken
like ibuprofen, two
shots of espresso,
and testosterone.

Mold me
into ropes, shibari and
bitter licorice—
in powdered sugar,
draw me
from memory.

GENERATION DEAD/HIGANBANA DOLLS: GLUTTONY DOLL
By: Cookie Calyx

Seattle of Generation Dead encounters Akira Hachijou searching for another of the Higanbana Dolls, and the two end up in a creepy house during a rainy night. Features weight gain and body horror. Explicit (sorta).

Disclaimer: Generation Dead's owned by DNA Comics, Higanbana Dolls by Kumiko Sayuri.

Author's Notes: I doubt anyone expected a crossover like this. I'm probably the only *Gen Dead* fan who's read *Higanbana Dolls*. I love weird crossovers and hoped to find one about these two. I realized I had to stop waiting for someone else to write this story and make it myself.

Before I go further, I wanna be upfront. I've decided to admit I like weight gain in stories and art. I like guy characters who aren't normally fat either being fat or getting fat and enjoying it. I'm tired of feeling like that's something to be ashamed of. I didn't feel comfortable saying it outright, even as a *Sumoboarding* fan, because I haven't encountered a lot of supportive people in real life. It took a lot for me to admit I'm nonbinary, but it was through talking and commissioning an artist I consider a dear friend that I was able to say I have a kink.

Akira and Seattle are my faves, so naturally I want them BIG. The fact they're asexual like me means a lot.

M*other was especially hungry tonight. Sally knew Mother was always hungry, but tonight she was gripped with a particularly ravenous craving. Sally wasn't sure what Mother craved exactly, so she made everything. Maybe there was something in the air. The seasons were changing; the nights getting shorter and warmer affecting a person's mood. And what affects their mood affects their hunger.*

Sally did her best to accommodate Mother's hunger. She worked her fingers to the bone, if her fingers had bones, preparing the dining room for mealtime. It's not like she had anything better to do. Sally was thankful she only needed to create a meal for one. She disliked having guests. Baking was hard enough when it came to pleasing Mother, but it had to be done.

Almost every square inch of the once grand dining room was covered by an incredible array of baked goods. Across the table, on the chairs, inside the cabinets which once held fine China, along the windowsills, inside the fireplace, even on the mantle above the fireplace.

Two spots were bare of sweets; the floor and the glass case atop the mantle where Sally resided. Sally knew better than to leave food on the floor. She wasn't raised in a barn.

And she didn't need to give Mother another reason to open her case.

Ever.

The door to the dining room swung open with a bang, slamming against the wall with such force the room shook. A few cookies fell from their resting place and crumbled on impact with the floor. Mother paid no heed to the broken treats as she crawled in on all fours, but Sally knew she'd get to the broken cookies soon enough.

Mother never left a single crumb behind.

Safely in her case, Sally wished she could look away as Mother fed. No matter how many times she watched Mother cram sweets into her maw, Sally always felt pure disgust. Her jaw unhinging as she swallowed cakes and pies whole. Teeth grinding as jam and custard and cream spilled from Mother's mouth, down her arms and onto the floor like blood.

It wouldn't be long until Mother finished devouring the treats along the walls and the surfaces of the room. She'd then focus on the splatter on the floor. Mother never cared to chew with her mouth closed.

Though she couldn't close her glass eyes, Sally felt tears running down her porcelain cheeks as she heard Mother slurping up partially chewed morsels from the ground. Running her tongue along the floorboards until they were licked clean. Paying no mind to whatever mess Mother dragged into the room with her on her grimy hands and the soles of her blackened feet.

The sound of a sandpaper tongue being dragged against wood drove Sally mad.

She thanked God they were alone this night, in this house so far away from civilization.

As bad as this *was, Mother was* **worse** *when she had company over for a bite.*

"What a wild and crazy vacation that was!" Gina "Rainbow" Vivaldi suddenly declared as the bus pulled out of the station, heading in the direction of Roswell Falls, Nevada. "I can't believe we survived a week at Terrorville amusement park AND helped a ghost chicken solve a murder in a small Southern town."

"Gina, *why* are you talking like that?" Salli-Ann "Winter" Maza was put off by the odd way Gina described what their friends already knew. Like she was doing exposition for the people on the bus who weren't members of Generation Dead, the team of college student superheroes who gained fantastic powers after being killed and resurrected by alien scientists.

"The farther away from that psycho chicken, the better," Maximillion "Airgun" Thibodeaux groaned as he applied balm to the cuts and scrapes covering his muscular arms. A band-aid concealed the spot on his chin where his goatee had been pecked off. The Cowboy hat that usually rested atop his blond head resided on his lap. "That bird was fucking mad about something, and I don't know what."

"Don't you mean *clucking* mad?" Gina joked, her rainbow-colored tresses bouncing around her head as she laughed.

"Bridger, *please* save the puns for home," Salli-Ann groaned while pinching the bridge of her nose. "It's been a long couple of weeks."

"Wrong one, Sal," Max pointed out.

"Sorry Gina, force of habit. Hey," Salli-Ann looked around, her shoulder length black hair swaying as she did. "Where IS Bridger?" Gina and Max joined their Hopi housemate as she craned her head into the aisle, looking for where Bridger "Seattle" Warren sat.

"Dunno," Max answered as he peeked over his seat, hoping to spot a familiar, scruffy-headed Spokane slacker with his face buried in a trashy comic or horror novel.

"I thought I saw him getting on," Gina recalled, tapping her nose ring with her index finger as she so often did while thinking. "I *definitely* saw someone carrying a skateboard."

"But are you sure that was Bridger?" Max inquired. Gina did a poor job hiding her uncertainty, not helped by the embarrassed shade of red appearing her usually pale face.

Salli-Ann turned to Alice "Pose" Vane on her right, slumped against the bus window, and asked, "Do you know where Bridger's sitting, Alice? Alice?"

The only response Salli-Ann received was gentle snoring as the tall, blonde leader of Gen Dead slumbered.

"Uh-oh." Salli-Ann turned her attention to Max and Gina as they stuck their heads over their seats, gesturing towards the snoozing, statuesque white girl. "Our tireless leader's on an impromptu trip to dreamland."

"More like Coma Land," Max sighed. "Al's impossible to wake up if she don't want to."

"I'm not surprised, this vacation took too much out her," Salli-Ann frowned. It was very rare for the inhumanly durable Alice to need a nap. Seeing her dozing was slightly unnerving for Salli-Ann and the others. "I didn't think she was that exhausted."

"And I don't see Bridger anywhere," Gina fretted, looking sickly green.

"Place your bets," Max announced. "What should we be more worried about? That we left Bridger at the bus station? Or how mad Alice is gonna be when she wakes up to learn we left Bridger at the station?"

The three superheroes involuntarily shuddered. While they knew Alice was a sweetheart who wouldn't dare consider hurting a fly for any reason, she also had a terrifying temper coupled with her fierce desire to protect her friends at all costs. She wasn't the type to leave someone behind, not even if you held a gun to her head.

Which some learned the hard way.

Salli-Ann quickly deflected blame. "You know what Bridger's like. He probably got distracted playing those obnoxious arcade games you have to spend five dollars' worth of quarters on. Or he stuffed himself with as many gas station nachos and donuts as he could afford and made himself totally sick." Salli-Ann thought for a moment. "Or both."

"Sal, you know Bridger's gut is tougher than gas station nachos," Max chuckled.

"Maybe we should ask the driver to turn around or just get off here to find him," Gina proposed. "We can always catch another bus."

"No way, the sooner we're home the sooner this vacation can finally end," Salli-Ann declared. "With Alice out of commission, that makes me acting leader. Bridger can catch up. He's a big boy and can take care of himself for a few hours."

Gina looked appalled. "Wait a minute! Do you hear yourself?"

"Yeah!" Max joined in. "No one voted you leader, Winterbutt. If anyone's leader while Al's not, it's me!"

"What about me?!" Gina demanded to know.

As Rainbow, Winter, and Airgun argued over who got to be Gen Dead's temporary top dog, the rest of the bus's occupants decided to ignore the bickering 20 somethings. While Pose blissfully slumbered, ignorant of the discord among her teammates while nestled in dream time, she had no way of knowing Seattle was careening into the path of something not even his iron stomach could handle.

Probably.

"*R*azzafrazzing bus razzafrazzing vacation ...*"
Miles away, a scruffy, stocky Spokane student sulkily skated. Bridger "Seattle" Warren couldn't believe it. Not only had the bus left without him AND his so-called buddies in Generation Dead hadn't waited for him, someone managed to buy the last package of sticky buns from the gas station before he could! Was there no justice in the world?

"No respect, no respect I tell ya," Bridger complained in his best impersonation of Jabberjaw (which usually drove Salli-Ann crazy; she HATED sharks). His stomach grumbled; he knew those nachos and donuts weren't as filling as they appeared. With a backpack slung over one arm and a tote bag slung over the other, he maneuvered his board down the deserted road hoping to reach his friends. An avid boardhead, Bridger had no problem keeping his balance despite the heavy load he carried. But it wasn't doing any wonders for his mood.

"Was this payback for suggesting we check out Terrorville in the first place?" Bridger wondered aloud. "It wasn't my fault we couldn't find Zoo Gardens. Max is the one who was supposed to bring the map!" He ran a hand through his black hair and groaned, asking himself, "And whose fault was it spending all that time trying to get a high score on *Hydrothunder* in the bus station, Bridgeboy?"

Bridger wiped sweat from his brow as he continued down the road. Looking up, he saw the blue sky slowly shifting into shades of yellow and red. The white clouds faded to black. He didn't like the looks of how many clouds there were. That wasn't a rumble of thunder he heard, was it? Gazing behind him, there weren't any approaching vehicles. He was flanked on both sides by thick trees.

"Ah to Hell with it."

A geyser of water manifested beneath Bridger's skateboard, lifting him into the air. The water rose higher until Bridger levitated above the trees. Unfortunately, the added height did little to help the situation. All he saw for miles was an empty stretch of road, trees, and a rapidly darkening sky.

"How fast was that bus going? Was Keanue Reeves driving?" Bridger groaned at such an obvious reference. He really *was* in a bad mood. "I didn't even *like* that movie."

The body of water extended outward, becoming a tunnel Bridger rode atop with the forest beneath his board. As long as Bridger concentrated, the water would remain for him to travel on, similar to how Max would ride the wind. Or Gina's rainbow bridges, and Salli-Ann's icy pillars. Sometimes the four raced to see who was faster, but Alice always outran them with her superhuman legs.

It was weird, being by himself as he skated along the water created by his mind.

He didn't like it.

Bridger never liked being alone.

He'd been dead once. In that moment he discovered *real* loneliness.

"Let's live our lives heroically, let's live them with style," Bridger sang to not feel so alone with the sky growing redder. *"Just a long, long time..."*

Singing and skating above the trees, doing tricks on his board to try and lighten the mood as he searched for signs of civilization, Bridger thought, *I hope Al ain't mad at me.* He hated ever seeing Alice upset for any reason. Out of everyone in Generation Dead, the two were probably closest. Not like *that.* Even if Bridger wasn't asexual, he couldn't imagine wanting anything other than the special friendship he had with Alice Vane. Bridger understood the vulnerable parts of Alice, and she trusted him as the most reliable part of their little group.

Yeah, reliable. That's me. I'm so reliable I let them leave without me.

If it hadn't been for Alice, the five would've never escaped the aliens at Area 52 when so many others had died and *stayed* dead. He'd follow that woman into Hell if she asked.

Maybe what they had was love, just a different kind of love. Friends could love each other, couldn't they? But then, Bridger didn't think it was fair to not love Gina, Salli-Ann, and Max the same way. Even if Alice trusted him more, he felt that sort of love for all his friends.

"Even though we dream, even though we cry, even though we get-huh?" Bridger gasped when he noticed something in a clearing near his righthand side. A dark structure. A house?

Levitating on his miniature wave, Bridger said aloud, "Okay, even from here I'm guessing that house is bad news." He could roughly make out the house in question must've been huge and probably run down. Something felt wrong just by looking at it. "Considering my lack of options, I'm gonna have to take a chance and hope for the best."

Famous last words, a voice in Bridger's head said.

Pushing forward, Bridger directed the water towards the house and wondered if it was abandoned, haunted, or home to a clan of inbred serial killers. With the way his life went, it was surely going to be one of the latter two.

I'll take haunted over inbreeding, he thought. *Especially after helping that ghost chicken solve that mur-*

Bridger's thoughts were cut short when a flock of black birds flew towards him from out of the trees.

"Ah! Hey! Watch it!" Bridger swatted at the winged creatures, trying to keep himself afloat. "Out of the entire freaking sky you had to fly into my face?! Rude!"

Sadly, his concentration boke and the wave dissipated beneath Bridger's board. It took him a moment before he realized he was falling through the trees, their rough leaves and branches scratching his brown skin and tearing up his already torn jeans and oversized "Hydrocity Zone" t-shirt.

"Ow! Ouch! Ow! Damn it! OW! MotherFUC-"

THUD!

Impact smelled suspiciously like a bouquet of flowers and for a moment, Bridger's world turned red.

"Owwww…" Bridger groaned, thinking he was staring up at the evening sky. He'd never seen a sky so red before.

"Um, hi?"

"Huh?"

After a few seconds of recalibration, Bridger realized he wasn't looking at the sky. Nor was he on the ground.

"I hate to bother," a muffled voice spoke. "But if it wouldn't be much trouble, could you please get off me? I'm inhaling a lot of dirt and it's not a pleasant experience, thanks."

"Ahh!" Bridger scooted off the other person with lightning speed, backing up against the trunk of a tree. The initial fright over, Bridger stood and went to help the other person off the forest floor. "Shit, I am so sorry! Are you okay, dude?"

"Well, I can't say you're the first person to fall for me," the stranger said as he rose with Bridger's assistance.

"I didn't fall for you, I fell ON you," Bridger corrected. "Seriously, are you okay? I didn't break anything did I?"

"It'll take more than that to put me down for good," the stranger revealed as he dusted off dirt from his baggy khakis. Brushing his red bangs out of his face, he then said, "Shit, my hair's loose. Give me a moment."

Bridger couldn't believe the color of the other man's hair. He'd never seen anyone with such a shade of red, unless it was dyed. He recalled Gina coloring parts of her hair a similar red for Valentine's Day.

Now that he wasn't on top of him, Bridger saw the other man looked roughly around the same age as him and his friends. In the fading daylight, he looked as though his skin was tanned. The sort of tan one got from being under the sun all day. He was about a head taller than Bridger with broad shoulders and well-toned arms sticking out of a silver and green tank top with the number "83" on it.

As he tied his hair back into a messy ponytail, with his bangs Bridger thought the guy looked like he stepped out of an anime.

And still he smelled of flowers. Was he wearing perfume?

"That's better," the man said as he flipped his ponytail over his shoulder. "Well, if you'll excuse me."

"H-hey!" Bridger stammered as the stranger picked up a backpack and started walking through the forest. Looking around, Bridger quickly grabbed his own bags and his beloved skateboard before running after this guy who smelled like flowers.

"I don't mean to be rude, but I've been on the road for a week now and almost at my destination," the man said without stopping his stride.

"But you might have a concussion or something!" Bridger argued. "And aren't you even wondering why I fell out of the trees?"

"I'm used to weirder things happening," the man replied. "I go to Ivy Falls University."

"I don't know what that means, but it just so happens weird things happen to *me* all the time, too!" Bridger huffed. Who *was* this guy?

Sighing, the man stopped to face Bridger. "Look, you seem like a nice guy, falling-out-of-trees notwithstanding, but it would be better if you headed back for the road. There's something potentially dangerous in these woods. For transparency's sake, I don't know how dangerous, but I might be more equipped to deal with it than you."

"Then it's a good thing I dropped in, because *I*," Bridger proudly struck a pose as he paused for dramatic effort. "Happen to be a superhero."

"Okay."

"That's it?" Bridger wondered. "You're not gonna say that's impossible or tell me I'm cuckoo for coco puffs? Aww, man, that's no fun. Usually, I get to do a little demonstration with my superpowers to show I'm not crazy."

"ARE you crazy?" The man asked.

"Ah, hmm." Bridger thoughtfully rubbed his chin in contemplation. "That's a good question. There's a chance I could be crazy AND have powers. Never thought of that before."

That got the man to laugh, and soon Bridger was laughing too.

"I'm sorry, I didn't tell you my name." The man stuck his hand out. "I'm Akira Hachijou."

"Nice to meetcha." Bridger vigorously grasped Akira's hand. "I'm Bridger Warren."

"Is that your superhero name too?"

"Nah, it's Seattle."

"Why Seattle?"

"Seattle-Man sounded too clunky."

"Fair enough."

Bridger fell into step alongside Akira as they navigated the woods. Bridger told Akira how he'd been left behind at the bus station and got lost when he spotted the house.

"I've been trying to find that house for a while," Akira explained.

"Why?"

"I'm looking for a doll which belonged to my sister." Akira stopped himself. "Actually, it's better to say she created it. Making dolls was one of her hobbies. That and gardening." Chuckling, he added, "One sort of led to the other."

"Must be some doll to wander out here by yourself," Bridger wondered.

"All of her dolls are special," Akira sighed. "And there are a lot of them."

"How'd it end up here? Your sister lose it or something?" Bridger continued, until he saw the dark look on Akira's face and assumed the worse. "Shit. Sorry."

"It's fine, just, it feels like I'll be looking for them my entire life," Akira ruefully mused.

"How long have you been looking for them?" Bridger asked.

"A long, long time."

"...exactly how old are you?"

"Well..." Akira thought of how to answer that. "It's been quite a few years since I was a kid, but I'm not ready to call myself an old man just yet."

"Tell me about it," Bridger sympathized, placing a reassuring hand on Akira's shoulder. "I feel like I've been 20 for over two decades since I got my powers." Under his breath, he muttered, "Those goddamn aliens."

"Ran—my sister—her dolls were taken from her and there was nothing I could do to stop it." Akira reminisced about his sister with a tone of frustration. "She had so many of them sometimes I'm not even sure which doll I'm heading towards until I get there. I never really know what to expect."

"Bummer," Bridger shook his head. "But hey, you've got a veteran crimefighter by your side today. You need someone's ass kicked, just point me in the right direction."

"You mean like there?"

Bridger looked towards where Akira pointed.

From a distance, the house looked like a mess. Up close, it was terrifying. The storm clouds did nothing to make the mansion look inviting. It was the sort of house Bridger read about in Verdona Klemp's *Heart Attack* books to frighten kids. He'd been to houses like this before. Being in Generation Dead made him and his friends a magnet for places like this.

He had no doubt people died in this house.

Akira fished around in his pants pocket, removing a miniature lockpick set and a flashlight as they approached the front door. "I prefer to get in through a door instead of the windows, to avoid broken glass." He started scowling as he removed a piece of plastic that was stuck on the lockpick set. "Dammit I got frosting on-"

"What is THAT?!" Bridger exclaimed.

"You've never seen someone pick locks before?" Akira asked.

"Not that, THAT!" Bridger pointed to the sticky plastic wrapper.

Akira looked at the rapper. "Oh, yeah. I stopped at a bus station a few miles back to load up on supplies. Normally I stay away from gas station baked goods because they can be kind of sketchy, but I had a craving for cinnamon buns." Grinning to show off two rows of perfect teeth, Akira added, "I've got this monster sweet tooth."

"*You're* the guy who swiped the last of the sticky buns?!" Bridger couldn't believe it. Out of everyone he could've stumbled across...

"If it makes you feel better, they were stale," Akira added.

"Whatever, let's get inside and get your sister's doll," Bridger said. As Akira worked on opening the massive front door, Bridger observed, "This place reminds me of the house from *Granny's Gruesome Graveyard Garden*."

"Huh?" Akira asked. "Whose granny?"

"Uh hello? *Granny's Gruesome Graveyard Garden*?" Bridger incredulously asked. "The game where you're trapped in a house full of homicidal plants grown from a cemetery? It's like one of the best horror games of the century."

Akira suddenly turned pale for a moment as he imagined the scenario Bridger described. Of flowers growing out of someone's grave. From someone's remains. A sight he was all too familiar with from watching his sister craft her dolls.

"Dude?" Bridger didn't like the look on Akira's face.

"Huh?" Akira blinked. "Oh. Oh! Sorry, it's, I-I've never heard of it. I mean I've never heard of that game." Trying to sound calm, Akira blithely added, "I don't like video games."

"You, you don't, *dude!*" Bridger clutched his chest. "First you bought the last sticky buns, and now you say you don't like video games? You are KILLING me. Knife to the chest."

"I just don't have the patience for them. They give me a headache with all the blips and bloops," Akira defended himself.

"'*Blips and bloops?*' What was that about not being an old man?" Bridger quipped.

"Eh what's that?" Akira cupped his hand over his ear. "You say something about horseradish being a delightful condiment, sonny?"

Well, at least he's able to laugh at himself, Bridger thought with a grin until his stomach suddenly grumbled. *But he owes me a pack of sticky buns.*

CLICK.

Akira pushed open the front door into the dark house.

From deep inside, something smelled sweet.

CRACK!

BOOM!

And so came the rain.

iles and miles away, Alice Vane's eyes fluttered open. "Mmm," she said as she stretched her arms. "Goodness," Alice yawned, wiping away tears and bits of sleep crud from her eyes. Outside the bus all she could see was darkness and rain. "Are we home yet? Guys?" She turned to notice Gina, Max, and Salli-Ann furiously playing Rock-Paper-Scissors.

"Would you two stop doing paper, we can't all do paper!" Salli-Ann shouted. "Redo!"

"This is the 38th time, Sal, just admit I won the first round!" Max demanded.

"Redo!" Salli-Ann reiterated as she held her hand out.

"Can't we use the fortune teller I made?" Gina begged, holding a folded piece of paper with numbers and symbols.

"I am not interested in knowing how many children I'll have with Mary Elizabeth Winstead, Gina!" Salli-Ann shouted.

"Excuse me for providing a little variety to the answers!" Gina huffed.

"REDO!" Salli-Ann shouted.

"Can I play?" Alice asked.

Salli-Ann, Max, and Gina all went pale as they realized Alice was awake, slowly turning to face their friend and leader with identical mortified expressions.

"I had the most wonderful dream," Alice sighed. "I got these neat ruby slippers and a little dog in a basket as I went to meet a wizard in a city of emeralds." Laughing, Alice pointed at each of her friends to continue the bit. "And Gina, you were there! And you, Max. And Salli-Ann. And Bridger, too." Looking around, she asked, "Where's he sitting? Guys?"

The other three members of Gen Dead looked at each other, wondering who'd be brave enough to tell Alice what happened.

Salli-Ann said, "You're gonna laugh, I swear."

But as it turned out, Alice *didn't* laugh.

Alice didn't say *anything*.

Not even when she burst through the roof of the bus, dragging Salli-Ann, Gina, and Max with her in her iron grip as she ran down the road with her superhuman speed to relocate her missing friend.

"You've never played ANY kind of video game?" Bridger asked as he navigated the dark halls of the abandoned house with Akira, following the sweet smell that greeted them at the door.

"Never," Akira answered. He held the flashlight, dispelling some of the darkness as they walked past open doors. It seemed the house truly was abandoned, save for the smell. It smelled familiar, and Akira began to narrow down the identity of the doll that must've been in the house.

"What about *Sumoboarding*?" Bridger asked.

"No."

"*Candy Crow*?"

"No."

"*Zandalee 64*?"

"Saw the movie." Akira added, "That woman deserved a better film."

"She really did." Bridger agreed. "*Lovely Waitress Fights*?"

"Please tell me that's not a thing."

Bridger laughed before his stomach growled again. Even the furious pelting of raindrops on the windows did little to mask the sound. The sweet smell made his hunger worse.

"Are you going to be okay?" Akira asked. "That last one almost sounded angry."

"I spent most of this afternoon skateboarding after a bus, I can't help feeling peckish," Bridger defended himself. "Maybe if SOMEone hadn't bought the last sticky buns..."

"Well, I think I might be able to make it up to you," Akira said as they stopped in front of two double doors. The sugary sweet aroma was at its strongest when Akira opened the doors. The beam of the flashlight revealed a switch on the other side of the door.

CLICK.

An overhead lightning fixture and lamps built in the walls flickered on.

"We have power so that's good," Akira said. "I wasn't sure with how old this place is. There must be a generator somewhere." He turned to notice Bridger's jaw hanging open, his brown eyes wide with shock at what the light revealed.

"Dude, you didn't tell me this was a fucking Hansel and Gretel house!" Bridger cried, his vision filled with images of cakes and cookies, pastries and pies, on almost every square inch of the room. While the rest of the house felt cold, this room was warm from the confections on the tables and chairs and everywhere else save the floor. Like they'd just come out of the oven.

Bridger tried to keep track of all the goodies. Standards like apple pie and chocolate chip cookies, jelly donuts and chocolate cake. Brownies with and without nuts. Key lime and lemon chiffon pie. Velvet cakes in every color. Those cookies with the rainbow sprinkles you always see in

Italian bakeries. Frosted cupcakes and scones. Tarts and tortes. There were more sweets than the room should've been able to hold.

While Bridger tried to comprehend the goodies before him, Akira focused on the fireplace mantle.

"Sally!" Akira cried as he ran towards the glass case on the mantle, ignoring the goodies. Inside the case was a porcelain doll with chocolate brown hair, in a faded dress once a bright cotton candy pink. "As soon as I could smell the baked goods, I figured it was you."

"Sally?" Bridger echoed, taking his eyes away from the array of delights.

Akira opened the case and carefully removed the doll as Bridger joined his side. Upon closer inspection, he noticed the doll's eyes were sugary pink. There were dried stains on her cheeks. Tears?

"You poor thing." Akira held the doll up, gazing into her eyes. "How long have you been stuck here?"

Bridger wondered if the doll talked, but it seemed she lacked that ability as she remained silent. Akira's expression turned remorseful as he said in a low, quiet voice, "I'm sorry. I can't tell you how sorry I am. Ran didn't mean for any of you to be taken away. I've been trying to find everyone, but I-I didn't mean to take so long to find you. I'm so, *so* sorry."

Bridger took in the sadness he heard in Akira's voice. He could sense the gentleness in his touch as Akira held the little doll close to him. He couldn't imagine what Akira's travels must've been like, but he was getting a good idea of how personal this must've been for the guy. The way he spoke, it sounded as though he genuinely knew Sally as an old friend. It made him wonder about the other dolls

Akira's sister created. He wondered about his sister Ran and what kind of person she was.

Looking around the room, Akira asked, "Did you hear us come in? Was all this for us?"

"So, all this was the do-I mean, Sally? Sorry," Bridger apologized. He could tell from the way Akira spoke to her that Sally was alive in some capacity and wanted to respect her autonomy. "She makes candy?"

"That's what my sister gave her," Akira said. "To make up for how she died."

"How... I mean," Bridger tried to ask.

Akira's face turned grim as he said, "Sally's parents starved her to death. They thought she was a burden, so they refused to feed her. When they caught her trying to steal a cookie, they sewed her lips shut."

Bridger looked at the doll, at her eyes.

"They did it on purpose," Akira suddenly said. "Left it out to tempt her. They liked doing that. A sick little game to see how far she'd go to eat in order to survive. When Sally died, she was so thin there was barely anything left to bury. They cremated her. My sister planted one of her seeds where they spread Sally's ashes. From the seed, a flower grew. From the flower came the doll."

"Why?" Bridger asked.

"It was her way to help," Akira sighed. "There are so many children out there who never got to live, and Ran, well, she wanted to give them another chance. She can't bring them back like they were before, but, it lets them do things. For themselves and others. It helps in a way. But not when they're left to rot in cases and cages and attics. Ran never meant for that. I didn't..."

Bridger didn't know what to think. He'd seen similar magic done, like when the Stump Woman killed a bunch of college students to turn them into monsters. She tried to steal their humanity so they would destroy Generation Dead. They were free now, but those eight hated Bridger and his friends with a passion for losing their lives.

And there was his own resurrection. Him and his friends killed by the aliens. Killed to be revived with power. The five of them Area 52's only survivors.

Was Akira's sadness for the doll because she'd been abandoned, or because his sister brought her back as she did. Had he been complicit in the process? Was he showing regret? What did he plan to do with the doll now?

And why did those desserts smell *good*?

GROOOOOOWL!

Akira turned to a blushing Bridger, who clutched his stomach looking embarrassed. As he did, he noticed for the first time how good those desserts looked. And he hadn't eaten for a few hours...

A small smirk broke out on Akira's face. "Way to ruin the mood."

"I-"

"Excuse me a moment Sally." Akira gently propped Sally up against a triple layer cake on the table before picking up and handing Bridger a large cinnamon bun covered in icing. "You kept saying I owed you, right?"

"I mean, I dunno," Bridger looked around. "Are they safe?"

Akira said nothing as he sunk his teeth into the pastry.

"Hey!" Bridger said as Akira chewed and swallowed.

"You snooze you lose," Akira said before handing Bridger another one. Looking at the doll, he said, "Thanks Sally."

This time Bridger accepted the bun, placing it to his lips and almost biting down before he looked at Sally. "Thank you."

It was the best cinnamon roll Bridger had in his life, only until he ate another which tasted even better. And another while Akira helped himself to a sweet potato turnover. Soon the two were indulging in a little bit of everything as the storm continued outside. Bridger marveled at how biting into each dessert was like eating it for the first time, while Akira felt contentment in sampling Sally's treats for the first time in ages.

The two men chat and ate, Bridger seeing how Akira spoke truthfully about his monstrous sweet tooth while Akira found it funny that Bridger tried to keep up with him. The heaviness of the previous conversation was forgotten in the haze of sweetness, and the two acted like old friends while stuffing their faces.

While they spoke to Sally and tried to converse with them, under the spell of her goodies they failed to notice a glint of growing dread in her little eyes.

And that wasn't the only thing that was growing...

"That was the first time I've had starfruit cake," Bridger mentioned a good while later as he left the dining room with Akira feeling quite satisfied. Akira cradled Sally in his arms as they looked for a bedroom to hunker down in until morning. The thunderstorm got nastier, so they figured they might as well get comfortable. "How'd she even know how to make it?"

"That's Sally's specialty, she can create any dessert that's ever existed," Akira explained. He said to the doll. "You haven't lost your touch."

The floorboards creaked under their feet as Bridger added, "I think my fave were persimmon tarts."

"I haven't had chess pie since the last time I was in the South," Akira remembered.

Another old light flickered on as Bridger and Akira found what could've been the master bedroom once upon a time. Despite the dust and smell, it would make do for the night. As Akira gently placed Sally on a worn chair, Bridger tried to shake the dust off the sheets. He said, "This looks like it'll be big enough for both of us."

"You sure?" Akira asked as he noticed his reflection in a large mirror in one corner of the room. He'd been so focused on eating Sally's desserts he'd forgotten about their effects.

"Why? You a blanket hog?" Bridger asked.

"Well..."

"DUDE!" Bridger cried as he suddenly saw himself reflected in the mirror alongside Akira. There was just enough room for both of them in the glass. "We're HUGE!"

"You're exaggerating but, yeah, we're kind of... big."

Bridger looked down at himself. He couldn't see his feet with the way his stomach extended out and hung over the waist of his jeans. He was now realizing how tight they were, the pre-existing rips growing bigger against his thick thighs.

Akira's khakis no longer looked baggy on his plump frame. His tank top was stretched far, creating an outline of his large breasts resting atop his belly. Like Bridger, Akira was now noticing the tightness of his clothes.

The two had filled out considerably, sporting equally large, soft bellies poking out of their shirts that swayed when they moved. Their arms, legs, and thighs were all thickened out and meaty. Their faces were rounded out, cheeks softened with double chins.

They were very hard to miss.

"Did you know this would happen?" Bridger demanded as he turned to face Akira.

"Sorry, it slipped my mind," Akira groaned, feeling embarrassed at having gotten so sloppy. He was usually more guarded when it came to the tricks his sister's doll had in store. "Sally's goodies have that effect."

"SLIPPED your-?"

"I told you Sally starved to death," Akira reminded Bridger with a stern expression, turning to face him back. Their bellies bumped against each other as he said, Bridger feeling Akira press his weight against him as he spoke. It was not an entirely unpleasant sensation.

"My sister gave Sally the power to make sure no one would suffer like she did," Akira explained. For a moment his gaze darted over to where the doll sat. Darkly, he asked, "Do you know what actual starvation's like? To *really* starve to death? Not just missing a meal, but being told you're a selfish monster for wanting to stop the gnawing? Dying with your skin clinging to your bones as your organs shut down one by one?"

"Akira, it's cool," Bridger held his hands up. "I didn't mean to sound so mad. I mean I wasn't prepared to see," he gestured to their girth, "all THIS. I was surprised. You coulda told me before we stuffed our faces." Turning back to the mirror, Bridger placed his hands on his stomach. "I gain weight easy during the winter and it's no biggiee." Squeezing his gut, he added, "'Course I've never gained THIS much. Heh. Think my boobs are as big as Alice's. Cool."

"I know what you mean," Akira pinched at his arms to feel the muscles underneath the fat. "I joke about how I could never lose the Freshmen Fifteen, but this is a LOT more than fifteen."

"So, your sister gave Sally the power to, what, make people fat?" Bridger clarified.

"It's not permanent," Akira added. "It'll wear off in a few hours. Honestly, Sally's gift's one of the less extreme ones. My sister's sense of humor is… weird."

"This was bound to happen some point," Bridger announced. "As a superhero you're liable to get really fat at least once, usually from a meteor, or radiation, or evil girl scout cookies. Guess I was due."

"…evil girl scout cookies?" Akira repeated.

Placing his hands on his thick hips, Bridger said, "'Least we make it work."

"We do?"

"Yeah man, wear it with pride!" Bridger announced as he swung a plump arm around Akira's shoulders and drew him close. "I know a couple of dudes, Ahmed and Crunch, who're both on the big side and they totally rock it. Whenever I get curvy around the holidays, I know how to strut it around. If you got it, flaunt it."

Akira looked at the mirror as Bridger flexed his arms. "I guess we do got it."

Up close, Bridger noticed the flowery scent again when he suddenly frowned. "Aw, man."

"What?"

"Your boobs are bigger than mine that's not fair," Bridger pouted. "That's your third strike, dude."

CRACK!

BOOM!

CRASH!

"*GRAAAAAAAAAAAAAAAAAAAAAH!!!!*"

"The fuck was that?!" Bridger shouted.

"Was that your stomach again?!" Akira asked.

"*AAAAAAAAAHHHH!!!*" The howling intensified as the sounds of destruction worsened. Akira and Bridger covered their ears to drown out the shrieking.

"Like a fucking knife in my head!" Bridger tried to shout over the inhuman screaming. Akira fell to his knees, not noticing the sound of his pants ripping over the primal shrieks. He looked at Sally on the nearby chair and saw tears flowing from the doll's eyes.

The bedroom door was ripped off its hinges by a pair of claws. Spindly, mishappen limbs emerged through the open doorway. The sound of clattering bones and claws tearing through wood filled the room.

Akira didn't know what he was looking at.

Bridger remembered seeing something similar in a shitty American remake of a Japanese horror movie.

The creature's head was a giant lamprey mouth filled with circular rows open rows of jagged teeth, topped with wiry black hair. Skin clung to the bones, revealing the outline of every joint. Each limb moved with a cracking noise. The midsection was bare, revealing...

Before Akira could make sense of what he was seeing, the shrieking thing was pushed back by twin geysers of water out of the bedroom and through the wall.

"Put some fucking clothes on nobody needs to see that!" Bridger shouted as he propelled the water at the monster. Despite her decrepit appearance, the monster forced its way back against the water. Bridger gritted his teeth, increasing the pressure, when the monster ducked low and lunged at his fattened midsection.

Akira watched in horror as the monster towered over Bridger, leaned close, and seemed to... *drain* him. Bridger cried in agony as his new weight rapidly vanished, returning to his usual stocky build. The monster didn't stop there. Bridger resembled a water balloon shriveling up.

She was so focused on feeding off Bridger the monster didn't notice Akira pick up another chair and bash it against her head. Putting all his new weight into it, he throttled the monster.

Gasping for air, Akira dropped the broken chair where the monster lay. Bridger weakly moaned on the floor. Akira grabbed Sally.

"What the hell is this?!" Akira demanded. "Were you helping that thing this whole time, Sally?!" The doll continued to cry as he looked into her eyes. As he focused, all he could see was years of despair, a reflection of a black-haired woman furiously devouring sweets.

He saw a burial.

He saw a seed being planted.

No. Akira thought. Reaching down towards the monster, Akira placed a hand on its arm.

Like porcelain.

"She got a seed?" Akira said. "How did she get one of Ran's seeds?!"

The monster raised its other arm and tried to grab Akira. He dodged even with his added bulk, then heard Bridger moaning.

"Come on!" Akira dared the monster. "Why settle for an appetizer? I'm the main course, and I'm aged to perfection!"

As Akira led the doll creature away, Bridger dragged himself towards Sally. Every movement felt like agony.

"Hel... p..." Bridger whispered. "P, pl... es..."

A tear ran down Sally's cheek.

Bridger felt something heavy in his hand.

A cookie.

It took a lifetime to bring it to his lips.

Akira ran downstairs, the monster on his heels when the monster tackled him from behind. They crashed into the dining area, filled with some leftover sweets. Akira felt the monster's bony hands wrap around his thick neck when it drew him close to her head.

He felt the agony of losing himself as the monster fed. His body shrank like Bridger's, but it didn't stop there. He felt himself losing memories. Ivy Falls. His search for his sister's dolls. Helping with the garden. The monster was devouring his very being.

BOOM!

The ceiling was destroyed in a deluge. A large figure landed through the hole.

"You fucked with the wrong gamer, lady!" Bridger declared, standing bigger and fatter than before, his clothes torn to shreds. "You're messing with a guy whose logged a thousand hours on *Sumoboarding* and now I got the belly to match!"

The monster shrieked, threw Akira away, when Bridger barreled into her with a watery shield around his massive body. They went through another wall, out into a backyard garden gone to seed. Bridger grappled with the creature, avoiding her mouth.

"I got the highest grades at the University of the Buttslam, and it's time for a demonstration!" Bridger tossed the monster on the ground before propelling himself into the air with a blast of water. "As Rocky Waves would say, *CANNONBALL!*"

BOOM!

He missed.

"Uh oh."

The monster rolled out of the way and charged straight at him when another large figure hit the creature.

"Need a hand?" Bridger looked up to see Akira just as big as him, his clothes in ruins. "Good thing for leftovers."

"Dude!" Bridger cheered. "You got it-"

"Flaunt it!"

"AAAAAHHH!"

"***AAAAAAAAAAHHHHH!!!!***" The two men screamed back and charged at the monster. Suddenly they split apart before rushing the monster on both sides.

SMASH!

CRASH!

CRUNCH!

The creature lay in a broken heap on the ground. Bridger and Akira panted and sank down next to each other when the rain finally stopped.

"Nice moves," Akira said as he nestled next to Bridger. "But I prefer O'Connell McClover."

"I thought you didn't play *Sumoboarding*."

"I watched the cartoon. He's a redhead like me. We gotta stick together."

The two sat in the garden, the adrenaline fading from their bulky bodies. The rainy air smelled fresh. The two lay on the ground, cuddling next to each other, feeling more exhausted than they'd ever felt before.

"Any idea what that was about?" Bridger asked.

"Maybe."

"Do I want to know?"

"No. Poor Sally."

"Yeah. Poor Sally. ...Is this okay?" Bridger asked.

"Yeah, it is," Akira said as he nuzzled against Bridger's breasts. "I don't normally do this sort of thing."

"Me neither."

"Can I stay like this for a bit?" Akira asked.

"Yeah."

"It's not weird?" Akira wondered.

"My whole life's weird." Bridger pulled Akira closer. "But I like this."

"I'm asexual, so I'm not into-"

"Me neither, but, you can keep moving your hand like that," Bridger said as Akira rubbed his belly. "You smell good."

"Would it... could I...?"

Akira brought his lips to Bridger's.

"GRAAAAAAAAAHHH!" The monster suddenly screamed.

"Oh COME-"

SPLAT!

A pair of perfect, superhuman legs appeared from the sky and crushed the monster's head.

"*There* you are, Bridger!"

Alice Vane paid no mind to the obliterated skull or twitching corpse at her feet, nor why Bridger suddenly weighed over 350 pounds and was cuddling with an equally fat redhead.

Bridger saw Gina, Salli-Ann, and Max being held in Alice's grip, looking nauseous.

Akira had no idea what was going on.

"We've been looking all over for you, thank goodness you're safe!" Noticing Akira, Alice said, "Oh hi! I'm Alice. Bridger, who's your little friend?"

THE MATH OF LOVE [1+1=1]

By Ziaul Moid Khan

I want to touch you," I said, looking straight into Reshma's bizarre bright eyes. In the last two weeks, this was the seventeenth time I'd asked my newly found love this question in the hope of a positive response. The last sixteen attempts of my maneuver had proved futile, producing no concrete result. I was on fire, every atom of me crying desperately for her.

"You cannot," she said, and giggled like an innocent baby. Her blood red lips exposed her extra white teeth. Whiter than what they show in the toothpaste ads during those short commercial horrible breaks on television.

She was one of those rare looking girls fit for modelling, catwalk, the showbiz world. Slander, but with heavy bosom. Her tits shook heavily up and down as she walked giving a clear hint that she did not wear a bra, wittingly to draw more than usual attention.

"Why?" I said, perplexed.

"That I can't and won't tell you." She laughed again, giving me her usual response in mirth.

"Why not? Please…please Reshma, tell me!" I said pissed and pinched by her rude reply, "why do you always evade my questions, love?"

"Some other day, when the right winds will blow and bring around an opportune time," Reshma said, staring at the full moon that was trying to evade the dark clouds which were advancing towards her.

I fell silent. Looked up where she was staring—at the glittering sky. It was a perfect night with a circled moon and all galaxies of stars, adding to the beauty of the vast expense of the cosmos. We sat at our usual place—a hummock where the Krishna River flowed fifty meters below our feet. More often than not we came here after our first meeting-by-chance. Here it was peaceful, and both of us loved this place—away from the hustle and bustle of the city-life.

Last night at this same place she'd asked me if I really loved her.

"Of course, I do," I had said.

Then she'd said nothing. It seemed odd to me, but I did not nudge her lest she should be offended. A little short tempered was she. Truly I didn't want to lose her. I could not afford it.

"Are you OK, Nawaz?" she chirped. And I was back from my flashback.

"Yes. Why are you asking?"

"I guess you're hurt," she said. Her lips seemed to be the untouched petals of some new blossoming rose-bud. *I want to kiss these coral lips*, I wanted to say but did not. Sometimes it's safe not to say something your heart's crying to speak aloud.

"It's not like that," I said, looking sideways, "I think I have no right upon you."

"May I ask you one thing?"

"Yes."

"Which kind of right you want by the way? You mean physical!"

"All the rights," I said with possession in my tone, "physical and platonic, both."

"Of course, you'll have, Nawaz," she said with an I-know-your-intention-smile, "but give me some time. I can feel your feelings. But as for now—all the rights are reserved."

"Take your time," I said with sarcasm in my tone.

"Thanks," she said, casually this time, with no apparent emotions in her words.

The cupid shot his love-infected-bloody-arrow, as I got interested in Reshma the moment I saw her. Such peace on any mortal being I'd never spotted before. She was— oval faced, big eyes, good height and white as snow albeit not as beautiful as Snow White, but enough to spell a charm on a lad like me. She spoke the minimum words possible. Most of her answers were 'Yes', No', 'Maybe', 'Can't Say', and sometimes a faint 'Sure.' But I got, in her, a temporary refuge from my joblessness.

As I remember it now, I wanted to chat more on the very first day I met her. "I've an urgent piece of work, there." She pointed into the distance, the churchyard. And then she told—there was her father's grave. Mr. Goodfellow had died in a road accident, when he was on a high and could not judge the speeding truck, coming from the opposite direction near Vijayawada. I showed my sympathy, which she did not seem to have noticed or cared for.

A week later, she introduced me to this place, a small hilltop on the outskirts of my town—dangerous but pretty-looking, just like her. She insisted on coming here every evening if I wished to meet her. I had to agree. And thus, it became our regular rendezvous. She loved twilight and I loved her. So, I was always in agreement, to whatever she said, willy-nilly. One thing, among many things, startling about her was her hair ever-seemed drenched with dripping droplets of water as if she came out of a shower right then. I wished to ask about it but did not.

I could discern the rise and fall of her sizeable bosom. The white strip of her bra was peeping through her semi-transparent top that gave me a bizarre thrill, an excitement beyond words. I wanted to touch these tits. But her feelings seemed cold and indifferent to me. The night was illumined with a bare army of stars led by the shining moon. The howling of wolves could unmistakably be heard. But they must have been a far distance somewhere into the deep forest. I thought we were away from their reach, or it could be a misconception too.

"Don't you feel afraid to come here," I said, without looking at her, for I always resisted an urge to embrace her. That was what I always wanted. And that was what she always declined.

"What should I be afraid of and why should I be afraid of?" she said, still staring at the snail-moving moon. Her voice had a chime unexplainable.

"Those wolves in the woods," I said, "aren't they horrific?"

"They are the children of night," she said, "not something to be fearful of. I love their howl. You should too."

There was silence again. Only the gurgling of the river water, beneath, made its presence felt apart from the occasional voices of the wolves.

"Their spooky howling terrifies me," I said, drawing her attention toward my natural fear.

"That's background music, nothing beyond it. Just chill, Nawaz!"

Reshma shifted her glance from the moon to the current of Krishna River that was sprinting towards an unknown location. Every river finds its way to the ocean.

"You know swimming?" she said after a pause, looking at the tumultuous current of water fifty meters down our feet, where it formed several mini whirlpools. A fall from our place was a confirmed horrible death.

"No," I said, albeit it was a lie. I'd once been a state swimming champion, but that was years back when I was in high school. I hid this truth without any apparent reason, just to reveal it to her later. That was my weird habit—to surprise someone later by revealing the truth.

"Close your eyes," she said with a sudden glint of light in her eyes.

"Are you going to push me?" I said and cracked into laughter. The voice echoed from the woods.

"I'll save you, if you drown. Don't worry, I know swimming," she said and laughed, exposing her bare teeth again. Sometimes I felt some unknown terror when I saw two of them—her side canines—slightly longer than the rest in the set.

"Close your eyes," she repeated and chuckled. I was wedged in her charm.

Like an obedient child, I obliged this time, and felt a gentle push, at the same time, from behind. Her touch was ice-cold as if from a corpse. At first, I thought Reshma was just kidding, but realized in a few nanoseconds that I'd been literally pushed—to die—by someone I loved so intensely. Before I could calculate anything, I was airborne. The gravitational force of the earth pulled me towards the hissing waters. For a couple of seconds, I was sort of navigating in the space. I did not know when a squeak escaped my lips—*R E S H M A...!*

Then I heard a thunderous splash—the sound effect of my own great fall—as my chest hit against the foaming current. A terrible acute pain ran through my chest as though someone had pierced a long *Rampuri* knife into me. I writhed, convulsed in excruciating pain tinged with utter disbelief. I felt cheated, I felt deceived. I was still unable to digest the fact for being tossed into the river by someone I loved. To whom I was most likely to propose, with a red rose in hand and my left knee on the ground.

And I gulped water, a lot of water indeed, as my own painful body sank inside the devouring waters. The Krishna River was not indeed as polite as Lord Krishna (was). The water seemed to have conspired with my Girl — to kill me by drowning. Still, I was unable to figure out why the hell she wanted my annihilation, and as promised she did not jump after me. I jerked. *Was her love a façade? What profit did she have of my death after all?*

But putting aside all my philosophy on love for the time being, I suddenly recalled my swimming lessons. My hands and legs mechanically moved as though remembering the old methods I'd learned in my school's swimming pool.

Somehow, I managed to come afloat on the water-surface. My fearful eyes caught a glimpse of my Girl who still sat at the hillock with her feet dangling over the fast current of the river I was drowning in. I had no time to see whether her eyes were focused on me or drifted elsewhere. It seemed irrelevant now.

I peddled and side-stroked the water with all my strength, momentarily forgetting my terrible chest pain and the double cross that my lady-love had done to me. The priority now was neither to touch her nor to embrace her and not even to see her beautiful cleavage and her tight tits that reminded me of Britney Spears, but to save my life from the awful waters.

Luckily, I could manage to swim tonight though not like a champion, for I had left my practice years back, yet at least enough to bring myself to safety. The fast river flow was, however, hampering me to make headway. To bring myself out, I was fighting against the monstrous current. But it was not that easy given the circumstances. My body seemed too weak to swim with ease.

Under the moonlight, the water looked blue, but treacherous and not at all amiable. Within a minute I realized I could not move against the great force of the entire river. *Use the current to reach the side of the river,* shouted my mind. I gave the thought a fighting chance, took a sharp U-turn and swam with the flow of the river. Cleverly, I kept striving to come up close to the bank until I felt the side wall of Krishna.

My hands clutched at something. First it was the moss, but I tried again and again and then again. Eventually I gripped at some long side-grown grass and the deep rooted-hollow-reeds. I held fast to them and my body momentarily stabilized. I somehow crawled myself up clutching my hands at the higher reeds. I slipped thrice, but at my fourth or fifth effort, I succeeded climbing out of the hostile river. It was a welcome relief.

In my heart I thanked God besides my swimming coach Mr. Maitrey as I lay beside the river, breathing heavily on the dust-laden side path with drenched, cold, and torn clothes. I remained so for twenty minutes or so. Then I recollected all that had happened and stood up to thank my love for her attempted murder. With slow strides, I walked to the bridge, where-from was the route to the hillock she sat upon. From a distance I could see — she was still there, still staring at the full moon.

"Reshma," I said with rage in my eyes as I approached her, "what the hell was that? You almost killed me."

"The real life starts only after death," she said, taking a deep sigh that seemed to be a grunt as if nothing had happened. "You don't know the simple math of love; it's 1+1=1. Two bodies, but one soul," she said and giggled. Her laughter echoed in the distance. "You had to dissolve into me, if you wished to touch me or achieve me. And it was not possible unless you died or transformed."

"What the hell do you mean?" I thundered, my body still shivering, whether with cold or fury or both—I did not know.

"Relax Nawaz Khan, relax," she said her voice extra cold, "we're from two different worlds, you know. I think you don't know. What you call life is short lived, miserable and what you call death is—a stone reality, long and eternal. You call it life—the filthy world you live in. I was only trying to fulfill your desire—to touch me or make love with me, but perhaps Providence wants your presence more in the human world and least in ours—the cold world of Thin Airs."

I fumbled for the right words as I froze. Again, whether it was the effect of her stunning revelation that suddenly dawned upon me or the cold river water—still dripping off my clothes, I did not know. But I stood baffled, out of my wits and unable to speak as she made her lips round and whistled weirdly.

By now my love for her—for reasons unknown to me— had ceased substantially. The deep desire to take her into my arms was no longer there. The fever of love, that appeared earlier to be an eternity, was over. The threat of death made somehow drastic changes in my approach. But still I stood there confounded, my teeth rattling, while my shocked eyes gazing at her in utter disbelief, as she whistled again, this time clearer than before. What was she doing? Soon, I got the answer.

The dense forest had a sudden ruckus as if in response to her whistling. The thorns and hedges shivered like in a storm and came to a sudden animation, and then there appeared from nowhere before us—a big pack of wolves. My words froze in my mouth—surrounded by 40-50 wolves was a new experience for me. Every moment it felt like they'd attack me and tear me apart. Reshma stood up from her place and walked elegantly to them—like a princess towards her minions—and waved them to remain calm. But their blood red flaming eyes were still staring at me like they were waiting for orders from their mistress.

"We could be one, but alas we could not," she said, looking into my eyes and rubbing the neck of one of wolves that stood close in obedience to its mistress, "it's a pity that to my virgin love you could not enjoy. No need to fear now, live your life. Anyway, goodbye Nawaz!" she said. Then her ferocious troop moved behind her as she led them into the dark, dense, and moonlit whispering-woods to an unknown horizon. My eyes chased them as far as they could. My whole body shivered with goose bumps as now I was there stranded forlorn like a defeated gambler.

The retreating howling of the children of darkness somewhere in the deep jungle could still be heard. But their call did not seem as charming and charismatic as Reshma thought. The moon shone clearer now, for the clouds had parted off to let her move freely as she wished, over the forest and the treacherous Krishna River. I stood on the hillock trying to figure out the chain of events. My *Royal*

Enfield was still parked under the foot of the hill. *Go home,* said my sad heart.

Next evening out of curiosity, I visited the graveyard where Reshma's father was buried. Crossing the thorny hedges, I walked past the other crosses into the direction indicated by her the day we met here—first time. I did not have much trouble, however, in finding the old man's tombstone. But what astonished me more was— another grave on his left. The inscription on it read— *Reshma Goodfellow (1981-2000). Cause of death: Suicide by jumping into the Krishna River. RIP.* The earth seemed to give way beneath my feet as I realized whom I was dating.

Another flashback incident ran past my mind's eye — how the customers at the other tables were staring at me as we dined at the *Divine Restaurant* a few nights back near Church Gate, while I was talking to Reshma, and she was all ears with rapt attention. Were others able to see but me, alone? A chilling sensation ran through my spine and mixed into my blood—now as cold as was Reshma's touch when she'd pushed me into the deathly river.

Nawaz Sahib!" Somebody broke my reverie by calling out my name, as I was parking my Enfield in the courtyard. It was Rajendra, the postman. There was nobody in our entire colony who did not know him. He gave me his usual smile, alighting from his ancient Hero Bicycle. "A letter for you," he said, handing me a sealed yellow envelope. It was from The Third Eye Corporation. I recalled having appeared in an examination for Executive Investigator. I opened the seal and read. It said I'd cracked the written test, and the interview was scheduled for next Friday.

"Rajendra Ji," I said, "you've brought good news today, please come in to have a cup of tea." The old man came inside my drawing room to share my happiness. "You'll have to give me a full treat, once you get your final selection," said the silver haired postman, sitting on the couch. But some compartment of my brain was still busy calculating the math of love Reshma had taught me, for her pet wolves and the lethal affection still lingered there. But I thought I still loved her as my mind raced fast—first it said *yes*, then *no* and then a faint *let it go*.

SAINT VALENTINE

By Blue Sunshine

WE'RE IN BATON ROUGE,
and you're a mixologist
drinking the green sprinkles
off my king cakes,
baby dolls rollin 'round
inside your mouth,
turning them to emeralds.

You scratch your name
into my skin,
draw the syrup from within,
protecting me from
citric acid Romeos

who speak with their tongues out
and search for a certain
moisture of the interior—
fearing the exterior.

You crush me
into the powder
you set your makeup with,
and a halo blooms
'round your head,
germination,
soft and sticky
to the touch.

THE CREATURE

By Aiden E. Messer

Elio felt it again. Someone was watching him. He glanced around himself, taking in the dark street lighted by flickering lamp posts. Passers-by paid him no attention, and why would they? He ran a hand through his beard, taking a deep breath. It was just his imagination. He was passing. There was no way anyone could tell that he was trans, or queer in any way. He wasn't about to be hatecrimed. Everything was okay.

He walked into his building, letting out a breath of relief once he reached his apartment. He stepped into his messy room and grabbed his pajamas from under his pillow. Just as he removed his shirt, though, the feeling was on him again. Elio closed his eyes, taking a series of deep breaths. He was okay. He was safe.

Still, he closed his blinds just in case before finishing changing. He climbed under his covers and settled comfortably, ready to go to sleep, but a tingling sensation between his legs nagged at him. Elio sighed. Of course something like that would turn him on. He really couldn't comprehend how his brain worked, sometimes. He knew he really should go to sleep if he wanted to be ready for his hike in the forest the next morning, but he knew he wouldn't be able to until this was taken care of.

Oh, well. There were worse ways to fall asleep.

He reached under his pajamas, caressing his new cock lightly. No need to pump it this time, since he was alone. His other hand joined in, finding the small hole that remained of his cunt after surgery. He slowly pushed a finger in, wincing at the pain the unlubricated penetration brought him, but that was exactly what his body craved. Eyes closed, he let his mind wander.

A scene started to take form in his mind. Strong hands touching him, holding him down. He could almost feel them closing around his throat, choking him. A shiver ran up his spine, the impression of being watched creeping at the back of his mind once again. This time, however, instead of opening his eyes, he leaned into it, letting the anxiety invade him. He imagined a shadow in the corner of his room, shrouded in darkness, watching as he pleasured himself. A low moan escaped from between his parted lips, his left hand pounding harder and deeper into his cunt, his right one fisting his cock. Maybe the presence would wait until he was right at the edge of an orgasm before pouncing on him, grabbing his hands. Elio's breathing grew ragged, his chest moving up and down rapidly. It would impale itself on his cock, drinking in his pleasure like a succubus and leaving him drained of all vital force. Or maybe it would force himself in his tight opening, ripping him apart mercilessly, drowning him in a sea of agony and ecstasy. His walls clenched around his finger, his dick twitching at the thought. The orgasm ripped through him like a freight train, leaving him panting and satisfied. The feeling of being watched was gone.

Elio groaned when his alarm clock sounded, but he'd been looking forward to that hike the whole week. He stumbled out of his bed sleepily and made his way to the shower. The cold water finished waking him up. He put on comfortable hiking pants and a large shirt, and made sure his bag was ready. Once satisfied, he climbed into his car and drove to the forest. The morning air was still crisp, but the sun was already peeking through the trees, promising a warm day. Elio took a breath, enjoying the forest scent that filled his lungs. Birds sang, mingling their melody with that of the wind in the leaves. Elio walked at a leisurely pace along the dirt track taking him deeper and deeper into the woods. He had the whole day ahead of him, and he had every intention of enjoying the scenery. He was taking in the beauty of a particularly tall pine tree when he felt it again. The presence from last night. A shiver ran through his spine, and a tingling sensation crept between his legs. Elio shook his head. The only things watching him were birds, and maybe a squirrel or a mouth hiding in the distance. There was no sadistic killer hiding between the tree, waiting to jump on him.

Elio rubbed his legs together absentmindedly, then cursed himself as he noticed his reaction. Fuck! That wasn't supposed to turn him on either!

He ran his hand through his short hair in frustration. Living in fear for years could create some strange coping mechanisms. He kept walking, ignoring both the anxiety churning in the pit of his stomach and the aching in his groin, but the feeling of being watched only grew stronger. A crack sounded to his right, much too close. He turned his head to see a fur-covered form pouncing on him. His screams remained stuck in his throat. He fell to the ground, his back hitting the ground with a heavy thud. A few inches from him, a definitively human face stared at him. Definitely human, but wrong. Hair grew where it shouldn't have, his ears were too pointed, his nose too arched, his blue irises much too wide, and above all, he was holding him down with a force far too great for his size. Slightly smaller than Elio, he had no trouble keeping him pinned to the ground.

"You're scared," the creature said. It wasn't a question. "You're always scared, I can smell it on you."

Elio looked at him, frozen.

"But I can smell something else, too," The creature grinned, flashing its pointy teeth. "I can take the fear from you, make you like me. It will hurt, but you'll like it, won't you? And once it's done, no one will be able to hurt you again."

Elio's heart was racing inside his chest, and his groin was pulsing with need. He wanted to flee, wanted to run away and never look back. He wanted the creature to kiss him and devour him whole.

A hand crept under his boxers, brushing against his cock and making its way to his balls. The creature's fingers found the button to his penile pump, squeezing it. Is cock started to harden.

"Come on, say it," the creature purred, squeezing the pump once again. "You know you want it. You know you need it."

Elio's breath hitched. He couldn't find his voice, but his body reacted for him, his head nodding before he realized what he was doing.

"I knew you'd make the right choice," the creature cooed, squeezing until Elio's cock was fully hardened.

Elio didn't move when the creature let go of his hands to lower his pants, freeing his member. He remained on the ground, unmoving, blood pounding in his head. The creature removed his own pants, revealing his glistening cunt. He slowly lowered himself on Elio's shaft. Elio groaned, closing his eyes. *Fuck, it felt so good.* His eyes flew open again when a sharp pain invaded his clavicle, where the creature had sunk his teeth deep, shattering the bone. Elio screamed, yet he didn't try to push the creature away. The pain was mingling with the pleasure, creating a powerful mix he couldn't get enough of. The creature's lips came crashing with his, making him taste his own blood. Elio moaned, tongue swirling to get every single drop as his hips rocked violently.

"I'm going to destroy you so you can be rebuilt like me," The creature whispered in his ear. "Strong. Faster. Unstoppable."

His teeth sank in Elio's arm, shattering his humerus. The pain was beautiful, exquisite and all-encompassing. Already, the creature's teeth were on his forearm, destroying his ulna and radius both. Pain and pleasure were indistinguishable, and Elio didn't feel quite connected to this world anymore. All that existed at the moment was the bliss of his cock buried deep inside the creature's inviting cunt, and the burning that was invading all his bones one by one or two by two. Sounds reverberated in his mind. Moans, groans, screams, cracks, the pounding of flesh on flesh. He couldn't tell who was making them anymore. They were floating around, ghosts in an ocean of sensations.

Something exploded inside him, hitting him like a freight train. The most powerful orgasm he had ever experienced.

He wasn't sure how much time had passed when he opened his eyes again, but all that remained of the searing pain was a dull ache. He sat up on the forest floor, surprised to see that he could move. The creature smiled at him. Except, it wasn't a creature anymore. It was a young man, like him, all traces of unnatural features gone.

"I'll teach you how to control it," he told him, the gentleness in his voice contrasting with the violence of their lovemaking. "Together, we can turn others. Create an army. A community. Keep our brothers and sisters and all our siblings safe."

ANGEL OF THE NIGHT

By A.W.

A young woman lies on the altar. The church is filled with the dark sheen of a moonless night and wind hisses and billows through broken rafters. Dried blood that once dripped crimson from the altar to the floor, has now dried in crude patterns down the sides of the desecrated monument and onto the splintered wooden floors. Her body is maimed to pieces, wide hazel eyes, frozen in permanent fear stare up at the ceiling. Muscles have gone through the struggle against their bindings, and now they've long surpassed rigor mortis. She's begun to wilt and decay as if she never existed with only the birds in the rafters and woodland animals who've made their homes in this abandoned structure to sing her to her eternal sleep.

Like a good church always does, the perpetrators cleaned the altar before they tied her to it. They dressed her in expensive clothes and fed her wine and rich meat for days leading up to her slaughter. They were fattening the lamb of god for her slaughter, they said. They even dusted off the altar before they pinned her to it and wiped her tears as she begged to be spared. Then, when the deed was done. They were up and gone afterward, leaving their sacrifice in hopes that a cruel god would take pity on their pathetic suffering and grant them the glory they jacked off to.

The thought makes the watcher's lips curl into a snarl. Humans are the cruelest creatures; they prove time and time again. They are the divine's rejects, the lost children of flawed gods and sometimes, she takes pity on them, but not now. Not when she sees this.

And despite the rage, she approaches so gently. She brushes the hair from the senseless martyr's eyes and holds back her tears when she sees the rigor mortis has long been gone. No matter her magic, this woman will always be reminded of the violence forced upon her when she looks in the mirror. Still, the sinister thing works in the night with delicate hands and a hum. She lights the candles again with a flick of her hand and each one begins to glow warmly in the bleak and uncanny desecrated monument to a cruel god.

This is her fight, pushing back against a god that demands worship and control, who sees violence and does nothing. Who allows their followers to hate. She won't let another one of the fragile humans' lives be lost to a god drunk on rage and wine. In the flow of the candlelight, a dark ghastly silhouette glows on the cracked wooden walls. Bat like wings, a twitching tail, and beautifully curved horns grow from her body: a monstrous shape to the ghosts that haunt this place of pain, but to this person, she is an angel. She is a frightening and beautiful angel with her beautifully fanged, melancholy smile and uncanny flashing eyes. She is a savior without the visage of beauty in an attempt to find cruelty. She is.

Her eyes are animate, wide with fear. Her skin is marred with the scars of the knife and all too pale. The wound has filled itself with an undead, ghastly flesh. It is the beginning of the mosaic of this martyr's second life. No more is she a martyr and no more are they a victim.

"Why?"

The demon tilts her head, "I may be a monster, but I'm not cruel."

The Demon reaches out to help the young woman sit up. "Cyra. That's my name," the woman mutters after a moment.

"What a name," the demon purrs in response, a fanged smile flickering across her face.

"Do you have one?"

The demon pauses, taken aback. "Well, no one ever asks. I have a name, but not one a human can say." She tilts her head, "What would you call me, if you chose?"

Cyra looks at the creature before her, taking the being in. "Sophia," she finally answers. "It feels right?"

The demon quirks a brow, "What a smart girl. My peers call me Astaphaios, but you may call me Sophia, if you wish."

Cyra sits up now on her own, gaining more steadiness in this rejuvenated body. "Astra. Your name is Astra."

Astra grins again, "Oh, I'm special then, to receive a nickname right away."

"You did... save me."

"I do admit, it wasn't exactly all selfless."

"I don't care, really. Not anymore. Not after what they did. You did whatever you did for your reasons, and either way, I have a second chance."

Astra leans in at that, observing the person before her. She's been through a lot, so it makes sense she's so resilient, but that fact tugs at Astra's heart. Humans are so fragile and she hates to see them build callouses against each other.

"You're an intriguing human, Cyra. Or, well, now you're a bit less than human."

"What am I?"

"That is up to you," she grins, pulling back and pushing herself off the altar.

"Why?"

"Why what?" Astra quirks a brow,

"Why did you do this?"

For a moment, her expression darkens. Cyra sees the depths of darkness in the flickering pools of molten stone that Astra's eyes are reminiscent of. There's an anger that Cyra suddenly feels deep in her body. There's no more fear. They can't hurt her again, so all that's left is anger.

"They killed you for a god that feasts on blood and masquerades with kindness, wearing the flesh of his victims to seem more approachable. He's also selfish. You've read the book he supposedly wrote, yeah?"

Cyra blinks, opening and closing her mouth in an attempt to respond. Nothing.

"Well, before he pulled the wool over your eyes, there were other gods. The god that gluttonlously feeds off your pain is a god of war parading as a savior. It's his little divine experiment. Once you, humans, no longer amuse him, he'll end it."

Cyra's eyes meet the demon's eyes. "I won't be his pawn anymore. I used to believe, so fervently. I used to pray and now—" she pauses, standing up finally.

"I want to pray to a new god," she grins leaning up to kiss Astra on the mouth.

And who is she to resist? Astra has always had a surplus of entities lining up, but this? This felt... raw in a way the world hasn't felt recently. She kisses her back fiercely, wasting no time by forcing her tongue into Cyra's mouth to explore.

They part. "Tell me to stop if something is ever too much."

Cyra nods, a soft smile flashing across her face. "I will."

With that, Astra pushes Cyra down to her knees by the shoulders. "You said you wanted to pray to a new god? Well prove it. *Worship me.*"

Slowly, with shaky hands, Cyra begins to explore Astra's body, running her hands up her thighs. Astra is lean and her skin is cool. She's intoxicating in a way that a burning liquor is. And Cyra needs more. She begins to kiss up Astra's thighs, pushing aside the skirt.

"Oh dear. Clothes are so impractical," Astra huffs, waving a hand so both of them are now bare in the moonlight. "Shall we continue? Perhaps we can make this place sacred again."

Cyra grins, "I think we can."

"What do you want? I can have any parts you like."

Cyra's grin widens, "Well, I have no preference, but I do enjoy the idea of you bending me over the altar and fucking me until I'm screaming your name."

"For someone who used to be so prim and proper, you're very willing to spread your legs. And for a demon of all things."

Cyra's grin morphs into a coy smile, "Well, like I said this is my second chance. Why not start it off with a bang?"

Astra's eyes flare with a sudden hunger and her body is beginning to buzz. "Literally a bang." With a hand and some magic, her body morphs. "Suck me off." The woman stares hungrily. Astra's sudden large cock is enough for the wetness in between her legs to become noticeable. She leans forward to take Astra in her mouth, staring up at her all the while.

Cyra's probably virginal mouth feels electric on Astrid's cock. And who knows really, with a mouth like this, maybe Astra is a freaky church girl. She knows they exist and they're her favorite demographic to liberate. Regardless of what the situation is, Astra's body is alight. Astra's hands go to grasp Cyra's head, holding her closer, pulling on her perfect hair. She can't avoid the intoxicating pools of copper staring up at her with a seduction that only a truly living person could conjure. Cyra is Astra's perfect masterpiece, her Frankenstein's monster. Though, this monster is far from a monster. She's proof that the lies and violence of the world don't have to triumph. She is proof of what beautiful creatures humans can be, on her knees worshipping a false god. Maybe Cyra could deify Astra. She's certainly trying. She takes her fully in her mouth, gagging each time Astra's cock hits the back of her throat.

"Yes, perfect. Good girl. Like that," she groans, bucking her hips into Cyra's mouth. "I'm so close." She is. A few serendipitous moments later she screams as she falls over the edge. Astra pulls away, wiping her mouth with a grin. "I did good, I take it?"

Astra nods rapidly, staring down at the woman again. The mere sight of her on her knees, cum on her chin is enough to light the fire again. "Stand up," she breathes. The girl complies and before Astra can command her, Cyra leans up to kiss Astra hard. She never imagined a demon's lips would be this warm, but then again, Cyra never imagined she'd be kissing a demon. She thinks that kissing a demon in the church where she died is retribution. This little act of rebellion doesn't account for the millions of people who suffered in places like this, but it seems to return Cyra's soul to her body.

Astra pushes Cyra away only for her to push Cyra against the altar. "You'll get what you wanted, sweetheart," she breathes in her ear. Cyra grins down at the altar. "Good." With that, Astra positions herself behind the woman and lines herself up. "There we go."

She slides in, inch by inch. With every movement, Cyra's whines grow louder. Her hands grasp at the edges of the altar for stability. As Astra begins to fuck into Cyra, her moans and whines mix with the harsh ghasts of wind that blow through the holes in the rafters. Tears well in her eyes as Astra fucks her. Astra is her angel. She has to be. This demon is the guardian angel she always wanted, begged for. Now, she doesn't have to beg anymore, unless Astra tells her to. Then she would. With each second Astra is in her, her body lights up more and more fire. Astra's cock is bringing her body back to life once and for all.

Their fucking is all too brief and all to glorious. As Cyra finally comes down from her orgasm, Astra pulls out. "You were so good for me, Baby."

A few seconds later through breaths, Cyra replies, "I need more.

Astra chuckles, "Not tonight."

"Some other night?"

"Yeah."

Astra smiles and puts a piece of hair behind her ear. She summons a soft sweatshirt and a pair of leggings for Cyra. "Go home. Rest. You have your life back."

"Thank you, Astra."

Astra nods with a small smile, a genuine smile this time. "We'll meet again my angel of the night."

APPETITE OF THE RUTHLESS VIRTUOSO

By Sirius

There are three stages of being invited to dine with Count Evelyn Blythe, each of which must be observed with the utmost veridicality and with the same religious fervor as is usually reserved for the Son of God. For Evelyn Blythe, whose withered heart is fed by a thick aristocratic vein, counts himself as much an artist as he is a perfectionist. Every part of the evening ritual, from invitation to farewells, is as vital as the seven-course affair laid out between these observations.

To be invited, and to flounder, often has more devastating consequences than simple social disgrace. The count has noted himself to be a pristine judge of character, and any spot on his record must be removed as a stain from an expensive tailcoat.

The first stage that must be observed is the invitation itself. The courier will arrive on the dot of noon. Not a moment before, and they will not linger a minute past. It is expected that you will greet them at the door and offer some refreshment. Limeflower water or Earl Grey is proper. They will decline, and you must exchange no further words. Note that the count's communications will always arrive on a Thursday, and no one will think less of you if you find yourself waiting in the foyer ten minutes before the stroke of noon. Although have a care not to pace in front of your windows, as this may attract attention to your anticipation and excitable state.

Upon receiving the invitation, it is permissible—and expected—to feel a flutter of joy. Some anxiety is also expected, for anyone who is not both elated to be part of such an exclusive event and ardent to make a good impression is not worthy of a seat at the table. It is customary to allow oneself an afternoon. The invitation, which will be written in flowing red ink on a simple crème-colored card, may rest on your desk as you pull out your diary and ruminate over a midday cup of tea or coffee. If you have any appointments, it is expected that you will move them—and take the necessary steps to secure your evening's schedule before submitting your response.

You will accept, of course. A crème-colored card with black ink is customary. It must compliment the impeccable style of its sender while being none bolder, and it must be a measured response of enthusiasm and restraint. To fawn over one's host is considered overzealous.

The second stage is to dress properly for the occasion. It is expected that one will wear red. A deep carmine shade is preferred, for crimson is too garish and burgundy is too dour. There is no need to bring anything with you. In fact, it is forbidden to carry in anything that can be used to identify your person. The count takes great pains for discretion and is jealous of his privacy, and so he extends that same courtesy to you. Family crest rings and other expensive statement pieces are best left in one's jewelry box. The count prefers to purvey clean, unadorned flesh. Sparkling gems and expensive furs will only rub, sully, and obscure the skin. One must bear in mind at all times that the count chose you for a reason. Likely there is no flaw or mark upon your skin that he would deem unsightly or unworthy. It is not worth risking the evening with a rash or a black dermographism, no matter how small it may all seem.

On such matters, the count is the virtuoso.

The third stage is selection. Here is where you must court him. You must consider why you were invited and appeal to his discerning eye. You will be in the room with a dozen other choices, and so now is the time to make yourself stand out. To know and cater to his idiosyncrasies will grant you the best chance at tantalizing his taste.

You must allow yourself some ease of mind. The menu has already been planned. Count Blythe would not serve mint jelly with a dish that paired better with tamarind, and he would not select a dry red wine over a sweet white if he did not believe it would complement his guests. These evenings are planned over the course of months. Each recipe is curated as carefully as the hands that prepare them. For your part, you need only recognize the honor that has been bestowed upon you. This grand, delightful privilege has been withheld from kings and queens. Just as many have tried to grovel, beg, and cajole their way to the count's table. And yet, the invitation came to *your* door.

Do not smear your skin with oils or douse your wrists in bitter perfumes. The count's nose is sensitive and favors the body's unhindered redolence. Avoid both and have faith in the temptation of your own flesh. A baring of your shoulder or a daring glimpse of your calves without stockings are hardly unprecedented events in the count's parlor.

When the count approaches you, it is of the utmost importance to keep your eyes fixed downward. You may be enticed to meet his gaze, particularly if he presses the round ball of his golden handheld rod against your chin and tilts it up. It has nothing to do with deference, so do not allow yourself to be resentful. Having been invited, he very well knows what sort of spirit you possess and what sort of person you might be. That has already been noted and categorized. There is nothing new for him to learn about you. Your eyes will only serve as a distraction for what is actually of importance in that moment. Likewise, one must swallow their words. The utterance of a single, undesirable sound could mean he turns his head away and leaves you in disgrace. And disgrace, as it has already been mentioned, is a devastating fate.

You may open your mouth, but only if you are prompted. The count cares very much about the state of one's organs and muscles, and a glimpse at your tongue will tell him all that he needs to know. Everything is dependent upon what else is being served, which will not be disclosed until the places are set and the platters are lowered.

There is a fourth stage of being invited to dine with Count Evelyn Blythe. One that can only be speculated upon and whispered about, for it is a far more fastidious ritual—and so closely tailored to the individual that to assume would be as deplorable as sin. Accounts have been written—various letters have been intercepted and diaries have been confiscated bearing notes on the subject. Through these, and by example, it is possible to piece together the proceedings of the fourth stage—although nothing is ever certain.

When the count chooses you, he will lead you away from the other guests and into a private room. This room will be no less elegant or lavishly decorated than the others, although it will be a great deal colder. There will be no fire in the hearth, and there will be a sheet draped over the settee. The count will release your hand and instruct you to sit upon the sheet.

He will apologize that he is unable to give you anything for the pain. It is best not to ask. To do so would imply that the count is inconsiderate in any way, or that he may have overlooked the detail of your inevitable agony. This is not an oversight on his part, rather a strenuous judgment call. The integrity of the flesh cannot be compromised, or the entire selection process would have to begin again, and you would be disgraced. Laudanum, chloroform, and opium alike cause similar disturbances to one another and cannot be risked. Rest assured that he has plenty on hand.

The count will ask you to remove your clothing and he will provide a second sheet for you to conceal your modesty, if that is of a concern. He will then instruct you upon a favorable position to remain in for the duration of his ritual. Out of kindness, he will place a piece of wood or a bit of sand-filled leather between your teeth—unless it is the tongue he desires.

There are many usual cuts of meat for the count to take. Most often he cuts from the back, the thigh, or the buttocks. Rest assured that he is not the sort who will amputate a limb without much prior discussion. He studied underneath a surgeon and uses only the finest, sharpest blades that can be purchased. Even so, and even with the aid of a bit, you are likely to lose consciousness. This is the best outcome, for time will fly quickly under the influence of darkness.

When it is finished, he will dress your wounds and clothe you. He will use smelling salts to revive you, and then he will give you cognac or gin to drink and some opium to take away the pain. He will apologize for his soiled state, as there will be blood on his clothes, and he will implore you to take a moment before rejoining the other guests. He will dismiss himself, with regrets, to change his own clothes. The part of you that went under his knife will have already been whisked away to the kitchens, giving it no time to spoil. The count employs a house cook of great delicacy and skill who will prepare the meat precisely as it is meant to be to suit the evening's menu.

It need not be said that you will eat everything that is presented through all seven courses. And when the main dish arrives, steaming hot and freshly prepared, it is your prerogative to sample it at the same time as the count, a fraction of a second before everyone else. And it will taste better than anything you have ever tried before. Everything after will pale in comparison, and you will be left longing for the buttery, tender meat that you may never relish again, but you will dream of swallowing every night.

You may find it strange, after these proceedings, to return to the world untouched by the count's hand. No one will quite understand what you have been privileged enough to experience. They will ask you for details, but you will give them nothing. Even if you have the words, you will not be able to describe everything that transpired that night. You will remember almost nothing, except for what it felt like to walk through the count's doors and be treated like royalty. You will have vague memories of how everything tasted, and you will wish you could have it again. You will bear his scars, of course, and that will set you apart. You will come to learn how to recognize others by their scars, as well.

If, by chance, you meet another who has shared this sacrament, you may exchange a knowing glance. Your secret will simmer between the two of you, acknowledged only by a quirk of your lips or the slightest inclination of your chin. Of course, you will still find yourself unable to speak of it—guarding jealously the details and hoarding every moment—from invitation to departure—as a dragon over gold. You will suck that feeling, that desire, and that longing dry until you are left empty, with only your scars. Bitterness may overcome you and divide you from such companions. It is natural to drift apart. The count's favor is a lonely boon to possess.

And you will find it difficult, but you must not continue to wait in your foyer. You must not stand alone at the door ten minutes before noon, avoiding pacing in front of the windows and wringing your gloves in your hands. Such invitations are coveted, and the count values diversity in his palate.

So, practice grace, and do not despair when you are not invited again.

BORN FROM EARTH

By Jake Vanguard

Soft, moist earth is underneath my feet. Soon, I'll be part of it. My heart beats rapidly while I watch Callista draw the circle into the cleared area, the stick she chose easily gliding through the wet soil. Candles surround the circle, flickering in the soft breeze, illuminating her shape. Soft curves, dark curly hair, and a grace to her movements I couldn't think to copy.

She hums as she draws symbol after symbol, connecting the circle and star in the middle of it with the candles. A goblet stands in the center, next to Callista's grimoire and a dagger. My fingers curl up, uncurl, curl up—toes digging into the earth, the cool breeze raising goosebumps. The symbols call to me, urge me to come closer and lay down in their midst. I force myself to keep standing still, ignore the urge to pass them. This'll change me beyond imagination. Make me more. Make me like Callista.

"Mars?" I glance at Callista as she approaches me, carefully evading the lines she's drawn. "I'm ready. Are you?" Deep breath in, then out. Callista didn't tell me everything about the ritual, only *what* it'll do. How it'll change me, promising I'll become a part of the forest, as my true self. A part of *her*.

"I'm ready," I whisper, my voice almost carried away by the wind.

She smiles so softly at me, my fear has no place in my heart anymore. It's right, what I'm doing. Soft lips catch mine, curious fingers teasing my sides, coming to a rest on my ass. Heat rushes through me as I press closer to Callista, feel her hardening cock against me. I long for her, every single moment. We were made for each other, contrasting yet complementing. The cool breeze is forgotten, only warmth remaining.

A needy whine escapes me when Callista parts our lips and grasps my hand. "Come." She guides me closer to the circle, weaving through candles. "Be careful not to step on the lines," she reminds me.

I do as she says, following her steps closely, until we're standing in the middle of the circle. Callista urges me down until I'm on my back, gazing into the dark treetops. It's a new moon night, shrouding the forest in darkness.

Callista leans over me, a smirk on her full lips. Every single day, I'm taken aback by her beauty. She's the most gorgeous being I've ever encountered. Dark curls frame her angular face, long lashes almost hiding the flames reflecting in her dark brown eyes. A low moan escapes me as her breasts press against mine, catching me in a kiss once more.

"Just relax, my love," Callista whispers, her lips grazing mine. "Let me do everything." My trust in her is endless, so I don't mind her doing anything she wants with me. I begged her to change me, make me into what she is.

Slender fingers trace my form, drawing soft sighs as arousal flushes through me. My legs spread without thinking about it, inviting Callista between them, urging her to be united. She doesn't waver, pushing in until we're flush, our moans mixing. Being united with Callista, right here in the dark forest, feels amazing. Right. Like that's what we're supposed to be.

With every gracious thrust, my muscles tighten around Callista's cock, my pussy demanding more. Always more with her, never enough. Heat blooms under my skin, rising in waves that clash with the cool, damp press of earth beneath me. Callista's hands are all over my body, teasing, squeezing, flicking, until my high rolls over me.

Moans echo through the night as I ride my high, holding onto Callista, until she stops moving. "This was the easy part. From here on, it'll be painful. You won't die, even if it feels like it." Callista traces my side, making me shiver, then grasps the goblet and dagger. "From the earth, you will be rebuilt," she whispers, slicing her left lower arm. Blood drips into the goblet, appearing black in the candles' light.

My gaze is stuck on the drops, the fine line on Callista's arm, the dripping echoing in my ears. I'm tempted to grasp her arm and lick the blood right off her skin, but I control myself. I don't want to destroy the ritual with my primal urges. Only when Callista wraps a hand around the back of my head, urging me to sit up slightly, I look at her face. "Drink up, love," she whispers, holding the goblet to my lips.

Greedily, I gulp down the rich, thick liquid. It coats my tongue, tasting of iron and earth. So good. "More," I hear myself moan after the last drop is consumed.

Callista chuckles and pushes me back down. "You'll get more soon." Pouting, I look up to her, licking my lips to catch any lingering drops of her blood. With a flick of her wrist, roots creep closer, grasping my wrists and ankles, binding me spread-eagle. Callista still kneels between my legs, united with me, pulsing and hard.

She takes the dagger once more, kissing me softly. "Remember, you can't die," she whispers against my lips before she sits up, placing the tip of the blade against my collarbone. The blade dips into my skin, deeper and deeper. Pain shoots through me, my arms flailing—or they would, if they weren't bound. A scream ripples from my lips as Callista drags the dagger deeper, to my sternum, parting my skin.

I'm panting, my senses in overdrive. Another slash follows, opening up my other side, then a third, from my sternum down between my breasts toward my stomach. Tears spill over, and I'm choking, shivering, trembling. I've never been in so much pain. So open and vulnerable. "It hurts," I croak, trembling underneath Callista. Blood oozes from the open wounds.

"I know, my love. It'll be okay." Callista's soothing voice does nothing against the excruciating pain, the helplessness of being sliced open. My body is on fire, both numb and too sensitive to her touch.

Callista dips two fingers into the cut, a pathetic whimper coming from me, and starts drawing symbols onto my skin. My own blood decorates my neck, my hips, symbols painted upon my breasts. All while Callista slowly rocks her hip, softly humming as she moves within me.

"May the earth claim your body and protect your soul," she sings, bliss on her face as she comes. Pain and arousal battle inside me, every sensation too much and not enough. The breeze cools the hot blood still pouring from my parted skin.

Callista smiles at me, then leans down and licks across the long laceration up my stomach to my chest. Her chin's coated in deep, dark red, glistening, barely visible on her dark skin. I manage to crane my neck enough to see what she's doing—peeling my skin back, revealing my rib-cage. Bony white, covered in blood red. Disbelieving, I stare at my open chest, Callista's fingers caressing my ribs.

I wonder—don't I feel the pain anymore? Or is my body getting used to it? Has my brain decided to shield me from it? There's only a dull, pulsing ache coming from my chest now, even as Callista's fingers wrap around the lowest rib.

Crack.

My eyes widen when she triumphantly holds up a piece of the rib, broken off cleanly. "You're doing so well, Mars," she coos, gingerly laying the bone aside. Then breaks off another. And another. Taking me apart. "There it is," Callista murmurs, dipping her hands into my chest.

This time, pain shoots through me once more, blackening my vision. My throat feels raw. Did I scream? My ears are ringing, and my heart's beating frantically—but it's not where it's supposed to be. No. I can *see* it. "C-Callista." My voice is so raw, so small.

She holds it. My heart. Right above my chest, cradled in her hands. "Hold it close to you, my dear Mars. Protect your heart." Without being able to think or give my limbs orders, they move, guided by roots still wrapped around my wrists, toward my chest. "Uncurl your fingers," Callista says, and I oblige. My fingers wrap around my heart, its steady beat pulsing against my palms. "Very good." Callista places her hands over mine, holds them tight, and roots bind my hands together. Even if I wanted to, I couldn't let go of my heart.

Ba-dum. Ba-dum. Ba-dum.

It beats steadily in my hands. Calming. Reassuring.

I'm still alive. I'm here. I won't die.

My gaze is fixed on the small peek I get through my fingers, the constant movement. How fascinating such an organ is. Keeping me alive and standing all these years. Now, it's here, in my hands, unveiled from the depths of my body.

A laugh bubbles from my lips. People might think I'm crazy, but didn't they always think I was? A small girl from a small village, demanding she's not a girl but also not a boy. Not she and not he. Callista was the first to accept me as I am. Loved me, fully and without boundaries. I don't mind giving myself up for her, opening up and spilling my guts. It's freeing.

"What are you laughing about?" Callista asks, an amused smile playing on her lips.

I shake my head slightly, a strand of my dirty blond hair falling into my face. There are no words to describe how I'm feeling. Raw and vulnerable, but also so powerful and free. No social boundaries hold me back, not anymore.

Callista shakes her head, surely bedazzled by my strange behavior, and hoists me up on her arms. She's strong, cradling me against her chest, and I look up to her. So beautiful. Smeared with earth, blood and cum, we're one with the forest. One with each other.

Together, we approach the shallow grave I dug out myself. Excavating my own grave—how ironic. A smile plays at my lips while Callista places me in the hole. Moist earth surrounds me, mixing with my blood.

Callista kneels at the edge, looking down at me lovingly. "Remember—you can't suffocate or die. Don't panic." She stretches and places a soft kiss on my lips. "I'll be with you the whole time. I love you, Mars."

She loves me. My heart sings between my fingers, beating more rapidly. A broad smile covers my lips as I gaze up to her. "I love you too," I whisper, unable to speak any louder. Callista nods softly and stands up, only partly visible to me now.

I take a deep breath, preparing myself for the next part. "May earth rebuild you," Callista sings, throwing the first shovelful of dirt down onto me. More and more follow, covering my body.

Thunk. Thunk. Thunk.

The mud presses down on me, heavy like a thick blanket. It feels secure. Cool. Refreshing even. The moistness soothes my aching chest, until only my face is uncovered. "May you be reborn from earth," are the last words I hear from Callista before my head is covered as well.

It takes my breath, covers my eyes, presses me down into the soil. *Don't panic.* I have to remind myself, I can't suffocate. I can't die. Tentatively, I take a breath, ground filling my airways and lungs, but it doesn't suffocate me. What should have choked me doesn't, and instead, my heart begins to calm.

Silence is all around me. The longer I lie still in the darkness, the more my senses sharpen. There, at my left foot, a worm moves around. The smell of damp earth, of soil and roots, is overwhelming. And a soft crackling of movement grows louder around me.

I twitch when something touches my side, but there's no space to evade it. After a moment of panic, I notice the familiar path the root takes. Over my side, up to my breasts. Callista. She's here, with me, as she promised. Joined with the forest.

More and more roots tug at me, wriggling around me, a few finding their way into my pussy. They feel so much like Callista's fingers, pressing against the right spots, all while more roots dig into my open chest. I want to scream, want to cry, want to moan. Torn between the foreign roaming of roots through my body, to the all-familiar teasing of my pussy and nipples, I can only give myself up to their will.

A shudder runs through me as I come once more, the roots not stopping at teasing me, even while they pierce and tear out my organs, one after one. First the kidneys, then the liver, one lung, the other—how am I still alive?—all but my heart, protected fiercely in my hands.

I'm taken apart, ripped apart from the inside, roots undoing me. More start ripping out my vocal cords, others flaying my skin on my chest and hip. My body is on fire, yet it's not really there. I know what's happening to me, understand it fully, yet the pain is dulled. My hollow chest and stomach cave in, filled with moist soil, as I'm only a shell of my former human self.

And yet, I do not fear. I'm where I'm supposed to be.

The roots that'd been teasing my pussy retreat, crawling over the remains of my body up to my hands. They wrap around my wrists, wriggle between my fingers. For a moment, I fear I'm doing something wrong, that they're not supposed to be there—but a calm sensation washes over me. The same one I always have whenever Callista smiles at me.

It's okay, the roots seem to say. *We're almost done.*

I don't fight back as they pierce my heart. A last gasp escapes me, then blackness welcomes me.

Darkness envelopes me when I take my first breath. I gasp, earth filling my mouth. It feels like home, like Callista. Like *me*. Connected to me, in a strange sense I can't grasp yet.

My fingers claw into the damp earth above me, digging into it. Adrenaline fuels me, lets me claw and dig faster and faster, until my right hand breaches the earth. A cool breeze greets my fingers, then they're enveloped by a warm hand. It tugs, pulling at me, helping me find my way out of my shallow grave.

Gasping, I stumble out of the earth, falling into Callista's embrace. "There you are, my love. You took your time." Her fingers caress my back, our chests pressed against each other.

Soil clogs my nose and throat, urging me to cough it all up. Only then, I glance up at Callista, really seeing her for the first time. Antlers peek from her hair, her eyes glowing in the dim moonlight. When she smiles broadly, sharp teeth become visible.

Wait, moonlight? I tilt my head back, staring into the sky. It's not a new moon anymore, but the first quarter filled. "How long did it take?" I ask, jumping at the sound of my voice. It's deeper, more androgynous. Exactly as I wished for it to be. My eyes widen at the realization, and I lean back, curious if all my desired changes were granted. Cupping my left breast, I grin broadly—smaller, as wished for. My hip seems narrower as well. Where Callista cut me open, faint red scars remain, but aside from it, no injuries are to be seen.

"Seven days." Callista reclines, her eyes hungrily wandering over my body. "You turned out beautifully. Every day of waiting was worth it." She leans closer once more, enveloping me in a hug, pressing her lips onto mine.

A soft sigh escapes me at the closeness, the intimacy. Our bodies have become one with the forest, connected in a deeper sense than humans can comprehend. I feel her hunger, her heartbeat and longing—and I'm sure she can feel mine. Biting her lower lip, I taste blood, rich and seductive—and Callista moans, pressing closer to me, her hard cock trapped between us.

Grinning, I push her back and watch her stumble, unable to catch her fall onto her back. So beautiful. All mine. The urge to be close, have all of her, rushes through me while I follow her down in a haste, straddling her. "Missed me?" I tease, taking her in.

"You have no idea." Strong hands grip my hip, holding me close while she thrusts up, fucking me deliciously. The overall scent of earth and soil clinging to us mixes with arousal, with blood as we bite each other in messy kisses, celebrating my change.

I've become more than human, more than I ever could imagine.

We're made of earth and blood and bones—and the fury of being forced to exist in a world not made for creatures like us. Why stay human, if humans are who shame us? No,

I'd rather stay in the forest for all eternity, with my dear Callista, fucking on my own grave.

I couldn't imagine anything better than being taken apart by my love, and put together by her and earth itself.